Scottish Relic Trilogy Box Set

Love and Mayhem

The Promise (Pennington Family)

The Rebel

Secret Vows Box Set

Borrowed Dreams (Scottish Dream Trilogy Book 1)

Captured Dreams (Book 2)

Dreams of Destiny (Book 3)

Scottish Dream Trilogy Box Set

Romancing the Scot

Sweet Home Highland Christmas

It Happened in the Highlands

Sleepless in Scotland

Dearest Millie

How to Ditch a Duke

A Prince in the Pantry

Jane Austen Cannot Marry!

Highland Crown (Royal Highlander Series Book 1)

Highland Jewel (Book 2)

Highland Sword (Book 3)

Ghost of the Thames

Thanksgiving in Connecticut

Made in Heaven

Marriage of Minds: Collaborative Writing *(Nonfiction)*

Step Write Up: Writing Exercises for 21st Century *(Nonfiction)*

Aquarian

Omid's Shadow

IT HAPPENED IN THE HIGHLANDS

MAY MCGOLDRICK

Book Duo Creative

Thank you for choosing *It Happened in the Highlands*. In the event that you appreciate this book, please consider sharing the good word(s) by leaving a review, or connect with the authors.

To our friends Betsy Mark and Rich Assenza

*Positive Proof of Second Chances
and Happily Ever After*

All the privilege I claim for my own sex...is that of loving
longest, when hope is gone.

—Jane Austen, *Persuasion*

❄   I   ❄

London
May 1802

"A CHILD'S birth should be a moment of joy, not misery." The words cut through the busy hum of chatter in the dress shop, reaching the young woman in the adjacent fitting room.

"*This* girl's origins are the most miserable, and the most abhorrent," a second woman trumpeted. "Our society has no place for those with such sordid beginnings, if you ask me."

The voices coming from beyond the curtained doorway cut Jo Pennington deeply, pricking open the wound that had been bleeding for her entire life. As she stared into the mirror, she had no doubt the two women knew she was within earshot. They had intentionally dispensed with any façade of courtesy. The volume and pitch of their conversation underscored their words.

"Indeed," the first woman agreed. "I have it on the

best authority that the girl's mother was a baseborn courtesan!"

The seamstress pinning the lace to Jo's sleeve was pretending not to hear, but her flushed face spoke of her embarrassment.

"'*Courtesan*' is too fine a term," the second woman replied. "I *know* what happened. I've tried to put the memory from me, but I was there. And I can tell you the girl's mother was from the lowest dregs of existence. I hesitate to use such disgusting expressions, but we must see the world for what it is, even though it shocks those of us with refined sensibilities. The woman was a slatternly doxy wallowing in a ditch. A stale and shiftless vagrant adding to the world's burden. A 'decayed strumpet', in the words of Dr. Johnson."

Jo squeezed her eyes shut. She knew only too well the identity of the second woman, though she struck a different pose in the presence of any member of the Pennington family. Lady Nithsdale had indeed been a guest at Baronsford's Summer Ball when the rain-soaked Countess Aytoun carried a hungry, mewling infant into the midst of society's elite, only hours after Jo's mother died giving birth in the mud beneath the cart of a kindly old woman.

But now Lady Nithsdale, loathsome and hypocritical, stood in the salon adjoining the dressmaker's fitting room, loudly proclaiming all she remembered and even more that she'd invented.

How quickly the clouds blotted out the sun!

Only an hour ago, Jo had been basking in the joys of lively Oxford Street, with its large, bright shops filled with hats and bonnets, slippers and shoes, ribbons and lace. Eyeing the latest fashions in the company of her adoptive mother and sisters, she'd been so happy. While her mind had been on her intended and her upcoming wedding, eleven-year-old Phoebe and eight-year-old Millie had been cheerfully cajoling Lady Aytoun into the absolute *necessity* of having matching dresses made for them from the colorful array of fabrics hanging in graceful folds behind the fine, high windows.

And now this. Again. Ten days before the wedding.

Jo forced herself to focus on the image of her fiancé's handsome face. On his dark blond hair, his smile, and his contagious laughter. On his broad chest and shoulders within his crisp naval officer's uniform. On his large, warm hands holding hers in the darkness of a carriage. But even that could not blot out the hurtful, penetrating sound of polished malice.

"And yet I hear she's to marry a baronet's son."

The second woman barked out a derisive laugh. "Your ears have not deceived you, my dear. She's to marry Wynne Melfort, a strapping navy lieutenant with more than a few eligible young ladies competing for his attention this Season."

"Melfort must be poor, I imagine. Second sons do need to make their way in the world, and the Penningtons are as rich as Croesus."

"I assure you money is the *only* motivation for this match," Lady Nithsdale asserted, the sneer in her voice clearly discernable. "The Earl of Aytoun has transformed a pauper child into an heiress worth twenty thousand pounds."

Waves of shame washed through her, leaving her cold and ill. The young seamstress continued as quickly as she could, pinning the lace to the silver-hued wedding dress. As Jo stared into the mirror, unshed tears welled up, clouding her vision, and the delicately embroidered shells and flowers blurred.

"I heard they managed to have her presented at court, and as *Lady* Josephine Pennington," the first woman continued. "I recall a day when money couldn't buy *that*."

Jo had been haunted by similar whispers since being presented in her first introduction to London society. Today's assault was only different in its openness and intensity.

Before this year, her parents had successfully deterred her from attending the salons and ballrooms of the Season. Knowing that her obscure parentage would surely be a topic for the gossipmongers of London, they'd never wanted to expose Jo to society's cruelty. Year after year, they'd persuaded her to stay at their estate in Hertfordshire or at Baronsford, the family home in the Scottish Borders. But at twenty-one years of age, with dreams of finding a husband, she'd won their anxious approval.

And then, immediately, she found Wynne. Or, he found her. Perhaps his initial attraction to her had been her dowry, but immediate sparks had flown between them. She knew they both felt it. Within a month Jo realized her weak-kneed reaction to the young naval officer was only partly due to his good looks and intense blue eyes. Their minds were in harmony. Their trust complete. The ability to bare their souls, reveal the long-buried aches, and celebrate the victories joined their hearts as one. And then there was his protectiveness.

The memory of their walk in Kensington Gardens this past Saturday came back to her. They'd been watching the military bands when Jo became aware of the feminine whispers. The voices made no mention of names, but it was perfectly clear that the topic of the conversation could only be Jo Pennington.

Recognizing her discomfort, Wynne had grown angry. Hints and vague innuendo and subsequent denial notwithstanding, he'd been ready to call out one of the husbands. During the few weeks of their engagement, she'd become more aware of his growing frustration. He was willing to confront and challenge anyone in defense of her honor.

But she couldn't allow it. It was not in Jo's nature to let him make a scene. Idle talk, she'd told herself over and over. It would go away. The gossips would find a new target. She didn't need any additional notice. And she'd rather die than have anything happen to him.

"Of course, what *else* should one expect of the Penningtons?" Lady Nithsdale scoffed. "The earl and his wife are no strangers to scandal. That family is quite fortunate that anyone in polite society recognizes them at all. You've surely heard the shocking tales of their first marriages."

"Tell me."

As the vile woman proceeded to expound on the Penningtons' family history, Jo's lip quivered. The pain cutting through her was sharper than anything the previous comments had inflicted. The lifetime of love and kindness she'd received at the hands of her parents, the affection she felt for her four brothers and sisters, as well as the extended family, made her wish she had the strength to tear down those curtains and claw the faces of the two women on the other side.

Her chin sank to her chest. Why couldn't they just go away?

"I'm not feeling well, I'm afraid," Jo said to the seamstress. "Pray, help me out of this and into my dress again."

"But, mistress, the modiste wishes to see you in it."

"I'll come back in a day or two to finish the fitting," Jo told her, retrieving a coin from her reticule and putting it into the young woman's hand.

A few moments later, she slipped through the curtained doorway. Refusing to look in the direction of Lady Nithsdale and her confidante, Jo could not escape hearing the snickers of the two women as she fled.

"Why, there she goes."

"*Lady* Josephine."

She didn't slow down as she passed a clutch of seamstresses standing around a bolt of scarlet silk, and went out into the front room of the shop. Since childhood, Jo had been taught that life was hard enough and that there was no place in it for such malevolence. But these women had grown up in a different school. Lady Nithsdale and her lot had no souls.

"What's wrong, sweetheart?"

Jo looked up at her mother waiting in the front of the shop with her two younger sisters. She'd promised to show them the dress once the lace was pinned to the sleeves.

"Where is the dress?" Lady Aytoun didn't wait for an answer. "Something has happened to upset you."

"Nothing has happened," Jo lied. "I think the pastries we ate aren't sitting well. Pray, let's go home and come back another day."

Millicent's gaze moved to the doorway into the salon. Jo thought for a moment she'd need to stop her from going in and demanding to know what happened and who was responsible.

"Please, Mother. I'd like to go now."

"As you wish."

Lady Aytoun acquiesced, but her dark frown reflected her true feelings as they left the shop. Her family, and now Wynne, wanted to protect her. But Jo couldn't bear the humiliation of a public confrontation. There could be no victory. She couldn't change the circumstances of her birth.

Settling into the carriage, Jo took a few steadying breaths to calm herself.

All the gossip amounted to nothing, she told herself for the thousandth time. The past didn't matter. Wynne had chosen her. He'd asked for her hand in marriage, knowing full well of her parentage. Her future with him didn't need to include the likes of Lady Nithsdale. She closed her eyes and tried to think only of him. Of their future together, away from London's ton.

Phoebe and Millie's chatter was a welcome distraction, and it served to keep Lady Aytoun from asking any more questions on their way back home.

By the time their carriage rolled to a stop in front of the mansion facing Hanover Square, Jo had buried the incident at the dress shop deep with all the others. A footman in gold-trimmed livery greeted them as he opened the door. Another servant escorted them up the wide marble steps to the front door.

Inside the mansion's entrance hall, Jo stopped to remove her gloves and hat, and her gaze was drawn to the semicircular alcove at the far end of the hall where she could hear men's voices.

"Hugh is back!" Phoebe shouted gleefully, running in that direction with Millie on her heels.

Jo smiled at their mother, feeling the same exuberance

as the two younger ones over the arrival of their brother. Only a year apart in age, Hugh and Jo had been inseparable since childhood, until his schooling required that he stay away for much of the year. And now he was serving as a cavalry officer for the king.

"I'm happy to see your upset stomach is already improving." Her mother smiled, heading toward the open set of doors.

Before Jo could follow, an elderly footman approached with a letter. "While you were out, m'lady, Lieutenant Melfort left this for you."

"Did he say anything?" she asked.

"Only that he was sorry you weren't at home to receive him."

"Thank you," she said, breaking the seal.

She wanted to see Hugh, but Wynne was not one to write her letters. She wondered if this had anything to do with this coming Thursday. His parents and brother were to join them for dinner.

She paused at the entrance to the alcove. The letter was brief. The lines danced before her eyes, but certain words and phrases came into sharp focus.

. . . wedding arrangements . . . misery for you . . . break off our engagement . . . Ever your servant . . .

"No." The room tilted. Her body became numb as she reread the words in a rush of denial. Wynne's face appeared in her mind. The moments they spent together were lies. His affection, his declaration of love, all lies. Jo's dream of her future vanished like a drop of rain on parched ground.

As her tears stained the letter, a strong hand took hold of hers, steadying her. Looking up through a blur, she recognized her brother Hugh's worried face.

To the east above London's steeples and rooftops, the sky glowed blood red, denying any promise of the sun's appearance. The green meadows and woods of the park remained vague, indistinct, reluctant to emerge into the murky dawn light. Nothing stirred, not even the low-hanging cloud obscuring the Serpentine. Hyde Park was quiet at this hour. Deadly quiet.

The stock of the dueling pistol felt smooth and cool in Wynne Melfort's hand. Tearing his gaze from the weapon, he looked across the dewy ground at the red-coated foe standing in the mist, silent and still, twenty paces away.

Hugh Pennington had come to kill him.

Wynne couldn't blame him. He was Jo's brother, and he was a man who would always defend her honor.

"Take your places, gentlemen."

The notion ran through Wynne's mind that neither of them should be here. He shouldn't have let it come to this.

But how else could he have made her understand? His orders had arrived yesterday. His ship was leaving for Newfoundland.

He loved Jo, but if they wed, what kind of life was he leaving her to? His own vile parents would provide a place for her, but what kind of place would it be? Their claws weren't any less sharp than the rest of the ton.

Wynne couldn't marry her because he couldn't protect her.

"When I drop my handkerchief . . ."

Too late for that now, he thought. Honor. Jo's honor was at stake. And Wynne knew what he had to do.

As the handkerchief fluttered to the ground, the two

men raised their pistols. In the distance, he heard the bell tolling in the tower above St. George's Chapel.

Wynne shifted his aim high and to the right of Jo's brother, and the muzzle of Hugh Pennington's pistol flashed in the morning mist.

The readers of the *Tittle-Tattle Review*, scouring the rag for gossip, found confirmation of what was already common knowledge in London. The third entry referred to the duel between Hugh Pennington and Wynne Melfort:

> It has come to our attention that on Saturday last, two well-known gentlemen faced each other with pistols in the misty dawn light beneath the tall and ancient elms in the northern environs of Hyde Park. Captain H.P. shot Lieutenant W.M. over a matter of family honor. W.M. was carried from the field. At the time of publication, it is unknown whether the wounded gentleman would survive the night.

$\approx$ 2 $\approx$

Western Aberdeen
The Scottish Highlands
April 1818

Sixteen Years Later

WITH THE MID-MORNING sun warm on his back, Wynne Melfort nudged his chestnut steed to a canter, following the grassy cart path along the banks of the River Don. He breathed deeply, filling his lungs with the strange, coconut scent of the brilliantly yellow gorse as his gaze was drawn along the sparkling waters to the crystal-blue backdrop of the round-shouldered Grampians to the west.

"Fine day to be out," he said aloud, expecting no answer from his horse.

When Wynne retired from the Royal Navy two years ago, he and his friend Dermot McKendry, who'd served as surgeon on his ships for almost a decade, had turned their steps toward this idyllic place in the Highlands. The majestic mountains and the mysterious lochs and the stretches of untamed coastline couldn't have been more different from the wide-open sea, or the lush green islands of the West Indies, or the crowded bustle of London and the West End. No place he'd ever been matched the beauty of the Highlands.

Not a mile along the river, Wynne turned his mount northward and rode up the rising tract through the newly tilled fields and stone-pocked grazing lands. Before long, the grey tower of the former Clova Abbey came into sight. Now known only as "the Abbey," the vast estate—with its farms and forests, mill, and fish ponds—belonged for centuries to Dermot's family, but the place had become the property of the Crown during the troubled times of Bonnie Prince Charlie. The McKendrys had a penchant for choosing the noble—and often losing—side of things.

The Abbey had offered the perfect situation for the two men. The good doctor, having inherited the wrecked estate, wanted to rebuild it and start a hospital—a licensed private asylum for those suffering from mental disorders caused by injury or disease. Prior to his years sailing with Wynne, Dermot had worked in an asylum in Edinburgh. Whatever he'd experienced there, it had been enough to drive the man to do this—to try to improve on treatment he found greatly flawed.

For himself, Wynne wanted a place to settle, so he put up his money in return for a portion of the estate lands. Now that his son had joined him here, Wynne's investment was even more important. Years from now, when he was gone, the tower house he was rebuilding and the land around it would provide a legacy, a home that Andrew Cuffe Melfort could call his own, with obligations to no man.

It was a sound partnership. Dermot served as director of the hospital, handling the medical side of things; Wynne served as governor, managing the business affairs.

Passing the fields that Dermot's aging uncle—known to all as "the Squire"—had designated as his golfing links, he soon reached the house. As he rode by the courtyard formed by two wings extending out from the main section of the building, he saw a number of patients and handlers taking advantage of the sun. The ground floor of a north annex, built by the army as a barracks during the campaigns to subdue the Highlands, now served as the ward for patients they were already treating.

Dismounting by the stables, Wynne turned at the sound of a shout coming from the direction of the kitchen gardens.

"Captain!"

He shielded his eyes as he looked toward the voice. With his bald head shining, Hamish was stomping toward him, hauling a scowling ten-year-old boy along by the collar.

This certainly didn't bode well, Wynne thought, peering at his son's face as the two approached. Cuffe was sporting a welt over one eye, a bloodied nose, a swollen lower lip, and a torn shirt beneath his waistcoat and dirt-stained russet jacket.

Another fight. The lad had only been in Scotland for a month, and this was his fourth skirmish. Cuffe was living up to the warning his Jamaican grandmother sent when she'd written that she could no longer keep him.

Wynne knew nothing about raising a child, but he'd enlisted the aid of others to assist him. Cameron, the purser on his ship and now the bookkeeper at the Abbey, was to begin teaching the lad what he'd be learning in school. Hamish, lead man on the farms, was to instruct the boy about the practical side of managing the land, an education invaluable for a future landowner.

As post captain in the Royal Navy, Wynne had commanded a number of vessels and hundreds of men during his career. Lads younger than his son served aboard ship, and they all needed time to adjust to the life. He admired the ten-year-old's independent spirit, but Cuffe was beginning to worry him.

Wynne handed the reins to a stable hand as the two drew near.

"He's done it this time, Captain," the farm manager huffed. "This scoundrel of yers."

Hamish was known both for his patience and his stoical acceptance of the trials of farming in the Highlands. Whatever Cuffe had done now, it clearly had been enough to push the Highlander beyond his limits.

"What have you done, lad?" Wynne asked.

Thin but strong, with a ramrod-straight back, his son gazed steadily at the ground in front of him, his curly, collar-length brown hair falling partially across his battered face. He never looked Wynne in the eye or spoke to him—acts of rebellion, he supposed—but the boy would eventually come around. He had to.

"I'll tell ye, Captain," Hamish snapped, not waiting. "This loon of yers has turned the pigs out in the kitchen gardens."

Pigs in the garden. That was a first. He doubted the pigs did this damage to his face.

"Explain yourself," he ordered.

Cuffe's chin lifted and his deep brown eyes stared off at the mountains. He showed no hint of fear and certainly no suggestion of responding.

"I told the young miscreant to oversee the feeding of the pigs while I got ready for us to go out to the west farms. Next thing I knew, the porkers are running amok, the house is in an uproar, and Cook is rampaging, about as wild as I've ever seen her. Threatened to put yer son out for the faeries."

"How did he get the bruises on his face?"

"A fight, Captain." Hamish shook his head. "By the time we got the pigs back in their pens, we heard squalling so loud I thought the *Bean Nighe*—the demon washerwoman herself—was carrying off a bairn. Turned out yer lad was giving three of the farm lads a beating."

Looking at the injuries, Wynne wondered how bad the others must look.

"And two of them bigger than this one," the Highlander asserted. "Now, I know lads will scuffle from time to time, but we can't have the hospital governor's son beating up the very farm workers he's supposed to be overseeing."

There was no point in demanding answers. Wynne was well accustomed to the vow of silence Cuffe had obviously taken when it came to communicating with him. Over the past month, Wynne had managed the disciplining of the boy himself, but perhaps the chores he'd been assigning were not tough enough.

"I'll leave the issue of punishment for this infraction to you, Hamish."

Cuffe's face turned a shade darker, but he refused to look at Wynne.

"Take him," he ordered the Highlander. "My son needs to understand that if he refuses to present a reasonable defense for his actions, there are consequences to be paid."

The farm manager led Cuffe off, muttering about mucking shite out of the stables. According to Dermot, Hamish believed that tough, physical labor was the best way to teach and discipline, and maintain self-respect.

Walking along the side of the building toward the north annex, Wynne tried to remember what he'd been like at that age. As a second son, he'd endured the dreary routine of tutors at home while his older brother was away at Eton, and those men had never spared the rod in teaching him discipline. With the exception of developing an aversion for corporal punishment, he'd never questioned his life or the decisions that were made by his parents. He'd always accepted that those in authority knew best.

Years later, a duel fought on a grey London morning—and the long weeks of recovery that followed—had served to awaken him. He was twenty-two then and had been fortunate to see another sunrise.

As Wynne entered the north annex, the bookkeeper, Cameron, appeared at the bottom of a stairwell.

"Dr. McKendry is looking for you, Captain. He's in his office."

Telling the former purser that Cuffe would likely be absent from his afternoon lessons, Wynne then ascended the stairs. He walked past his own office—an oasis of order and calm—and entered Dermot's chaotic workplace. Regardless of the constant nagging of the housekeeper during the weekly cleaning, every surface of the spacious room was covered with papers and folders, and the floor was little better. Textbooks and medical journals were scattered about and piled in corners. Volumes lay open on every available chair and on top of stacks of paper.

Each man had his own method of managing his affairs, and neither interfered with the ways of the other, though Wynne was often sorely tempted by the sight of Dermot's mess.

Standing at a tall desk by a window, the doctor was inscribing notes in an open ledger. He turned around and tossed the pen on top of the book when he heard Wynne enter.

"You're back." He smiled, satisfaction evident on his face. "The most extraordinary circumstances have developed with our new patient."

"Charles Barton?" Wynne asked. "A change in his condition already?"

"Come and see for yourself." Dermot came around his desk.

Ten days ago, Charles Barton, fifty-six years of age, arrived at the Abbey emaciated and unresponsive, delivered for permanent care by his aging mother, a local landowner. Her son, Mrs. Barton explained, had arrived home at Tilmory Castle in this condition after sustaining a head injury during an explosion aboard some merchant ship months earlier.

Though the old woman had provided generous financial support to make certain her son would be well cared for in his final days, Dermot believed that Barton's demise was not imminent.

"I heard an uproar of some kind coming from the

direction of the gardens," the doctor said, as they started down the stairs to the hospital ward.

Wynne nodded. "I understand the pigs had some extra greens in their diet, thanks to Cuffe."

The men exchanged a look. Nothing more needed to be said. Wynne's struggles with new parenthood weren't lost on Dermot. "Well, I'm certain Hamish will have everything back on an even keel in no time."

"I hope so," Wynne replied. "I took your aunt's recommendation and stopped down at the village and spoke to the vicar about providing Cuffe with some religious instruction. It was agreed that an hour a week would—"

"You should have asked Blane McKendry about *golfing* instruction instead." Dermot shook his head. "I happen to know that old heathen can teach Cuffe more about niblicks and longnoses than he can about Psalms and Beatitudes."

Regardless of the weather, the Squire and his brother the vicar met every day to chase their golf balls across the fields.

Wynne and Dermot entered the nearly empty ward. He'd seen many of the patients outside. At the far end of the long and spacious room, two handlers were settling Stevenson, the only unpredictable patient in the hospital. Still in his twenties, the former dockworker from Aberdeen had been diagnosed with "furious mania." Highly disturbed, he had occasional bouts of violence, and any irritation could upset him. Even now, he was upbraiding the handlers with loud obscenities and clutching his tam protectively to his chest.

Wynne knew it took a special temperament and character to treat lunatics. Dermot would not permit the use of shackles, though they were commonly used elsewhere, and only Stevenson was restrained at night. The doctor believed attempts should be made to cure these men, and short of that, they should at least be allowed to live decently.

Charles Barton, their newest patient, was sitting by a sunny window halfway down the room with a secretary's desk on his lap. Thin fingers moved a pencil lightly over paper.

"He's conscious!" Wynne exclaimed.

"More or less," the doctor said. "He has yet to speak a word."

The two men crossed the ward to the window, but Barton didn't look up or acknowledge their presence. The man's greying curls were bound in a head wrapping, and his pale, sunken cheeks sported a thick beard.

"His mother made no mention of it, but we've discovered that Mr. Barton is an accomplished artist," Dermot told him. "But the fascinating thing is that he likes to draw the same face, the same young woman, over and over."

The old man's eyes were fixed on a sheet of paper, his fingers becoming more insistent as he finished with a drawing and reached for a clean sheet.

"I'd like to know the subject of this man's obsession." Dermot handed the recently drawn sheet to his friend. "It might help with the patient's recovery."

Wynne gazed at the drawing in his hands. He'd seen those dark curls before in a thousand dreams. He'd seen them swept up, and he'd seen them falling gracefully over those slender shoulders. He'd seen those eyes, so precisely angled above the high cheekbones. The delicate nose, the set of the mouth. Those lips.

Recognition struck him like a bolt of lightning. He felt the blood drain from his face. It can't be, he thought. Alarm and hope battled for dominance.

Wynne picked up another sketch. And then another. He stared at each one in turn. All the same woman. There was no question.

It was only yesterday, the first time they met.

The flushed faces of dancers in their gowns of gold and blue and green, and their evening suits of black, and uniforms of red and blue. Around him, his fellow officers were joking and pointing out prospective brides and conquests.

And then he saw her.

They'd never been introduced, but he knew her by name. She was unlike so many of the young women being presented at Court for the first time, who fought for every glimmer of attention. Even now, standing by the punch bowl, she had a quiet reserve that hinted at sadness. He wondered if she was affected by stories that were beginning to circulate. He didn't put any stock in gossip, but the talk of her origins was spreading like flames in a dry August meadow.

Groups of partygoers milled about, and several young women halted beside her.

Wynne knew the moment something was said. The warm blush drained from her pretty face and her back stiffened.

Suddenly, she was off, darting through the crowd with the deftness of a bird in flight, until she disappeared through the doors opening onto the terrace.

What possessed him to go, he'd asked himself so many times. He only knew she was upset, she was alone, and he went after her.

. . .

"I . . ." Wynne began to speak, but the words were too slow to keep up with his drumming heart and his racing mind. "The woman in these drawings is Josephine Pennington."

❦   3   ❦

Baronsford, the Scottish Borders
May 1818

THE DROWSY INFANT'S contented sigh caressed Jo's heart like a summer breeze. Holding her niece on her lap, she gazed at the long lashes and the round cheeks and pursed, red lips. She didn't think she'd ever seen a child more beautiful than the Honorable Beatrice Ware Macpherson Pennington, born just two months ago to her brother Hugh and his extraordinary wife, Grace.

"The resemblance is astonishing."

Jo tore her gaze from the angelic bairn and watched her sister-in-law peruse the portfolio of sketches that had arrived only yesterday from a private asylum in the Highlands.

"These must be drawings of you at a younger age," Grace asserted, holding one of the pages up to Jo's face.

Relief rushed through her. Her sister-in-law confirmed

what she too had seen. The image definitely bore a close resemblance to her.

"Look at the tilt of the eyes. The shape of the brow. The reserved smile. Even the expression on her face as she looks away. You do the same whenever you're the center of attention."

Everything Grace said was true. Upon opening the parcel, Jo had been dumbfounded. She couldn't recollect when these sketches might have been done of her. But she'd quickly noticed the differences. The loose curls that draped over the woman's shoulders. The dated style of her dress, long before Jo's own time. One of the drawings depicted a worn mountain peak in the background. At no time in Jo's youth had she ever visited such a place, though of course, it might have just been a whim in the mind of the artist.

But the similarities were undeniable, and Jo was struggling to repress the buoyant feeling of hope rising in her chest. The possibility existed that these sketches might lead to an answer she'd been pursuing all her life.

"But you don't think they're pictures of you?"

Jo shook her head. "No, I'm certain they're not."

Grace paged through the drawings, looking at each one. "And these were sent by whom?"

"A physician named Dermot McKendry," she replied. "He writes that he's the director of the Abbey, a licensed private asylum near Aberdeen. His letter refers to an elder gentleman under his care. The man doesn't speak, nor does he acknowledge anyone around him. He simply spends his waking hours rendering likenesses such as these."

"Of other people as well?"

"No. His mind is apparently fixed on this particular woman."

Grace laid the pictures aside and leaned toward Jo to adjust the soft blanket framing the baby's face. "Did Dr. McKendry mention the name of his patient?"

"No, he didn't."

Jo's nerves were getting the better of her. Grace, well aware of her friend's need to move when she was troubled or thinking, took her daughter back. Jo immediately rose to her feet.

"But what made this doctor think that these were likeness of you, aside from the obvious resemblance? Do you know him?"

"I don't believe so. But even though he doesn't explain in his letter, we've had many women who've come through Baronsford, staying at the Tower House until they were able to find employment. Many came from the Highlands and returned there. Any number of them could have found a position at the Abbey."

Jo began pacing across the brightly lit library. Aberdeen. Thirty-seven years ago, her own mother had been in the company of cotters who'd been cleared off the land in the Highlands and were passing through. Perhaps she was from the area. Perhaps Jo's origins lay in Aberdeen. After crossing back to Grace, she picked up one of the sketches.

"You're hoping that the young woman in these drawings is your mother," her friend said.

There were no secrets between them. Grace was one of the only people that she had ever opened her heart to. Regardless of the years that had passed and all the philanthropic projects Jo had used to give her life purpose, the mystery of her birth was as painful today as it was when she first recognized the ramifications of her dubious origins.

"Write back to the doctor," Grace suggested. "Ask for more details. Perhaps he'll reveal the name of this patient."

Jo shook her head. She'd tried to learn more about her mother before and had run up against blank walls. This was the first potential clue ever, regarding the woman who gave birth to her. Perhaps these drawings would lead her to a family connection. No, she couldn't leave it to chance. She couldn't allow Dr. McKendry's patient to slip away.

"I need to go there. I want to meet this elder gentleman."

"But what do you know of Dr. McKendry?" Grace asked. "Or this asylum, the Abbey?"

"Nothing. And I do understand that I'm building a castle of hope on a foundation of sand. Still, I can't waste this chance. I'll not err on the side of caution. Not this time."

No woman Jo had ever met had lived through more dangers than her sister-in-law. No one in her acquaintance was more courageous than the young mother seated before her. Grace had seen the bloody battlefields of France and Spain, and endured a sea crossing between Antwerp and Baronsford trapped in a wooden crate. She was a survivor. Jo prayed that her friend would see this for what it was, a simple journey to the Highlands.

"You know your brother," Grace said doubtfully. "Hugh will insist that you delay such a trip until he knows everything there is to know about Dr. McKendry, the Abbey, and his patients."

She was correct. Hugh would try to stop her. Jo loved

her brother, respected him. And in his view of life, knowledge was always empowering. As Lord Justice of the Commissary Court in Edinburgh, he never acted impulsively. Add to that the protectiveness he felt for her, and she knew he would make this trip impossible.

Jo recognized she'd created a dilemma for her friend by telling Grace her intentions. She didn't want to drive a wedge into the bond of trust between husband and wife.

In Sutherland, a few days' ride north of Aberdeen, their younger brother and his wife were expecting their first child. Jo had planned to go and help them. She'd simply stop in at this asylum en route.

"Hugh knows I'm going north to see Gregory and Freya at Torrishbrae," she said, taking a seat beside Grace. "I'm leaving a bit earlier, and I'll be perfectly safe. I'll be traveling with a maid and a driver and a footman."

"You promised Phoebe that you'd wait until she arrives from Hertfordshire before traveling north. She's planning on coming with you."

"My sister is unreliable when it comes to her plans. Any day now I expect a letter from her containing a long list of excuses of why she is delayed. She might not get here until that babe is walking."

With secret dreams of being a writer, Phoebe lived in a world of her own. The realities of ordered schedules and family obligations held little importance.

"Aberdeen is on the way to Sutherland," Jo said. "My stop at the Abbey will be brief."

"I still think you should tell Hugh about the letter and the sketches," Grace insisted. "And your intended visit to this asylum."

"You can tell him," Jo told her. "But wait until I am already on the road."

$\ast$ 4 $\ast$

With each Thursday market, the sleepy Highland village of Rayneford came alive, drawing cotters and tradesmen and vendors from the entire region. The market was especially busy this time of year, with the agents of coastal merchants crisscrossing the Highlands to buy newly shorn wool.

So when the Squire mentioned he'd seen Cuffe traipsing across the fields toward the village, Wynne told himself that he shouldn't have been surprised. Market day certainly offered more to interest a boy than Cameron's lessons and his long columns of sums.

Still, as he rode toward the village, he reminded himself that he had a responsibility to keep his son on the right path. But doing it was becoming more difficult all the time.

Nearly two months had passed since Cuffe's arrival, and a single week didn't pass now without some complaint about him from Hamish or Cameron. The lad was becoming quite proficient at dodging his lessons. He simply didn't show up, disappearing during the hours designated for instruction. It was the same for his time with the vicar.

Whatever admiration Wynne once had for his spirited nature, that feeling had gradually dwindled to discontent and annoyance. But whatever complaints the others voiced, they paled in comparison with his own disappointment regarding their father-and-son relationship. Or rather, their lack of it.

Wynne continued to be a blank space in his son's world. Cuffe didn't speak to him—not to complain or to engage in the most mundane conversation. He could draw no response of any kind from him—no reaction to praise or to discipline, no acknowledgment whatsoever that he even existed. The ten-year-old ignored him entirely, and that was more irritating than he would ever have imagined.

A cart approached from the direction of the village, the piles of wool fleece it had delivered to the market replaced by supplies for the Abbey's kitchen. Wynne exchanged a few words of greeting with the driver and his young helper. The lad was about the same age as Cuffe.

Seeing the boy opened another door of worry. Since arriving from Jamaica, his son had made no friends at all, as far as he could tell.

Cuffe's mother Fiba was of African descent, and Wynne had made certain everyone knew the lad was his son and heir. This hadn't helped him make friends with the younger farm hands, to be sure. He fully intended him to grow up as a gentleman, and his name and wealth made Cuffe the superior of anyone his own age within miles of the Abbey.

To remedy this, the vicar had made numerous

attempts to introduce him to other boys of his rank in the area. Cuffe hadn't shown up.

He was a loner, an outsider, an elusive spirit who preferred to retreat rather than try to accept his new role in this society.

As Wynne rode along the river toward the stone bridge leading into the village, he realized he was not only thinking of Cuffe. Two people matched that 'loner' description. His son was one and Jo Pennington was the other.

Her letter to Dermot had arrived yesterday. Jo was expected to reach the Abbey tomorrow or the next day.

Wynne tried to turn his mind to the hills, to the lowering grey sky, to the passing folk who demonstrated the liveliness of fairgoers. But it wasn't working. She was on his mind.

He owed her, even after all this time. If a connection existed between Jo and Charles Barton, she had the right to know. He wanted her to know.

Dermot had been excited about Wynne's suggestion of sending off the drawings. It could be of immense help to his patient if Lady Josephine were indeed the woman depicted in them. And he'd asked no questions when Wynne told him it was necessary that he remain anonymous and even absent himself during her visit. Each man respected the judgment and privacy of the other. While she was here, he would go to Dundee.

The patient had showed no further improvement. The elderly gentleman still could not care for himself. Barton had yet to speak a word or show an understanding of anything being said to him. Nonetheless, day after day, as long as he was in possession of pencil and paper, he drew. And the sketches were all the same. They were a depiction of Jo Pennington or someone who looked eerily similar to her.

When Wynne first saw Barton's drawings, years had folded in on themselves like a paper troublewit puzzle, forming and reforming memories in the blink of a moment. Even though he'd spent the years after their broken engagement sailing the seas and fighting the French and the Americans, he still knew a great deal about Jo and the life she'd led. She never married, instead, devoting her time to a number of benevolent causes, even starting a facility that housed destitute women and their children.

Wynne's older brother and his wife had purchased an estate in the Borders, only a short distance from Baronsford. The Penningtons were frequently mentioned in his sister-in-law's letters.

He didn't know the nature of Charles Barton's relationship with Jo. Friend, lover, fellow philanthropist? Of course, the possibility existed that Wynne was seeing something that wasn't there at all. Perhaps the woman in the drawings wasn't even Jo. Still, vividly recalling the agony caused by the mystery of her origins, he had no choice but to give her the opportunity to pursue this if she chose. Obligation weighed on him, and informing Jo about Barton might lift the burden he'd been carrying.

As Wynne crossed the bridge, shouts of vendors hawking their wares reached him from the open area around the market cross, and some pipers were striking up a fanciful Highland tune. Deciding to search out Cuffe on foot, he dismounted and left his horse with a tanner's boy by the edge of the river and started into the village, passing a pair of housewives sitting out on stools in front of an open door. The smell of sweet oat bread and honey cakes hung in the air.

Rayneford and the Abbey wouldn't be places to hold much interest for someone of Jo Pennington's station. He assumed she'd spend no more than a day, see Barton, and then move on. He'd already spoken to Dermot's aunt about looking after Cuffe while he was away, but he hadn't yet mentioned it to his son. As if his presence or absence would make any difference at all.

The Squire's wife was one of the only people at the Abbey his son had not alienated, and Cuffe spoke to her with the note of deference she was entitled to. Mrs. McKendry, small and round and maternal by nature, was close in age to the lad's Jamaican grandmother, and Wynne wondered if some similarity between the two women had struck a chord in Cuffe.

Looking past an old man carrying a large basket with a score of heather-brush brooms, Wynne spotted his son crouched in front of an abandoned cottage. Beyond him, a row of fishmongers had planks laid out with large salmon on display. Cuffe had four brown trout lined up on a coarse bag on the ground.

A stab of annoyance immediately gave way to worry. Fishing was not against the law, but if he had success at this endeavor, what was to stop him from trapping pheasant or duck or brown hare to sell next? He could easily find himself in trouble if someone didn't know he'd gotten the game from Abbey grounds. The assumption might be made that he'd poached them, and the difference in his skin color from the pale and ruddy faces of the native Highlanders wouldn't help him.

Any remaining confidence Wynne had in the lad's ability to stay out of trouble and to adjust to this new life slipped away. There was nothing he hadn't provided. Food, shelter, education, and a great deal of freedom to do as he wished. Last week, he'd selected the best horse in the stables for Cuffe when he appeared to show an interest in riding. His son wanted for nothing, and yet here he was, selling fish at a market.

A woman approached Cuffe with three little ones clinging to her skirts. She glanced over at the line of fishermen and exchanged a few words with the boy. *Taking pity on him*, Wynne thought. One of the brown trout went into the basket she was carrying, but before the coin could change hands, Wynne intervened. Snatching the money, he gave it back to her.

"The lad is not selling them," he said sharply. "They're free. In fact, you can take the rest too, if you can use them."

Cuffe's expression hardened, but he said nothing, refusing to acknowledge Wynne's presence.

"See here. I don't know what business it is o' yers. This wee fellow has every right to earn his . . ." She stopped abruptly when she looked into Wynne's face.

Wisely, she said nothing more, but sent Cuffe a look of commiseration. Gathering up the remainder of the trout, she quickly scurried off in the direction of the market cross with her children in her wake.

Wynne believed he was a reasonable man. As a captain in the navy, he'd prided himself on issuing rational commands even in the midst of the strongest gale or the fiercest battle. Noncompliance wasn't an option. He expected others to carry out his orders, whether it was on board his ship before, or at the Abbey now. He didn't know how he'd managed to let slip all the rules he lived by in dealing with his son.

"We need to talk. Come with me."

The words had not left his mouth when Cuffe started walking away from him.

Wynne caught hold of his arm. "Don't make this worse."

The ten-year-old was strong and quick. Tearing his arm free, he started to run, but Wynne reached out and caught him again, this time grabbing the shoulder of his jacket.

"I'm giving you the opportunity of addressing this with me in private," he warned. "You and I need to talk about what you've done. And you'll tell me—using your words—why you felt the need to sell those fish. What is it that you don't have?"

Wynne might as well have been talking to those trout. Cuffe's sole interest was to pull himself free. They were beginning to draw the attention of others, so he took a firm hold of his son's arm and started toward the tanner's, where he'd left his horse.

"I know what you're doing," he said as they walked. "You're trying to make money for your escape. You think you can buy your passage back to Jamaica."

A brief pause in the struggle was a sign that he'd hit the mark, though Wynne didn't need any confirmation. He already knew. He wasn't about to stand by and see the boy getting battered week after week and not learn the reason. A few questions of the right people, some help from Hamish, and a clear pattern emerged.

"Every fight you've been in since you arrived has been over money. Last month, you let the pigs into the kitchen gardens because those farm lads had made a wager with you to do it. Afterwards, they reneged, so you fought them. Am I right?"

His son stopped, and Wynne knew he was right.

"Listen to me. Regardless of how much money you lay your hands on, you can't go back. Your home is here. Your place is with your only living parent . . . me."

The boy tore his arm free, but didn't try to run.

"Talk to me," Wynne ordered.

Cuffe backed away suddenly, stumbling into the road just as a carriage came out of the village.

The two lead horses in the team reared up as the driver reined them in sharply. The confused sound of horses and shouts mingled with the scream of a woman nearby as Cuffe fell backwards. Wynne sprang after him, grabbing his jacket and hauling him to safety as the horses plunged forward, carrying the carriage past them before stopping.

A woman was peering back at them with concern through the small window at the rear of the carriage. Her dark eyes met his with recognition. Wynne felt a kick deep in his gut. They were face-to-face.

Jo Pennington had arrived a day early.

Their time together had lasted only a few months. Her family believed Jo's suffering had subsided after a short while, but it never had.

After the duel, regret over the loss of Wynne's affections cast an impenetrable cloud over the remaining days of her youth. Occasional suitors presented themselves, but she allowed none of them within the circle of her affection or trust. No one she met could compare with the young naval officer as he remained in her memory.

. . .

Another ball, another stroll through the gauntlet of hushed whispers and embroidered tales. Another round of introductions to shallow young men and their hollow, well-rehearsed charm. Would-be suitors who didn't see her at all, but were well acquainted with her name and her dowry.

Jo was quickly growing tired of the charade. She was exhausted by the gossip of the ton.

Shame. Disgrace. Indignity. That was what they whispered. She didn't belong here.

They pursued her to the refreshment table; she was certain of it. But when she heard the tasteless reference to her family and the titters, she'd had enough. She had to escape.

Slipping through the crowd, she saw the open doors and made her way onto the dark balcony and the refuge it offered.

The façade of composure she'd been maintaining since the start of the young Season cracked and fell away. Tears coursed down her cheeks. She was shaking with anger and unhappiness and frustration. Her parents had warned her, and they were right. Her presentation at Court and her coming out had been a mistake.

Wallowing in misery, she heard a man's deep voice behind her. "Which hand?"

She'd assumed she was alone. Panic and embarrassment overwhelmed her as she tried to wipe away the tears.

"Pray, tell me which hand."

He was persistent. The balcony was dark. She turned and saw the tall naval officer standing near the trellis. His face lay in shadow, and he was holding out his closed fists.

"Have we been introduced?"

"No, Lady Josephine, we haven't. But you can still tell me which hand."

He was playing a game and she went along. "The right."

He turned his hand over and opened it. Empty.

Jo glanced toward the doors to the ballroom. "I really must be getting back."

"Which hand?" he asked again. His left hand was still extended.

"The left," she said, trying to finish this foolishness.

He opened the hand. It was empty.

"I realize you're teasing me, sir, but I'm not in any mood for it. I need to return to my friends."

"I'll give you one more chance. Which hand?" he asked, holding out only his right hand again.

He was not giving up.

"The right one," Jo said, smiling despite herself. "And this is my final answer."

His fist slowly turned over and opened. A delicate red rose bud lay in his palm. "For you."

Later that night, Jo and Lieutenant Wynne Melfort were officially introduced.

He was Captain Melfort now. Secretly, she'd followed his advancement and accomplishments in the ensuing years, combing through the war news for every mention of him.

As Jo stared out the rear window of the carriage at the man and boy standing on the edge of the lane, a thousand feelings rushed through her, but she clung to one. As painful as their separation was, time had softened much of her sorrows.

Tall and confident as ever in his stance and gaze, Wynne showed no trace of aging. He looked just as she still saw him in her dreams. The years had been kind to him. If anything, he had grown even more handsome.

Her eyes met his, and she nodded her head. He bowed but did not approach.

A blur of voices and market sounds filled the carriage, but none of them penetrated her thoughts. Then, the surprise of the incident gave way to panic. The urge to run, to escape from him, propelled her thoughts and actions.

"Have the driver walk on," she whispered to Anna, her maidservant.

She forced herself to take a breath, then the next and the next. Her heart was drumming in her chest, and any sense of composure was slow to attain. She willed herself to be calm; clear thinking was a necessity right now.

They'd finally met again. And the worst was over. What once existed between them was over. It was over, Jo kept repeating to herself. It was over.

"Did you know him, m'lady?" Anna asked. "A braw, handsome gentleman, to be sure."

At the time of Jo's engagement, the maidservant had been working at Baronsford. She guessed if Anna knew Captain Melfort at all, it was only by name.

"Perhaps. He looked familiar," Jo replied vaguely. "But you were saying you have cousins who live somewhere near Aberdeen."

As Anna rattled on, Jo considered what had just occurred. According to directions they received in Rayneford, they were very close to the Abbey. And Wynne was in the village. Perhaps he had a connection with the hospital. That would explain how Dr. McKendry identified her from the patient's sketches.

The vagueness of the letter she received now made sense. She wouldn't have come if she knew Wynne had anything to do with this.

She could still go back. Turn the carriage around and continue the trip north to see Gregory and Freya. But the

Abbey was real. She'd known that before she left the Borders. Her sister-in-law Grace wouldn't allow Jo to leave until she'd made inquiries in Edinburgh with the help of one of Hugh's law clerks. They'd learned Dr. McKendry had established the asylum as a reputable facility in only two years of operation. Whether her brother was aware of the actions of Grace or not, Jo didn't know, but she'd left Baronsford assured that she wasn't walking into some ruse or fraudulent situation.

The patient and the likenesses to Jo in the sketches had to be real too. There was nothing to gain, no purpose to be had, no advantage that she could think of that would prompt someone like Dr. McKendry to formulate such an elaborate deception.

Jo reminded herself of the reason for coming here. Her mother.

"M'lady, that must be the Abbey," Anna said, motioning out the window to the building rising in the distance above the fields.

She wasn't going back, Jo decided. And when it came to Captain Melfort, the most difficult part was behind her.

At least, this was what she needed to make herself believe.

WYNNE WASN'T ABOUT to go to Dundee. He wouldn't go as far as the village until he was certain Cuffe understood the potential consequences of his behavior. Safety and discipline had to take priority right now.

Selling fish to make a little money wasn't what was pushing Wynne to the edge. Nor was it his son's refusal to acknowledge or speak to him. Wynne was angry because Cuffe backed directly into the path of the carriage. He could have been trampled beneath the hooves of those horses. He could have been killed.

Words like *careless*, *irresponsible*, *selfish* spilled out of Wynne all the way back to the Abbey.

"You'll remain in this room and think over what you've done until I decide your punishment. There is a penalty for willful stupidity."

No word of complaint came from Cuffe. Still wearing his muddy boots and clothing, he threw himself on the bed, tucking his hands behind his head and staring morosely at the ceiling.

Wynne went out and shut the door with more force than he intended. He was very close to losing what little restraint he had left. Punishment. Consequences. He'd never imagined how frustrating it could be making a headstrong ten-year-old listen to reason and act in an acceptable manner.

His old life offered little insight as to how to proceed. Admittedly, halfway back to the Abbey, he'd momentarily entertained the notion of signing his son onto the crew of a warship. Many wayward boys became men of value on the high seas. But he dismissed the thought. He couldn't do it. The realities of such a life were harsh, but they were especially hard for someone of mixed race.

Wynne simply didn't know how to proceed.

Maybe he'd made a mistake plucking the boy from the place he'd grown up and trying to resettle him in a life so entirely foreign to him. Maybe he should have increased the grandmother's allowance, insist that she move down from the mountains to a house in the Jamaican port of Falmouth. If he'd made these arrangements, perhaps she could have kept Cuffe close and out of trouble.

Wynne ran a hand through his hair, frustration weighing on him. Whatever was required of him as a father, he was failing at it. During the first eight years of Cuffe's life, he'd had the excuse of being away at sea. During the past two years, he'd shrugged off his responsibility, telling himself he was building a future for the two of them here in the Highlands. His son was here now, and Wynne had no more excuses.

As a child, Cuffe was safe growing up with his grandmother, who still lived in the Maroon village of Accompong. Protected by its isolation and the rugged Cockpit Country above Falmouth, he'd been away from the outbreaks of violence that broke out between the Maroons and the sugar plantation owners. The evils of slaveholding still haunted the islands, and peace was tenuous, at best. But the number of clashes was on the rise.

Cuffe's grandmother confirmed the reports in her letters to Wynne. She feared that the growing boy was being drawn into the increasingly volatile situation. Open conflict on a large scale seemed imminent, and she couldn't hope to keep Cuffe out of it.

Wynne agreed. He admired the Maroons and their fight, but he didn't want his son involved. There had been no other viable option but to bring him here.

"Excellent!" Dermot's voice from down the hall drew Wynne out of his thoughts. "You didn't go to Dundee after all."

The suite of rooms he and Cuffe occupied while his tower house, Knockburn Hall, was being renovated, was on the same floor as their offices.

"Do you have an hour to spare? I need your help."

Before joining the doctor, Wynne frowned one last time at the closed door. No point in locking it. No doubt Cuffe could go out a window and climb down the side of the building if he chose to leave. Punishment. He still didn't know what to do to get his son's attention.

"Lady Josephine Pennington has arrived," Dermot told him as Wynne drew near. "You were right to contact her. She's the spirit and image of Barton's sketches."

He already knew she was here, but her arrival—and whatever sentiment it evoked in him—was secondary to the problem he was facing with Cuffe.

"She asked about you," Dermot told him. "She wanted to know the nature of your connection with the Abbey."

"You told her, I assume."

"I couldn't very well lie. I told her that you were the hospital's governor," Dermot replied. "I hope that causes no trouble for you."

"It's fine," he said, resigned to the situation. Knowing he was here, Jo would assuredly not be lingering for any length of time.

"Good, because I need your help."

Wynne glanced back down the hallway toward his rooms. He needed to deal with his son, but that could wait for a bit.

"Barton was awake drawing for much of the night and was sleeping when she arrived," Dermot told him. "So I brought her over to the east wing. She's taking refreshments with my aunt and uncle right now."

Wynne imagined Mrs. McKendry and the Squire would be pleased to be entertaining such company. People of distinction rarely visited the Abbey.

The doctor paused by the door to his office. "But to complicate matters somewhat, I received a note this morning from Mrs. Barton. She and Graham are visiting our patient today."

Graham Barton had made more of an impression on Wynne than the mother. The surly uncle of Charles Barton had been running the estate at Tilmory Castle for many years, and was clearly accustomed to making the important decisions.

"And they're coming today?"

"They're waiting downstairs while my attendants rouse Barton and prepare him to receive his visitors."

"Have the Bartons and Lady Jo met?" Wynne asked, entertaining the idea that maybe the families were acquainted.

"I thought I'd wait on that. I'd like them to meet in

the ward itself, at Barton's bedside," the doctor told him. "The experience of unexpectedly seeing them all at once might shock him and possibly create a positive reaction in him. I was reading a paper about it that Dr. Ellis, down in West Yorkshire, wrote regarding . . ."

As Dermot shared the details of the study, Wynne tried to imagine the Bartons' reaction to the patient's improvement. The last time the family had seen him was the day they brought him to the Abbey. They thought his death was imminent.

"Even if the meeting produces nothing," Dermot concluded, "I don't want to miss the opportunity."

Several arguments came to mind opposing the doctor's enthusiasm, the most logical one being that Jo and the Bartons knew each other. Such knowledge of one another might also explain why the two parties arrived at the Abbey on the same day. But Wynne remained silent on that score, not caring to cast a wet blanket on his friend's optimism.

"I'll accompany Charles's family to the ward. But I need you, my friend, to go to the east wing, drag Lady Josephine from the clutches of my aunt and uncle, and escort her to the patient's bedside."

His immediate inclination to protest died before he voiced it. There could be no avoiding Jo. They'd seen each other. She'd asked about him. And she'd decided to stay and see the patient instead of leaving. Wynne already knew he'd regret it if she left and they hadn't exchanged at least a few words.

Their shared history was dead and buried, he told himself. He no longer carried in his heart the affection, or the feeling of protectiveness, that he once had. What remained now was accepting this opportunity to satisfy his curiosity about her character. He wanted to know how much Jo Pennington had changed, if at all.

***

The Squire and Mrs. McKendry glowed more like proud parents than uncle and aunt. Their enthusiasm for the hospital and its director illuminated every word that came from their mouths. And they were quite fond of Captain Melfort as well.

Seated at a table in an antiquated, oak-paneled drawing room, Jo sipped tea and listened to stories involving Wynne and Dr. McKendry during their days in the navy. The tales went far beyond the reports and accolades she'd read about in the newspapers in the early days.

The conversation turned from the past to the hospital and the estate.

"The Abbey would have gone to ruin if it weren't for their partnership," the Squire asserted, spooning sweet apple butter onto another thick slice of warm oat bread. "With the exception of King George's construction of the north annex to house his army during the Rising, no work was done on this place since my grandsire's day."

From the little she'd seen of the massive structure, it appeared that a great deal of renovation was currently in progress.

"Our Dermot always knew what he wanted to do with the Abbey—that is, making it into a fine hospital—once his father was gone," Mrs. McKendry said. "But he could never have done so well without the captain."

"So right, darling," her husband agreed. "It was a blessing they both decided at the same time that they were done with their traveling the world."

"True." The Squire's wife nodded, pouring more tea for Jo. "And the captain . . . well, he needed to find a suitable home for Cuffe."

"Cuffe?" Jo asked.

"His son," Mrs. McKendry replied, sending a quick glance at her husband.

His son. A pang of disappointment slid into her heart like a needle. She placed her cup and saucer gently on the table. Of course, he'd be married, she scolded herself. Time had taken her youthful bloom and left her a spinster. But not so for him. The passing years had not only improved his looks, they'd given him the opportunity to fill the pages of his life with happiness.

"The lad's mother—" the Squire started.

"He married her," his wife interrupted. "Cuffe is the captain's son and heir."

Jo's mind returned to the incident, little more than an hour ago, when her carriage had to make a sudden stop on the lane leading out of the village. A young dark-skinned boy was standing beside Wynne, and she wondered now if this was the son they spoke of.

"The lad's mother died giving birth in the Indies," Mrs. McKendry confided in a low voice. "Cuffe was raised by his Jamaican grandmother until just two months ago, with the captain paying for everything. She must have saved enough money, because suddenly she didn't know how to control him any longer."

Perhaps it was because gossip had been the bane of her own existence, Jo bristled instinctively. She had no right to be hearing this. She was no more than a stranger to these people.

"The lad must get his wildness from his mother, for Captain Melfort is the most disciplined of gentlemen."

"How old did you say Cuffe was?" Jo asked, interrupting her host.

"Ten years old."

"Before we lay blame on a mother who is no longer here to defend herself, or a grandmother who has raised him from infancy, I should say that wildness in a lad his age is fairly common. We needn't attribute it to the nature of a parent, especially one none of us have met," Jo asserted firmly. "You said Cuffe has only been here for a mere two months. Now imagine how anyone would struggle to adjust to completely new social expectations. And he's so young. Everything he knew, all of his previous routines, replaced by customs and courtesies that we see as natural, but are actually only natural *to us*."

Jo was ready to continue, to challenge the couple to take back not only their words, but to acknowledge the prejudices they were harboring against the child. But her hosts were looking past her at the doorway.

"Captain, join us," the Squire said, standing. "Allow me to introduce our guest."

❧ 6 ☙

THE TIMIDITY that he had known in Jo's character was gone. In its place, Wynne saw a lioness ready to pounce in defense of his son.

The notion warmed his heart. With the exception of Dermot, Cuffe had very few champions at the Abbey. Many of the farm folk ignored the lad. Others tolerated him politely out of deference to Wynne . . . at least in his presence. And there were some, like the Squire and his wife and the vicar—genuinely good-hearted people—who had the best of intentions but managed to say the wrong things at the wrong time.

A faint blush colored Jo's cheek as she stood and turned to him. She'd changed. He had always thought her very pretty, but she now had a handsomeness about her that took him aback. The perfect symmetry of her high cheekbones, the confident set of her mouth, the soft curves of her hips and breast. She was a flower that had bloomed, but had retained in maturity the best qualities of youth.

Wynne gazed into her grave, brown eyes. Beneath the well-defined eyebrows and the long lashes, the shadows of sadness still dwelt there.

As the Squire started to make the introductions, Jo spoke.

"Captain Melfort and I are acquainted."

Curious looks passed between the husband and wife as bow and curtsy were exchanged, but they asked no questions. No explanations were offered either.

"Take some tea with us, Captain?" Mrs. McKendry asked.

"I am afraid I can't, ma'am. I'm here to steal your guest away and escort her to the ward. The doctor believes his patient might be ready to accept visitors." He turned his attention back to their guest. "That is, if Lady Jo is ready."

"Yes, I am. Absolutely," she said in a rush before thanking her hosts for their hospitality.

Wynne waited by the door, listening to the lilt of her voice, watching her movements, and feeling the years drop away.

Their parting was back. He owed her an apology. Whatever words he wrote to her were meaningless because he'd never had the chance to explain himself more fully. But she wasn't at home, and his cowardice made him leave the hastily written letter.

The duel with her brother the next morning had ended any chance of them meeting until today.

Wynne thought the years had dulled the sharp edge of their past, but he was wrong.

" . . . and our invitation stands, m'lady," Mrs. McKendry was saying. "If you decide to stay the night, or a fortnight, or as long as you desire, you're welcome here.

We have any number of rooms in the Abbey that we keep in readiness for the families of the patients when they visit."

"That is very kind of you, but my brother Gregory and his wife are expecting me at Torrishbrae in Sutherland. I was hoping to be back on the road by mid-afternoon."

Gregory married, Wynne thought. The last time he'd seen Jo's younger brother, he was only slightly older than Cuffe.

Jo avoided meeting his gaze as she approached, and Wynne recalled a time when she'd rush across a room to take his hand and demand to know what he was thinking.

As they maneuvered through the corridors out of the east wing and into the old great hall, he broke the silence lying heavily between them.

"I need to apologize for inadvertently eavesdropping," he said. "I entered the drawing room a moment before my presence was noted. I was impressed by your knowledge of children's manners and behavior, and your sense of conviction in voicing your views."

She glanced back over her shoulder. "I'm afraid I've developed a failing in being too abrupt on this topic. My tone was a little strident for the occasion, I believe."

"Don't worry about them. The Squire and his wife are not ones to carry a grudge," he told her. "They are kind-hearted people. Truly. At the same time, they're unfamiliar with how to deal with anyone, adult or a child, who looks different or behaves differently from people they're accustomed to. Unlike your own broad-minded family, they lead a provincial life here in the Highlands. I'm quite sure Cuffe is the first person of African descent that they've ever met."

Wynne's gaze was drawn to her face as she tucked a

strand of loose hair behind an ear. The blush rose again into her cheek, and he wondered if the mention of her family was the cause of it.

"I heard your son is only ten years old," she said, stepping past him as he paused in a doorway to allow her through. "With enough time and patience—and the right amount of encouragement—I'm certain he'll come to embrace his new home."

"One would hope." Wynne wasn't about to rail at her about the impracticality of idealism. Her words made the situation sound far simpler to resolve than the reality. They'd nearly reached the north annex. "But have you ever been in the position of dealing with a child in such circumstances? Or been exposed to the difficulties that can present themselves?"

"I have. But I grant you, not in the role of a parent. However, I've been involved with many horrific family situations, and I've provided whatever was needed to help."

Seeing the footman standing by to let them into the ward, Wynne motioned for him to wait.

"Where was that?"

"At a shelter we refer to as the Tower House, near Baronsford."

"Was there ever a child wholly under your care?" he asked.

"Never wholly. The residents share in the responsibilities. It's part of the mission of the place. But I imagine you too must have the help of tutors and any number of people to help you with your son."

The argument simmering within him had no rhyme or reason other than Wynne wanted to believe that he'd done everything he could possibly do. He'd been patient, persistent, generous, and still there was a boy upstairs who'd cut through all of his confidence and made him feel like a failure.

"I'm sure raising and educating a son who must already think himself a man is not easy. Children can be complicated creatures," she said gently. "I've come to believe that no two are the same. But as long as you're willing, and you value your son as the treasure that I'm certain he is, the path will reveal itself."

The kindness and compassion, the calm temperament, the reasonable approach. She could always change the darkness to light and chase away any rain cloud. Her voice warmed him even now with its quiet assurance. During the time they had been betrothed, they never argued. Jo knew his moods, recognized his moments of sadness, read his thoughts when he was troubled.

"Shall we go in?" she asked.

Wynne trailed after her, realizing that already the weight of dealing with Cuffe's behavior was lessening. He didn't need to decide on one ultimate punishment. There was no one solution to fix what was wrong. He shouldn't second-guess the decisions that were made in the past. Today was simply another day amid many more days of challenge.

The ward was busy, with most of the patients having returned from activities that took them and the attendants outside. While a few sat by windows, staring out idly, most were joined in a number of social pastimes, with games of chess and draughts and backgammon being played at tables.

Wynne watched Jo taking all of this in. When a patient named Fyffe—a harmless fellow from Nairn— waltzed around them as he played his imaginary fiddle, she smiled sweetly at him and waited until he'd danced away.

She showed no fear or awkwardness at all about the strangeness of the place.

He gestured across the room.

"That's Charles Barton in the bed," he told her quietly. "The two older people across from Dr. McKendry are his mother and his uncle, his only living family. They live at Tilmory Castle, not four miles from here."

Jo looked across. "I don't recognize any of them."

Dermot paused in what he was saying when he saw them.

As Jo and Wynne started across the ward, the relatives standing at the patient's bedside looked at them.

For a moment he thought they'd turned into pillars of salt. Like Lot's wife, they stood like statues, gazing at Jo with expressions of shock. Slowly, Mrs. Barton's mouth opened, and a confused and horrified look came into her eyes. Graham shook his head, as if to shake off a vision that he could not account for. As if seeing a ghost that had suddenly appeared in broad daylight, the two stared in disbelief.

Then, Barton's uncle regained control of his features, the customary hardness returning to his face. But his mother was slower to recover her composure, weakly reaching out and clutching at the old man's hand as she sank down heavily onto a chair.

They knew her.

The seeds of hope cast upon her heart when Jo first saw the drawings at Baronsford sprouted and took root, sending up shoots and spreading tender green leaves. Mrs. Barton's bloodless face, the trembling fingers pressing a handkerchief to her lips, the hooded gaze constantly flitting from her son to Jo to the old man standing beside her, every movement indicated familiarity, recognition.

Jo forced herself to breathe. This woman sitting in an asylum deep in the Highlands, and the man standing rigidly beside her, held the key to the mystery of her past. The mere possibility that her lifelong pursuit of her mother's identity could end with a simple introduction to these people nearly overwhelmed her.

Excitement buoyed her as she neared the patient's bedside. The years of speculating where she'd come from, the never-ending mission of defending her late mother could all come to a close in the next moment.

"Lady Josephine Pennington, may I introduce Mrs. Barton and Graham Barton," Dr. McKendry said.

The courtesies were exchanged, but the young tendrils of hope and anticipation were immediately knocked askew by the old man's icy glare. Mrs. Barton's response was no warmer. A mask had descended over her pallid features. And after the introductions were complete, the woman shifted her gaze toward Charles, effectually shutting out everyone else.

A hard, tight knot of panic began to form in Jo's chest. Those seedlings of hope wilted, their growth arrested by the rough cold wind of the Bartons' response. A silent cry rose in her throat. She wanted them to look at her again, to give her some sign that they shared a tangible relation, a connection, something hard and fast and true. Instead, she was facing a wall of stony disregard. They'd hastily covered their involuntary moment of surprise and recognition with a cold veneer of indifference and hostility.

But Jo saw through them. She'd faced rejection her entire life.

"As I was saying before Lady Josephine and Captain Melfort joined us, this new development offers great promise," Dr. McKendry explained. "Since we reduced the dosage of laudanum, Mr. Barton has displayed a distinct desire to communicate with us, in his own way, through the sketches."

He reached behind him and fetched a portfolio from a nearby table, presenting it to the mother.

"This is all his work. Drawings of the same person. Someone who closely resembles Lady Josephine."

The doctor made a vague explanation of how, through a mutual acquaintance, he was able to identify Jo as the possible subject of the drawings before corresponding with her.

That mutual acquaintance he referred to stood beside Jo, his grey coat brushing against the sleeve of her dress. It was true they'd been alienated for years, but at this moment she felt no strangeness about Wynne's presence, stalwart and steadfast as the oldest of friends. And she welcomed his company. He, perhaps more than anyone, understood the significance of this connection. She had no doubt he was the reason Dr. McKendry reached out to her.

"Is it possible you've all met before?" the doctor suggested. "If you'll take a look at the drawings, you'll see the resemblance is astonishing."

Mrs. Barton opened the portfolio, paged carelessly through a few of the drawings, and closed it. Her face showed nothing as she glanced up at her brother-in-law.

Jo waited for an answer, too anxious to speak, still clinging to her fading hopes.

"Never have," Graham said, speaking for the two of them.

Jo could not gather herself enough to say anything; the knot in her throat precluded it. Their faces, when they saw her, conveyed a clear sense of recognition and then dismay. But why would they deny that now? They were holding back, hiding behind a façade of aloofness. There was some hidden history that these two were reluctant to address.

They knew her mother. Jo had no doubt of it.

Mrs. Barton handed the portfolio back to the doctor. "These drawings suggest no individual person. They could be anyone. They're images conjured by a delusional mind. I believe you've allowed a *very* slight resemblance to your friend Lady Josephine to influence your opinion." She pointed at her son. "It breaks my heart. But look at him, staring at nothing, completely disconnected from us and the world. You're wrong if you think he's improved, and I fail to see why you've involved her ladyship in a family tragedy where she has no business."

They were dismissing her. A light had flickered beneath the door to her past, but Jo had no power to push it open. The sketches were significant. They had to be. The doctor told her when she'd first arrived that Charles Barton was fifty-six years of age. Of the little Jo knew of her mother, she would have been fairly close to him in age.

Mrs. Barton's sudden change in demeanor, Graham's hostility, and Charles's sketches were enough evidence of some connection. But she couldn't find a way to challenge them. Their denials slammed the door on her, shutting her outside.

She'd come all this way for nothing. Old, familiar feelings of helplessness jabbed her like an iron fist in the gut. She felt ill, defeated in what had to be the last chance she'd ever have of reclaiming her identity, of knowing who she was. Tears burned her eyes and threatened to break free.

A pressure of a firm hand in the small of her back awakened Jo to her surroundings. Wynne was there with her, supporting her. She took a deep breath and raised her chin.

"Perhaps, Doctor, you're asking the wrong people about Lady Josephine's connection," Wynne said before addressing the family. "Mrs. Barton, you said your son spent many years away from Tilmory Castle before the accident."

The old woman reached over and adjusted the blanket on Charles's chest. "Unfortunately, we don't know of his acquaintances during that time."

"Lady Josephine, perhaps you can shed some light on this situation," Dr. McKendry suggested.

Jo had already told the doctor she didn't know the name, and she'd told Wynne she didn't recognize the patient nor his family. Nonetheless, feeling her chance slipping away, she moved to the bedside.

All other sounds in the ward faded. The people gathered around the bed disappeared. Jo looked down into the patient's lined face. His breathing was ragged, and he appeared to be wrestling with demons, battling unseen shadows. His eyes moved restlessly as he scanned the ceiling above, running from nightmares. She was convinced he had secrets to divulge—secrets involving her mother—but he couldn't find the clarity of mind to grasp or convey them.

The sketches were distinct representations of the

same person. Every image depicted the same woman at the same age. She was someone he knew, someone locked in his damaged mind, but she didn't know how to pry that memory free.

"Charles," she said gently, casting propriety aside. "Charles Barton."

The patient turned his face toward the sound of her voice. He blinked and his eyes focused on her.

"Charles," she said again.

A lifetime of insecurity and self-doubt surged like a spring flood rising against the fragile wall of an ancient dam. Fear and hope and loss churned within her, threatening to break through the seemingly paper-thin walls of her chest.

Know me, she prayed, closing her eyes. Speak to me.

Charles Barton's hand slipped into hers, and Jo's eyes flew open. Warmth emanated from their joined palms.

"You've come," he whispered.

❦ 7 ❦

You've come. No more, no less. Those were Charles Barton's only words before he closed his eyes and released Jo's hand.

It was enough.

Wynne knew what those words meant to Jo. He felt the impact of them. Barton knew her mother. He saw her mother in her.

What she had to be going through was clear to Wynne. The flowing tide of emotion within her had been evident to him from the moment they'd walked into the ward. The prospect of answers looked to be within reach. But when Barton drifted away again, he felt her fear that all of this was coming to nothing. The possibility of a lifeline had been cast out to her and then snatched away.

Wynne had thought she meant nothing to him. He'd told himself it was only duty that drove him to do the right thing and arrange for her to come to the Abbey.

But it wasn't true. He still cared for her.

The strange behavior of Barton's family had caught

him off guard and then angered him. Their lack of cooperation in Jo's pursuit of a possible connection had driven Wynne to the edge of his patience. Years evaporated like a morning mist, and he was ready to go to battle on her behalf once again.

That was the moment he realized he needed to leave the ward.

As much as he worried about the outcome of the ensuing discussion with the Bartons, Wynne knew Dermot was entirely capable of handling them. And he was certain Jo would do better without an angry, unsolicited champion meddling in her affairs.

Before returning to his office, he stopped and spoke to Cameron and then went down the hallway to the suite of rooms he shared with his son. Cuffe was still lying on his bed, and he didn't even turn his head when Wynne directed him to report to the bookkeeper. He was to spend the rest of the day and tomorrow and the next day with him. He was confined indoors. No riding, no fishing, no roaming free, no going out at all. Cameron would see that he caught up with his lessons and then would provide him with more.

And anytime Cuffe wanted to talk, Wynne told him, he would make himself available.

Settling into his orderly office, he turned his attention to his work. He'd done what he needed to do immediately with his son. Now he had to push away any thoughts of Jo Pennington. And he might have succeeded if it weren't for Dermot coming in not an hour later.

"The Bartons have gone," he announced.

The question of Jo's whereabouts arose in Wynne's mind. He wondered if she was downstairs with the patient, or if she'd continued her journey to her brother's without saying goodbye.

"After you left, we nearly went to war down there," Dermot said, taking a book off the shelf and glancing at the title before placing it on the corner of Wynne's desk. "The mother became adamant about taking Barton back to Tilmory Castle. She continued to claim—in spite of what we all witnessed—that there has been no change in her son's condition."

"I assume you won that battle and Barton is still with us," Wynne said.

"As a matter of fact, I did. Graham stepped up as the voice of reason. Said he's far too occupied with running that estate. He has no wish to be responsible for his nephew's care."

In matters of inheritance, rich estates like Tilmory Castle were often the focus of investigations and court hearings after the passing of a laird or landowner. Wynne knew from speaking to the vicar that, as it stood now, Graham was next in line to inherit.

"And Mrs. Barton agreed?"

"She had no choice." Dermot pulled another volume off the shelf and studied the spine. "For good or ill, Graham obviously wants no shadow cast on him. He wants to be seen as doing what's best. He convinced Mrs. Barton, saying perhaps more frequent visits to the Abbey would put her mind at ease and they should allow Charles to stay."

Again, Jo and her whereabouts pushed to the foreground of Wynne's thoughts. Growing impatient, he glared at his friend placing the book on the wrong shelf and reaching for yet another volume.

"And Lady Jo?" he asked as casually as he could.

"Yes. There's the matter of Lady Josephine," Dermot responded, turning his back to the bookshelves. "Mrs. Barton was quite distressed by the sight of her when you escorted her in. I know I wasn't alone in seeing it. You surely did too."

The older woman clearly knew Jo—or someone of similar appearance. Whether the link was familial or social, Mrs. Barton was a poor liar. Her reaction was too sudden and too pronounced. She would have collapsed to the ground if that chair hadn't been behind her. And even afterwards, it took her a great deal of time to regain her composure.

"I saw it."

Dermot pulled another book from the shelf. "And then when Barton said—"

"Where is Lady Jo now?"

The doctor glanced over. "I believe she went out to the stables to speak with her driver and manservant."

"Why? Is she leaving?"

"Leaving?" Dermot echoed vaguely, paging through the volume. "No. In fact, she asked if she could take us up on my aunt's invitation to spend the night here at the Abbey. Told me she'd be grateful if she could visit with Barton without the distraction of his family. And I think that is an excellent idea, considering how positively he responded to her voice. He spoke—for the first time—and minor as it might seem, to me it was a monumental step."

Jo was still here, and he felt a weight lift from his shoulders. After all this time, they'd met again. They'd spoken about Cuffe. Now he wanted another chance to see her. Perhaps they could both successfully close a door on the past.

"Why are you frowning like your ship just hit a sandbar? The recovery of our patients should make you happy." Dermot dropped the book on a chair. "Unless your sour look is attributable to the fact that Lady Josephine is staying. Do you disapprove of her spending the night at the Abbey?"

"Of course not. Why should I?" Wynne shot back. "This is your hospital. Barton is your patient. If you think her staying here will aid in his recovery, why ask me?"

Dermot put both hands on the desk. They'd known each other for too long. The grey eyes challenged him to tell the truth. "I can arrange to get a room for Lady Josephine at the inn down in the village."

"She should stay here," Wynne snapped. "At the Abbey. I have no objection whatsoever."

The younger man studied him for a moment longer before straightening up. When he went back to the bookcase, Wynne knew they were not done with this conversation.

"What is it, McKendry? Say what's on your mind. Say it before every book I own has been scattered hither and yon."

"Very well." Dermot ran his fingers along a shelf and glanced over his shoulder at him. "What was the nature of your relationship with Lady Josephine?"

He was breaking an unspoken rule that had existed between them for years. One did not ask about the past. Everything each man knew about the other had been offered, never solicited.

"Why do you ask?"

"Because I'm impressed by her."

Wynne stared at his friend's back. "What do you mean, 'impressed'? You only met her today. How much time did you spend in her company to form such an opinion?"

"Are you saying she is not impressive?"

"Of course she's impressive!" Wynne replied.

"So it's fine for *you* to think she's impressive," he said, reaching for another book, "but not for me to think it?"

"Dash it, Dermot," Wynne said, slamming his palm hard on his desk. "Leave my books alone."

The doctor faced him. "What was your connection with her? And why did you wish to remain anonymous when we wrote to her?"

Wynne didn't think all Highlanders were as mule-like as his hardheaded friend, but he was certain that Dermot wouldn't give up until he had an answer.

"If you *must* know, we were engaged sixteen years ago. I broke it off."

He'd said it. It was out. And now perhaps he could bring it up with Jo and say the things she should have heard back then.

"She must have been a mere lass," Dermot observed with a note of accusation.

Wynne glowered at the younger man. "Save your charming Highland tongue for her. Lady Jo and I are only a year apart in age."

Dermot abandoned his harassment of Wynne's collection of books and walked to the window, gazing out. "You look old enough to be her father."

"I wouldn't recommend standing in front of an open window if I were you."

Though he was trying to keep his voice flippant, annoyance edged under the surface of Wynne's skin.

"So you were afraid she wouldn't come if you wrote to her yourself," Dermot surmised.

"No. I didn't think she would."

"And you wanted her to come." It was not a question.

"I didn't care if she came or not," Wynne lied. "I thought it would be important to her. And to Barton."

"Any regrets?"

"Regrets about what?" Wynne asked. "About bringing her up here?"

"That . . . or about breaking off your engagement."

Dermot McKendry was his friend, a man he trusted more than his own brother. But he was pushing his luck.

Before answering, Wynne paused, asking himself why he was finding this conversation so irritating. It should make no difference to him what Dermot knew about Jo.

"Well? Any regrets?"

He stood and made his way around the desk. Seizing a misplaced volume, he slid it back into the bookcase where it belonged. "You are *not* a spiritual advisor. You, McKendry, are the lowest, deucedest, maggot pie of a sawbones that I ever had the misfortune to sail with."

"So you do have regrets."

"None!" Wynne thundered, slamming another book back into the case.

"And now that you two have met again," Dermot asked, undeterred, "any renewed interest in her?"

Composing himself, Wynne crossed his arms over his chest. He could see from his friend's expression that the scurvy bastard was enjoying this.

"None," Wynne retorted. A thought flashed into his brain. One he didn't want to consider. "Why are you asking? Do you plan to pursue her yourself?"

"I? Pursue Lady Josephine Pennington? Let's consider that for a moment," he replied as if it had never occurred to him. The doctor leaned against the frame of the open window.

As Wynne watched him closely, he felt coldness settle in the pit of his stomach. It was the same sensation he felt just before the grappling hooks shot out and secured an enemy vessel. It was the moment before leaping with his boarding crew across the gunwales into battle.

"She's quite attractive, even pretty in an unpretentious way." Dermot paused, as if taking stock of the rest of her attributes. "She's educated, connected, and compassionate. She's told me already that she appreciates the humane way we're approaching our work here. She's a benefactor of charitable causes. And she's rich enough to support more than a few."

Dermot, consumed with his plans for the Abbey, had never expressed any interest in marriage until now. Younger than Wynne by six years and handsome in a boyish way, he was certainly an eligible bachelor, now that he'd made his fortune and inherited the Abbey. But only a certain kind of woman would forego the comforts of a normal household to live in an asylum.

Wynne's hands fisted as he realized Jo might just be such a woman.

"What are you going to do, sweep her off her feet with your renowned wit and charm?" he asked, charging his tone with all the irony he could muster. "Lady Jo is only here for one night."

"Say what you will, my friend. I know her visit this time is brief, but I'm told many romances begin with a single glance. We can write to each other." He started toward the door. "Perhaps I'll invite her for another visit. I might even leave you here to see to things while I travel up north and visit with her while she's staying with her brother and sister-in-law."

Wynne used to like Dermot McKendry, but no more.

"But I want you to know I would never convey such intentions if I thought you had *any* objection to this," the scoundrel said, pausing on his way out the door. "What do you say, old man?"

Wynne was responsible for her coming to the Abbey. She'd arrived not looking for romance, nor for a husband, but to find a connection to her mother's past. These were reasons enough to tell Dermot to veer off. But he couldn't say the words.

"Do as you please," he said finally. "But remember to treat her with utmost deference. And by God, your intentions had better be honorable. Don't start down this path even one step unless you're willing to stand beside her at the church door. Understand me?"

"That's all I needed to hear." Dermot smiled and bowed before going out the door.

Wynne finished putting his books back where they belonged. Life should be as easy to keep in order, he thought. Cuffe. His plans for the two of them. He shook his head. Nothing ever went smoothly. And now he'd need to accept Jo in the fabric of his everyday life . . . while she was married to someone else.

His eyes were drawn to the open window. He should have pushed Dermot out while he had the chance.

❧   8   ❧

"You haven't mentioned a word about dinner, m'lady," Anna complained as she ran a brush through her mistress's hair. "Pray, was the company pleasant enough? Did they have many guests? I can't imagine these country folk entertain quite the way we do at Baronsford."

Jo smiled. After a lifetime in service, the maid's benign snobbery was due to her pride in the Pennington family. In Anna's world, the places she traveled with Jo were not necessarily deficient in hospitality or comfort, it was simply that nowhere could conceivably compare in her mind with Baronsford.

"The food was delicious and well-prepared, Anna," she told her. "And the company was quite pleasant. We were twelve in number, and although most were strangers to me, the conversations were lively and very interesting. Everyone was kind to me."

"Well, I should think they would be, m'lady," the maid huffed. "A wee place like this in the middle of nowhere? I should think they're thanking their stars to be having such fine company as you."

Jo laughed. "The Abbey is hardly a 'wee place.' It may not be as grand as Baronsford, but I think it's lovely. Don't you?"

Anna nodded grudgingly and continued her brushing. "Well, all things considered, I suppose it's good enough, m'lady."

At dinner, she sat between Dr. McKendry and the vicar of the village kirk, the younger brother of the Squire.

The two men and the Squire engaged in witty banter all through the meal, ridiculing each other's ability to hit a golf ball or deliver a sermon or fix a hangnail. Even as she listened to the men and to Mrs. McKendry's efforts to shush them, Jo often felt the weight of Captain Melfort's gaze upon her. At the far end of the table, he was speaking with Mr. Cameron, the Abbey's bookkeeper. Wynne's son, Cuffe, was not present at dinner, but from the snatches of conversation that she could hear, much of the talk between the two men pertained to the boy.

"You came back early," Anna remarked. "No social doings after dinner?"

"Mrs. McKendry and I were the only females present. As soon as we left the dining room, I made my excuses and retired," Jo explained. "We had a long day on the road, and I'd like to be up early tomorrow. The doctor told me Mr. Barton is generally at his most alert and active first thing in the morning."

She'd spent more than two hours this afternoon in the ward at the older man's bedside. She'd spoken to him. Held his hand. But there was no other communication with the exception of an occasional glance in her direction. It was as if he knew she was there and was comforted by it, but couldn't sort out whatever it was in his muddled mind.

The mystery of their connection perplexed her. Now that she'd met him and seen his initial reaction to her, she had no doubt the answers to her mother's past would be found here with this man and his family.

She intended to accept the McKendrys' hospitality for only one night, but she already knew it would be terribly difficult for her to walk away now. Even before going down to dinner, she'd been considering the possibility of taking a room at the village inn for a few more nights. She could easily come up to the Abbey each day and visit with the patient. She'd simply send a letter off to Gregory and Freya, explaining that she'd be delayed in arriving. With her family knowing her whereabouts and that she was safe, she could stay the extra time.

Wynne edged into her thoughts. Sailing men were supposed to grow wrinkled and old from the ocean's winds and the sun, but not him. His face was etched with the lines of responsibility, but his eyes were still bright and alert. Though he didn't smile easily, when he did, the room brightened. Dressed for dinner in his navy-blue coat and cream-colored silk waistcoat, he appeared taller, broader across the shoulders than she remembered. And he had a manner of holding himself, a confidence in the way he spoke, that reflected years of command.

She pushed his image from her mind, focusing instead on the sounds of birds drifting in from the darkness outside her open window. Two sedge warblers were calling and answering, but grew suddenly silent at the hoot of a distant owl.

Jo wasn't about to tell her maid, but Wynne was

another reason she needed to escape after dinner. To sit around the same table was one thing, but to socialize in a drawing room and carry on casual conversation was quite another. And she never imagined her reaction to him would be so strong. Staying at the Abbey, even for one night, was difficult enough. The apartment where Jo was situated was on the floor above the patients' ward and adjacent to the rooms Wynne and his son occupied. He was too close.

Jo's brother Hugh assumed she was ignorant of what the family had been doing for years, but she was well aware that he and the rest of them had cast a protective circle around her. All Melforts were kept out, excluded from interaction with the Penningtons, even when Wynne's older brother and his wife acquired an estate near Baronsford.

Her gaze lingered on the bedroom wall separating her apartment from his. A soft breeze wafted in, carrying with it the scent of cigar smoke and gorse and pine. The warblers started up again, and a nightingale joined them. She would make no mention of Captain Melfort in any letters to her family.

"I'll say this for them. They have a household staff here that is nearly that of Baronsford's," Anna continued on. "Though not the tradition of family we have, of course. I'd wager there's not a second generation of servant folk here. And don't you know that many of the menfolk are *sailors*, m'lady?"

"I didn't know that," Jo replied.

"They're always looking for more help too, I'm told. I'll need to make mention of it to my Aberdeen cousins the next time I wri—"

A sharp crash and a furious roar from the ward below silenced the maid.

The two of them sat frozen, listening to more shouts and cries for help. Jo's head turned to the window as she heard footsteps running toward the house. The second crash of a heavy object brought Jo to her feet and scrambling to pull on and belt her robe. She rushed toward the door.

"You can't go out there, m'lady."

"Stay here in the room, Anna. I'll be right back."

"But this is an asylum!" the servant cried out. "There could be madmen or killers on the loose!"

"Stay here," Jo repeated, going into the hall and closing the door firmly behind her.

The hallway was dark. A door slammed. The shouting was now accompanied by wails. More shouts from a distant part of the house, and running footsteps. Quickly, she made her way to the stairwell and started down.

Responding to the occasional crisis was a necessity at the Tower House. Jo wasn't reckless. She knew whatever was happening in the ward wasn't her concern. Still, having met Charles Barton, she couldn't remain in her room and not worry.

When she reached a landing at a turn of the stairs, she startled a small, thin figure hiding by the railing and listening to the confusion below. With a cry, the boy stepped back and Jo reached out, catching his arm before he went backwards down the steps.

"I didn't mean to!" he burst out in panic. "I . . . I didn't know he would hurt him."

Jo recognized Wynne's son. He'd shed the russet-hued jacket he'd been wearing earlier. He was shaking, and his head turned at the sound of the continuing commotion downstairs.

"What happened, Cuffe?" she asked quietly, releasing him. "Has someone been hurt?"

The boy spun away and rushed past her up the stairs, disappearing into the darkness above.

He'd done something wrong, something that brought on this chaos. And he was sorry for his part in it. She kept to the wall and slowly descended.

Three men were standing by the door into the ward. One was carrying a candle. Even with his back to her, Jo could see it was Wynne. Loud shouts and sounds of objects being thrown about could be heard coming through the thick door.

"Stevenson was secured for the night, Captain, sure as I'm standing here," one of the men hurriedly explained. "I watched the lads fasten the straps myself, same as always. We all know how difficult that one can be."

Jo went down another step.

"Aye, Captain," the other man said. "Two years we've had him here, and everyone knows he's the one needs watching most."

"I came out here after checking on everyone," the first man continued, raking a hand through his hair. "That was not an hour ago. They was all sleeping. I sat at my post here like I always do, night after night. Maybe I shut my eye a wink, but I was right here."

"And Stevenson's tam," the other jumped in. "What do ye make of that? How do ye think the other one got it? He never stirs once he's abed, and we all know to leave it be."

Wynne was asking no questions as the men went back

and forth in their explanations. Jo looked again to the door. The noises coming from the ward were subsiding.

"I'm thinking this was no accident, Captain. Someone was causing mischief in there."

"Maybe the rogue slipped past me. Or more likely came in through a window."

"I'm thinking they wanted Stevenson to go after Barton."

Jo didn't think she made a noise, but she must have. Wynne's head snapped around and he peered in her direction.

"Who's there?" he demanded, holding the candle up and coming toward the stairs.

Knowing it would be foolish to run away, she stayed where she was. She clutched the front of the robe, closing it tightly against her pounding chest.

Please, she prayed silently. Don't let Mr. Barton be hurt.

Wynne's face softened with recognition. "You shouldn't be down here."

"Is he hurt? Mr. Barton?" she asked, unable to keep the trembling edge out of her tone. She had to know.

"He'll have some bruises, I expect. The doctor is seeing to his arm right now to make sure he hasn't broken a bone. But considering everything, he's doing well."

"What happened?"

Wynne looked around them and motioned to the stairs. "This is not the best place to be speaking. Do you mind if we go up?"

Jo turned to take a step, but as she did, the hem of her robe tripped her. She felt his hand grasp her elbow, steadying her until she found her footing. Though his action was an innocent reflex, his touch caused her face to catch fire and her pulse jump. With his hand still on her arm, he lighted their way up the stairs. As they ascended, his closeness filled her head with the scent of night air, whiskey, smoke, and the man. This was the second time he'd touched her after a very long time. It was the touch of a friend, she told herself.

At the top of the stairwell, she paused in the hallway and turned to him.

"Pray tell, what happened?"

As his eyes washed over her and took in her face, her lips, her hair hanging loose around her shoulders, she saw a fleeting expression of reminiscence. Then the look was gone.

"We only have one patient at the hospital that we consider potentially dangerous to himself or to others," he explained. "The man's name is Stevenson. He's tended to closely during every waking hour. During the night watch, he's secured in his bed. And we have attendants who walk the ward regularly throughout the night."

She began to envision what took place in the ward, but waited for Wynne to expound.

"Stevenson somehow got free of his restraints and attacked another man. The rest of the patients in the ward raised the alarm with their cries."

"And Charles Barton was the victim of the attack," she reaffirmed what she'd already heard. "But no one else?"

He nodded. "One or two others tried to intervene, but Stevenson directed his violence at Barton. The victim will be fine. Thankfully, the night attendant entered the melee and others quickly arrived to help. You can visit Barton yourself in the morning, if you like."

"What was all that about a tam?"

"Stevenson is extremely attached to his hat. Carries it around like a baby. The tam was put on Barton's bed."

Cuffe's words came back to her. She recalled the distraught and fearful expression in the dim light of the stairwell.

At the Tower House, Jo had seen and spoken to many troubled children. Many were entirely capable of inflicting harm on themselves and others. But there was real remorse in Cuffe's tone. And his obvious shock at the way the events had unfolded indicated that there was a great deal more to this than simply a youth intent on doing mischief.

"Those attendants downstairs are responsible men," Wynne told her. "We've never had an incident like this at the Abbey. My guess is that none of it was accidental. It may have been intentional. Someone slipped into the ward, freed Stevenson, and moved the hat to give him a target for his rage. Why someone would do such a thing is hard to fathom."

Jo remained silent, unwilling to offer anything. She already knew the identity of the culprit.

Wynne's gaze moved past her shoulder down the hall-way. She imagined Cuffe could be hiding in the shadows there.

"When you came out of your room earlier, did you see anyone?"

She knew he had a right as the father to know, but she couldn't bring herself to say the words. Cuffe was already feeling the grave significance of his actions. Still, she imagined there was something more behind the child's actions.

She opened her mouth to convey to him what she knew. She had every intention of at least telling Wynne she'd encountered Cuffe in the stairwell. But different words spilled out.

"No, I didn't see anyone."

***

Wynne saw a movement by the door to the rooms he and Cuffe shared. After the afternoon lessons with Cameron, the lad had been directed back to his room, where a supper tray was waiting. He was not to stir until tomorrow morning, when he would return to the tutor.

A thought crossed fleetingly through Wynne's mind whether Cuffe could have had anything to do with what happened downstairs. He immediately dismissed it. In the two months since he'd arrived here, the ten-year-old had shown no interest in the hospital or the patients, despite Dermot's repeated invitations. And getting tricked into letting the pigs into the garden had been the extent of any damage he'd caused. Wynne was fairly certain his son would never do anything to injure an innocent person.

Jo turned and followed the direction of his gaze. "I was hoping to meet your son while I'm here."

Her gentle words startled him and drew his attention back to her. Jo's face was calm, pensive, concerned. She was an exceptional woman. Wynne had ended their engagement less than a fortnight before their wedding. He'd never been able to find the opportunity to apologize or explain, other than in a brief note. He'd left her alone to deal with the aftermath. Much later, he'd married another woman and had a child. But in spite of it all, here she was expressing an interest in meeting Cuffe. She'd always been patient and kind, but Jo Pennington carried within her a dignity he'd been too young to truly appreciate all those years ago.

"Is there a chance we might be introduced tomorrow before I leave the Abbey?"

"I'll be sure to make the arrangements," he declared. "I'd like him to meet you."

Before I leave. The notion of Jo leaving so soon did not sit well with him. Even though the question of the drawings and the reaction of the Bartons had not been resolved, a door had been opened. She could pursue it on her own.

He admired Jo's face in the flickering light of the candle. He watched the gentle pulse along the pale column of her throat.

She'd be better off going, he told himself. They'd all be better off. His conversation with Dermot earlier had left him strangely unsettled, and he didn't like the feeling. He didn't like the way he needed to monitor them as the young scoundrel tried to entertain Jo over dinner. Wynne wanted his deuced life back to normal.

And yet, memories of the past continued to flood back to him.

He remembered sitting with her on a warm night in a wooded lane by the Cascade in Vauxhall Gardens. The taste of the soft skin beneath her earlobe mingled with the scent of summer flowers. His own wonder at her innocent, wide-eyed response as she tried to make sense of the desire charging the air between them.

She pushed a stray ringlet behind an ear and he struggled not to touch the waves of gleaming dark hair falling nearly to her waist. He'd lost count of how many times as a young man he'd imagined seeing Jo's silky hair spread across his pillow.

A handful of kisses. Only once, in the shadow of a rose trellis during a ball, had those kisses led to a passionate whirlwind of caresses. That was the extent of the liberties he'd taken. He wouldn't make love to her, though he knew she would have given herself to him. But the malicious whispers had already begun, and in those moments of youthful gallantry, he wouldn't risk adding further damage to her reputation.

But in the end, he'd wounded her more deeply than any malevolent backbiter.

"Must you leave so soon?" he heard himself asking. "After everything we saw today, it's clear Charles Barton's progress could be dramatically improved if you were to extend your stay."

And it wasn't only for Barton's sake that he was asking.

"I've been thinking the same thing." Her dark gaze met his. "Dr. McKendry mentioned the name of an inn at Rayneford Village this afternoon. I'll send my manservant down there tomorrow and make arrangements to stay for a few more days."

"There's no need to leave the Abbey," he said. "You're welcome to stay right here. If the rooms you're occupying now suit you, you can remain where you are."

Where he'd be able to chaperon that scurvy sawbones, Wynne thought.

"But I don't want to be a nuisance."

"You could be nothing of the kind," he insisted, already feeling better about the new arrangement. "Everyone at the Abbey will benefit and take pleasure in your company."

And *that* included himself.

❦   *9*   ❦

As Jo watched Wynne descend the stairs, she struggled to reconcile her troubled thoughts with a long-forgotten flutter in her heart. Her worry about the son battled with the fever she felt in the presence of the father.

Cuffe was responsible for what had happened in the ward, and she already regretted holding back the truth from Wynne.

She was a stranger in this place, she chided herself inwardly. She was certainly no parent. She was in no way qualified to hide what she knew and chance a greater disaster in the future. What did she really know about the unruly ways of a ten-year-old boy? Very little. What she *did* know was she'd allowed herself to be influenced by downcast eyes and a panicky and remorseful tone.

She knew what needed to be done, and she hurried down the hallway and rapped on a door. The footman who'd brought them up when they decided to stay, told her these rooms were occupied by the captain and his son.

No one answered, but she wasn't deterred. She knocked harder.

"Cuffe. Come to the door this instant."

Her friend Violet Truscott and the women who worked together in running the Tower House told her she had an excellent angry mother's voice when she chose to use it.

"Open this door *now*!"

Dark eyes appeared as the door opened a little. A shock of hair hung over his face.

"You didn't give me up to him," Cuffe said.

The tremble in his voice made her want to pull the child into her arms, but she held back.

"A man could have died down there," she said sternly, pushing the door open. "Mr. Barton was in no position to defend himself. Is that what you were after? Did you go down there to kill him?"

Cuffe stabbed at tears that sprang onto his cheeks. He shook his head. "No, I didn't. I didn't know that would happen. He told me it was a lark, to rile up the fellows who watch the ward at night. And he gave me this to do it. But I don't want it."

Jo stared at the coins in the boy's open hand. "Someone paid you to do this?"

Cuffe nodded.

"And he told you to put the tam on Mr. Barton's bed?"

He nodded again.

"The man who put you up to this is evil," she said, putting her hand on his shoulder. "This was no lark. He wanted to hurt people and he *used* you. He didn't succeed. But that doesn't mean he won't try again."

This was more dire than what she first assumed. Jo

deeply regretted not having Wynne there. It was important for Cuffe to go to him and tell him.

"This evil man could use someone else. Or even do it himself. We need to stop him," she told him in what she hoped was a stern tone. She needed to make him understand and do the right thing. "*You* have to stop him. You must go to your father and tell him who was behind this."

He shook his head. "I'll tell you his name, and you tell the captain."

"No," she replied firmly. "You did wrong, Cuffe. You put those men downstairs at risk. It's *your* responsibility to tell the truth."

He stood perfectly still for a long moment, staring at the floor before he finally spoke. "I don't talk to him."

Jo recalled the frustration Wynne expressed about his son. Whatever reason existed in Cuffe's head to make him want to punish his father, it was none of her business.

"I didn't give you up to him because I believed you would do right . . . on your own," she said. "You're not a child. You're a young man. I barely know you, but I see an intelligent, strong, and independent lad. And I think you already know this is the time to put aside your obstinacy and act as you should."

"The captain will be angry," he whispered.

"That's his right and his duty as your father. A man was hurt tonight," she reminded him. "A disaster will happen if you do nothing."

She dropped her hand from Cuffe's shoulder and looked directly into his eyes.

"You need to decide whether you follow the path that is right or wrong. But I trust that you know which one to take."

Cuffe's chin sank to his chest, but he faced up to his responsibility and stepped out of his room.

"Go find your father and tell him what he needs to know."

As Jo stepped back to allow him by, she glanced down the hallway to see Wynne standing at the top of the stairs.

He'd barely reached the ground floor when he heard the loud knocking and Jo's sharp commands to open the door. Retracing his steps, he stood at the top of the stairwell, watching her talking to Cuffe.

And Wynne heard every word that passed between them.

Cuffe's face was the very picture of misery as he came down the hallway to him.

"What is his name?" he asked brusquely. "The man who put you up to this?"

"Abram."

"Abram from the kitchens?"

Cuffe nodded.

"Wait in my office," he ordered. "I'll deal with you when I return."

Head down and feet dragging, his son went directly to Wynne's office. Down the corridor, Jo turned and disappeared into her own chambers.

The man had taken advantage of a naive lad to commit what was a deliberate attempt to injure or even kill Barton. As Wynne hurried down the steps, he seethed with anger.

He knew this Abram. An older man from the Inverness. They'd hired him fairly recently to work in the kitchens, deliver food trays, and help the attendants with whatever needed to be done. Because of his work, Abram was perfectly familiar with the peculiarities of the patients in the ward.

When Wynne reached the door to the ward and put the question about the man's whereabouts to the attendants, the last anyone had seen of him was when he took a dinner tray up to Cuffe.

Dermot came out as Wynne was sending two of the men to go and fetch Abram from the staff's quarters on the uppermost floor. Quickly, he explained to his friend what he knew, including what Cuffe had done.

"I hope you didn't punish the lad too harshly. He was manipulated."

"You don't need to make excuses for him," Wynne told him. "I've done nothing to him yet. He's awaiting his punishment in my office right now."

He started for the kitchen in spite of his doubts that Abram would still be there. Dermot fell in beside him.

"Having Cuffe free Stevenson and at the same time direct the attack at Barton was clearly a deliberate move," the doctor said. "Difficult to imagine why he'd do such a thing."

Wynne's thoughts immediately turned to the Bartons. "And how curious that all of this should happen today."

"You don't seriously think his own family would try to harm him."

"We both saw Graham and Mrs. Barton's reaction," Wynne retorted. "But we need to talk to Abram. He told Cuffe it was all a 'lark', but that's rubbish. Perhaps he harbors a grudge and saw this as an opportunity to get his revenge."

"He *was* hired at around the same time that Barton arrived," Dermot said thoughtfully.

"We'll know when we get our hands on the rogue."

Wynne could not get the Bartons' reaction to Jo out of his head, however. What exactly *was* her connection to the family? He worried if she could be at risk too.

"Don't forget, we know nothing of Charles Barton's years as a shipowner," Dermot reminded him. "We don't even know what caused the explosion that eventually brought him here."

Wynne knew very well the hard world of the sea, and the dark side of some who made their living on it. Smugglers who would cut a man's throat for an extra share. Slavers who vilely continued to transport human cargo in spite of the laws banning it. He'd fought against them and hunted them down from the Mediterranean to the coast of Africa to the West Indies. For shipowners, a line existed. On one side, honest living. On the other, violence, double-dealing, and the chance for greater riches. If Barton chose to do his business among the latter, his enemies would hardly be above seeing him battered to death in an asylum ward.

When they reached the kitchens, they found only two young men washing up. The rest of the staff had retired for the night.

"I'm guessing Abram is halfway to Inverness by now," Dermot complained. "But how can we keep Charles Barton safe when we don't know where the danger is coming from?"

"I should run away now," Cuffe murmured, looking out the window at the rising moon and the patches of forest on the mountains to the west.

This place wasn't home. He turned his back to the window and frowned at the open door. He could be gone, and no one would miss him.

Instead, he sat hard on the floor and slid back against the wall, cramming himself between two chairs.

Only an inch or so was left of the candle he'd lit on the captain's desk. The wax dripping down the side reminded him of the tears on his Nanny's wrinkled cheeks when she'd pushed him toward the solicitor who'd come to bring him here. She said she had no choice. She was getting on in years. Be dying soon. He had to go to his father.

Dying. Cuffe stabbed at the stubborn tears that kept finding their way out. They came every time he thought about her. How many nights had he lain in bed worrying about who was taking care of his Nanny now that he was gone? Bringing her water in the morning, moving the heavy pots hanging over her fire, fetching wood, fixing the roof when it sprang a leak during the hard May rains.

He took care of *her* as much as she took care of him. And their two-room cottage in the Cockpit village above Falmouth was home. Not this place with its houses of stone and its guards and lunatics roaming the gardens and living right beneath him. This wasn't home.

Twelve pounds. A bloody fortune. During the crossing from Jamaica, he'd heard the men working on the ship say that's how much it took to pay for passage in steerage. He had to come up with that or try to get hired on as crew. Even if he managed to find a ship sailing to the West Indies, hiring on was risky. He'd heard plenty of stories of free Jamaicans being abducted and sold as slaves to some passing trader. What was to stop a white ship's master from selling him on some sugar island along the way?

No, he'd be safer paying for his passage. But twelve pounds! He'd have to work for years to save that kind of money. And Nanny would tan his hide if he stole it or hurt someone to get it.

Cuffe wiped his face with a sleeve and stared at his hands. But that's exactly what he'd done tonight. He'd allowed himself to be tricked, and a man was hurt because of it.

The captain wouldn't believe him now if he said he didn't know.

Abram knew he was trying to make money. The dog had been there the time he made a deal with the farm lads. He was the one who separated them when they were fighting. He pretended to be Cuffe's friend. He even told Cuffe he'd help him leave the Abbey.

Liar. Cheat. Evil, she'd said.

That room, the ward. He'd never been inside it until tonight. It was the way Abram described it. The men the doctor kept there seemed normal enough when Cuffe saw them outside. Some talked a little loud or said strange things. A few never spoke at all. One just sat and stared at the bushes in the gardens. But none of them ever harmed another, that he'd seen. And when he'd slipped into the ward tonight, they were all sleeping.

He pulled his knees to his chest and rested his head. There was no one here who cared. No one liked him. He was nothing to them at the Abbey, but back in Jamaica an old woman loved him. To Nanny, Cuffe was the sunshine that warmed her ancient bones in the daytime, and the moonlight that showed her the road when her dim eyes struggled to see.

Man grow; wait 'pon man, she'd always say. A boy will eventually grow up to become a man.

Cuffe never knew his mother. Nanny was everything to him. To others, he was only ten years old, but to Nanny, he was her little man. And he needed to get back to her.

No matter how tight he tried to shut his eyes, fresh tears squeezed through. He missed her. He missed her songs. Her stories. He missed her scolding. Cuffe felt a fist tightening around his heart as he recalled the way she fawned over him when he did right.

It was getting late. The sounds from downstairs lessened until the house was silent again. His tears finally stopped, and he sat breathing in the country smells and listening to a family of foxes yipping in the distance as the moon crossed the corner of the window. Finally, he heard the captain coming up the steps.

He quickly stood. He'd done wrong and he expected to be punished. The captain had never laid a hand on him, but Cuffe almost wished he would. He couldn't bear spending another extra hour tallying sums in Mr. Cameron's dusty office.

The captain stopped in the doorway, and Cuffe kept his eyes on the dark floor between them.

He'd have to talk to him, though he knew it meant his last plan of getting back to Nanny was about to be destroyed. For weeks now, Cuffe never spoke a word to him. Since he'd arrived at the Abbey, he'd deliberately treated him as if he didn't matter. If the man grew to hate him, if he got tired of his surly ways, he thought maybe he'd pay his passage back home.

This morning in the village, Cuffe thought he'd won. The captain had never been as angry as he was after dragging him out of the path of the carriage horses.

But he couldn't play that game anymore. The guest,

Lady Josephine, ordered him to talk to the captain. In her hard tone and soft ways, she reminded him of Nanny. *Your responsibility*, she said.

The captain's silence made him jumpy inside. It was like the thick feeling of the air before a summer storm burst open. If he were a little boy again, he'd run and hide before the lightning began.

The coins he'd taken from Abram shone dully on the desk beside the guttering candle.

"It's all there." He pushed the breath from his lungs and the words rushed after. He motioned toward the coins. "The money Abram paid me. And I didn't think anyone would be hurt. He said it was a lark to get even with Robbie at the door for some daft prank in the kitchen this morning."

The silence continued to hang heavy between them, and Cuffe was too afraid to look up. He didn't know if the captain believed him or not. He pressed his hands against his thighs to keep them from shaking. He didn't want to cry. He didn't want to beg to be forgiven.

"I know I did wrong. Nanny always says if you follow a fool, you're the greater fool," he said, forcing himself to steal a look at the man at the door. His face was in the shadows. "I was a fool to believe Abram. I deserve whatever punishment you decide on."

If the captain had struck him with a rod, it wouldn't have been as painful as this waiting, but Cuffe had no choice except to weather it until his silence ran its course.

"Go back to your room. Tomorrow I'll talk to you about punishment."

Cuffe was surprised at the note of exhaustion in the captain's voice, but he was relieved at being dismissed. At the door, as he tried to hurry past the man, a large hand came down on his shoulder. For a moment he thought, this was it. The beating. He stood and braced himself.

"I need you to promise," the captain said. "I want your word that you'll stay in your room until I send for you."

My *word*, Cuffe thought. He was trusting in his honor despite what he'd done.

"I'll stay there, Captain," he said, meaning it.

$$\text{❦ \quad 10 \quad ❦}$$

NIGHT'S restless hours crawled ever so slowly over rugged ground toward the dawn, and when the earliest rays of the sun broke across the furrowed fields, Jo was already dressed. She had to get out and walk.

As she hurried past Wynne and Cuffe's rooms, the inner arguments that kept her pacing for much of the night once again ignited in her.

She'd lied to the father, but shortly afterward convinced the son to reveal the truth. What worried her was how Wynne perceived her interference. She was willing to argue her case if he gave her the chance. But beyond that, she was apprehensive about Cuffe and wondered what had transpired between the two. She'd been trying for hours to convince herself that none of this should matter, that she was here simply to learn more about Mr. Barton and his sketches. She was not staying for Wynne or his son.

Buttoning her spencer jacket and wrapping her shawl around her shoulders, she descended the stairs thinking of the attack last night. Charles Barton had an enemy. She'd overheard Cuffe mention the name Abram. She wondered now if the man had acted for reasons of his own or if he was only a rung of a ladder held by others.

Two attendants sitting by the door to the ward looked half-asleep but stood and doffed their caps to her as she went by. Jo understood there was no point in asking to see Barton. After last night, a visit to the ward would need the approval of the doctor.

Going out through the gardens, Jo followed a path toward the rising sun. Stables and a carriage house lay beyond groves of tall chestnut, and as she passed cottages of farm laborers, the smoke of wood fires rose above the thatched roofs. She exchanged greetings with a woman carrying a bucket of milk who stopped to watch her go by. Open fields lay beyond, and groups of workers were trudging toward their day's toil.

A few minutes later, Jo paused at the top of a small brae and looked south across the rolling landscape toward the River Don. Mist was rising from lower-lying pastures and along two brooks that snaked across the countryside toward the river. Though she couldn't see the village, she saw numerous cottages and sheds, as well as the fields used as golfing links by the Squire and his brother, the vicar.

Something about this place touched her with a feeling of familiarity, though she knew she'd never been here before. The Highlands was so different from the Borders, where Baronsford was located, and totally different from Hertfordshire, where she'd spent a great deal of time growing up. But the bracing air, the smell of the gorse, the way the light dispersed in the mist all affected her.

Turning her steps toward the hills rising to the north,

she walked along a path that followed one of the brooks and came upon a series of fish ponds formed by small dams. As she stood by a clump of willows, her attention was drawn to an ancient tower house nestled against a forest of spruce. She wondered who lived there so close to the old Abbey.

Her shoes and skirts were wet and stained with mud, but Jo strode on as questions about her mother again blotted out any other thought. Last night, she'd again paged through the portfolio of sketches Dr. McKendry sent her. Her birth mother. A woman she'd never seen, but who'd died bringing Jo into the world. For all the love she'd been blessed with in her life from her adoptive mother and father, holding the drawings in her hand still elicited a deep ache in her chest.

As the night wore on, Jo focused on details in the backgrounds of the drawings. A distinctive shape of a hill, a crumbling stone wall, a mill. Each of them seemed to represent a particular place, perhaps a specific memory in the ailing man's mind.

She wondered how Graham and Mrs. Barton would react if she paid a visit to Tilmory Castle, and whether she'd find those places in the drawings there. If their response to seeing her yesterday was any indication, she wouldn't be received at all.

A flock of geese suddenly took wing in a meadow beyond the brook, their pure white bellies a stark contrast against the brown feathers of their backs. The cause of their flight soon became apparent, and Jo immediately wished she too could escape as she recognized the man walking toward her.

Wynne saw her, paused, and then waved. She watched him as he strode across, his long coat open. He was hatless, and buff-colored buckskin breeches hugged muscled thighs above his high boots. All thoughts of escaping fled. For a prolonged moment, time flew backwards. Jo's skin tingled and she fought the urge to lift the hem of her skirts and run to meet him.

Instead, Jo pulled her shawl tightly around her as she stopped and waited for him to approach.

"You're an early riser," he said, after they exchanged greetings.

Not as early as he was, she thought, noting the hint of tiredness in his eyes. His hair bore evidence of fingers raking through it. Despite his obvious weariness, however, she thought he looked magnificent.

"Too many days trapped inside that carriage. I had to take the opportunity this beautiful countryside offered," she explained, looking in the direction he'd come. "I thought I'd walk that way if you think the people living at that house wouldn't mind me trespassing on their land."

Wynne looked back at the tower house. "I'll walk with you and make certain they don't."

Jo's intention was to go in the opposite direction of where he was traveling. There was no avoiding it. Wynne gave her no chance to object.

Regardless of what reason dictated, her heart directed her actions. They walked for a while in silence, and her recollections about their past continued. The way he walked with one hand tucked behind his back, his strides adjusting to match the length of hers, his distance courteous and yet close enough that she would occasionally feel the brush of his coat. She filled her lungs with dawn air, and made herself think of the present rather than the past.

"I must apologize for last night," she said finally. "I

should have told you right away I'd seen your son in the stairwell." Of everything on her mind, this was the least troubling of her thoughts.

"You have no need to apologize, especially to me," Wynne replied. "I'm the one who should express my remorse over every wrong I've done you."

"Please *don't*," she broke in, unwilling to dredge up the old memories.

The pained expression revealed his disappointment at being interrupted. Jo knew what she was doing. She was robbing him of a chance to confess, a chance to be absolved of the past. But she wasn't ready. She couldn't wash away the consequences of his action after a few words of apology. And she knew she couldn't trust herself. She could easily crumble before his eyes.

"I have a proposition," she said. "I should like to pretend we're two people whose history began yesterday. Could we do that, do you think? Begin again as strangers? Or perhaps as friendly acquaintances?"

"If you wish it, Jo."

Jo. Hearing her name on his lips was a contradiction to what she'd asked. He was challenging her. He was daring her to remember.

As they walked, she focused on the path, but the weight of his gaze remained on her face. She didn't want to revisit the day he'd broken off the engagement. That day and his duel with Hugh the following morning and all the days after were too painful. She didn't want to return to that time when she'd became a shell of a person with a heart wilted and dying inside. It hurt too much to remember.

She forcibly buried the ache once again beneath the sediment of the years, and glanced over at him. "Tell me.

Were you able to find the man who instigated the attack?"

"No. We searched the Abbey grounds last night. Abram was working in the kitchens, but he's definitely fled."

"Do you have any idea why he'd do such a thing?" Jo was feeling much more at ease when nothing of their own personal entanglement was a part of the conversation.

"It's difficult to say," he replied, shaking his head. "Charles Barton was a shipowner, as well as a local landowner. As you heard his mother say, that part of his life has been a mystery to her. It's possible he has any number of enemies. One of them could have been behind last night's attack."

Jo wondered how long Barton had been away from Tilmory Castle. If it was during that time he crossed paths with the woman in his drawings, she might never know more than she knew now. Unless he improved.

The path brought them to a log that crossed the brook. He climbed ahead and his hand reached out to assist her.

"I want to thank you for the talk you had with Cuffe last night. You were quite persuasive. He responded to you."

She slipped her fingers into his warm hand and climbed onto the log. The feel of their skins blending into one, the strength of his touch . . . it was all so familiar, as if she'd never lost him. History existed between them that refused to remain buried.

"Your son knew he'd done wrong before he saw me. His remorse and whatever apologies he made afterward were his alone. I was only the spark."

"He spoke to me. That was the first time."

As they reached the other side, he stepped down and grasped her by the waist and gently placed her on solid ground. It took a moment for the beating of her heart to slow enough to allow her to speak.

"What do you mean, 'first time'?"

"I mean, last night was the first time he'd spoken to me since he was a very small child."

Jo stared into his face. "But I heard from Mrs. McKendry that your wife died at childbirth. Didn't you and Cuffe see each other as he was growing?"

"My orders kept me busy at sea for years," he retorted, his tone indicating his irritation at having to explain. "Between fighting the French and the Americans, stopping over at Falmouth was very difficult. Of course, I saw him a handful of times that first year. But after that, his grandmother took him to live in the hills. I don't need to tell you about my parents. It wasn't as if I could entrust a mulatto son to their care. He was better off in Jamaica."

His parents. The past that she wanted to forget. The baronet and his wife. Intimidating people who managed to make Jo feel small and deficient from the moment she first met them. She couldn't blame Wynne for not taking his son to them. Cold and aloof, they could have never done an adequate job of raising Cuffe. Jo knew nothing of Wynne's wife, but right now warm feelings of empathy for the woman coursed through her.

"I provided for him. I urged Cuffe's grandmother to bring him to Falmouth or Montego Bay. She could have lived quite comfortably if she chose to do so. But her decision was to stay in a village in the hills among the Maroons. That was where the lad was raised."

Because of her adoptive family's lifelong work to abolish the evils of slavery, Jo was very familiar with the

Maroons. They were the unconquered fighters waging war from Jamaica's mountainous and forested interior. A constant threat to the government's efforts to further the interests of the plantation owners, for a century they'd been inciting periodic conflict, outwitting the military and spreading terror to the doors of the slavers. Never wasting a shot or an opportunity to inspire rebellion in the sugar fields, the Maroon communities of free men and women welcomed escaped slaves willing to fight for their independence. Not an army in Europe was strong enough to quell these warriors. And the Maroons continued to thwart island administrators and force them to negotiate for peace, securing agreements that successive governors would ignore at their peril.

"His name . . . Cuffe. What does it mean?" she asked.

A touch of a smile broke across his face. "Hot-tempered. His full name is Andrew Cuffe Melfort. But he doesn't respond to anything but Cuffe."

"A name befitting a warrior." She returned his smile.

They were getting close to the tower house, and Jo thought of Wynne's late wife. No doubt she was a warrior. How different she must have been from a timid and pampered adopted daughter of English aristocrats.

The brook they'd been following poured over what remained of a wide but ancient dam, and the broad pond extended past a ruined stable.

Jo had changed in many ways since Wynne courted her, but she was still not a fighter or a warrior.

As they climbed a rise and skirted the edge of an over-grown orchard, she was hesitant to go farther. But Wynne didn't show any sign of avoiding the house.

"We don't want to intrude," she said finally. "Perhaps it would be better if we turned back here."

"I know they don't mind," he said, motioning for her to continue. "I'd like your advice about punishment for Cuffe for what he did last night."

Jo was touched that he'd ask her opinion on such a sensitive and personal matter. "He *was* taken advantage of."

"If you please, don't make excuses for him." He picked up a fallen branch and frowned. "I'm not about to beat him. I don't believe that ever helps except to get a rogue's attention. Cuffe is no rogue and we already have his attention."

He was the same compassionate man she once knew. She recalled the conversations they used to have of someday having a child. And how he'd declare that he would be everything his own father failed to be. Empathetic. Fair.

"I want him to learn a lesson from the experience. But extra hours of arithmetic or Latin, or even mucking out a stable, is teaching him very little."

"Cuffe lives above the ward. Why not involve him with the care of the patients in some way?"

"Dr. McKendry has attempted that very thing, without success. He only wanted to get the lad to escort him as he made his rounds of the hospital, to get to know the patients." He tossed the stick away. "Cuffe shows no interest. And I don't believe forcing him would improve his relationship with them."

Her thoughts turned to her childhood and Melbury Hall, her family's home in Hertfordshire. Since before she was born, the place had been a refuge for freed men and women from the sugar islands. Ohenewaa. The wizened face of the serious old woman pushed into her mind's eye. Beloved and respected by all. As a healer, she helped the earl recover from injuries that nearly killed him, and as a teacher, she shaped the character of each of the Pennington children.

"Since he arrived at the Abbey, how is he doing with his tutors?" she asked tentatively, trying to decide if Wynne would take offence at what she was about to ask. He'd asked, and she was willing to help, but she didn't know if he'd listen to her suggestions.

"According to Mr. Cameron, my son doesn't have a great fondness for book learning."

"What is he being taught?"

Wynne explained the busy schedule that filled the young boy's day.

"You're giving him an English gentleman's education."

"He's my son. He's learning the things that befit his station."

"Pray don't mistake me," she said, hearing the note of defensiveness creep into his tone. "I congratulate you on all you're doing. You're preparing him to function as a gentleman in your world."

"Exactly." Wynne stopped and faced her.

"But Cuffe is more than an English gentleman, is he not?" she suggested. "What acknowledgment is being made of his mother and the world he has only recently left behind?"

His piercing blue eyes met hers and she felt as if he were trying to reach into her thoughts and read her mind.

"I take your meaning," Wynne replied. "He's rejected the name Andrew."

"And it appears he's rejecting the education you're providing for him, however valuable it will prove to be in his future."

"I want him to survive. Here. In Scotland and in

England. There's no life for him back where he came from," he argued. "How do I make him understand?"

"Talk to him," she said softly. "Negotiate, if need be."

"I'm not willing to forego giving him what he needs."

"You're showing him that you respect his Jamaican heritage by calling him Cuffe. Perhaps you can reflect that, as well, in his program of studies."

They were standing not an arrow shot from the tower house, and Jo looked at the massive stone structure. On the east side of the house, an addition was being constructed, though the building had not progressed beyond the foundation. There was no sign of life anywhere.

"What do you suggest? I've read Defoe's *Crusoe*, and I don't believe the man ever saw Jamaica or any island west of Guernsey."

Jo thought of Phoebe and the books at the Pennington libraries at Melbury Hall and London and Baronsford. "You might have him read literature written by Africans or those of African descent. The autobiography of Olaudah Equiano. Or the work of Phillis Wheatley, if you have no objection to an American poet. There are others. I'd be happy to compile a list for you. In doing so, you'll be showing him that you don't intend to strip him of an identity to which he is most attached."

"The lad is only ten years old. I don't wish to bore him out of his mind."

"What he may be feeling now is worse than boredom."

"I agree. But I'm at a loss."

"It's the gesture that is important. *Your* gesture," she said. "And he might surprise you as far as how advanced he is in comprehension and maturity."

Jo understood his frustration. He was willing to make a change. His commitment to his son was admirable.

"I'll make arrangements and buy whatever you suggest. But we began by talking about getting him involved with the patients."

"Have Cuffe read to them," she suggested. "Decide on a time each day for him to go into the ward and read aloud."

"And what would he read that would keep them engaged?"

"It's what keeps Cuffe engaged that matters."

Jo remembered the gift that she was taking to Ella, Gregory and Freya's niece at Torrishbrae. A volume of Ohenewaa's African tales that her sister Phoebe had collected over the years and written out for the next generation of Pennington children.

"I can lend you a manuscript edition of fables for him to read while I'm here. Unfortunately, I need to take the volume with me when I leave for Sutherland. They're Ohenewaa's stories from western Africa."

Wynne had never met her, but Jo had spoken many times of the wise woman during their times together. His blue eyes washed over her face and she knew he remembered.

His hold on her was back. The pull, the memories. They stood too close, the breeze making his coat dance with her dress. He brushed the back of his hand against hers in what could have been a silent gesture of gratitude for the offer. Warmth flooded though her. Her heart raced, her mind easing into the past and recalling how often he used to bring her fingers to his lips, turning her hand and kissing her palm. Butterflies danced in her belly at the mere thought.

She turned to the house, hoping to break the spell.

"Does anyone live here?" Jo asked, letting out an unsteady breath. She focused her attention on the grey and brown stonework and the unglazed windows. The slate roof appeared to be intact, however, and the foundation of the addition would be doubling the size of the house.

"No one at present."

"It looks much newer than the Abbey."

"It's older, actually," he replied, turning his gaze toward the structure. "Knockburn Hall was a hunting lodge of one of the old Stewart kings. He gave the land to some monks but kept the use of the tower house for himself. It's been sitting here for years, but it was recently purchased. The owner intends to move in when the new construction is completed."

Wynne offered Jo his arm and she took it.

They went closer, and Jo remarked about the lovely turrets and how the house was situated facing south. "It's so protected from the winds with the forest and hills behind and the open meadows before it."

"I believe the addition will have a great many windows and a terraced garden extending in this direction to take advantage of the view."

"You know a great deal about the plans," she noted suspiciously.

"I should. Knockburn Hall is my house. Or it will be when it's finished."

She shouldn't have been surprised. The living quarters of the Abbey was a McKendry stronghold. Wynne wouldn't want to raise his son in the home of others.

"Would you care to see the inside?"

They stood shoulder to shoulder. His free hand

pressed her fingers on his arm. A swell of yearning rose within her body.

She imagined the two of them alone in the house. The ancient oak floors. The morning sun streaming in the windows. There was a time when she dreamed of a moment like this, a time for the two of them. Alone. But that time was long gone. It was too late.

She pulled away from him, gathering the shawl tighter around her. "No, I should go back. I was planning on having breakfast with Dr. McKendry. I want to convince him to allow me to spend the day in the ward."

He bowed and she hurried away, retracing her steps to the path. The aching in her heart trailed her at every step. If only she could turn around, go in the house, pretend that they'd just met.

Only when she reached the brook did she look over her shoulder.

Wynne was still standing where she left him, watching her walk away.

"Me? Reading out loud in the ward?" Cuffe's face registered a curious mixture of horror and disbelief upon hearing Wynne's announcement.

"I said I would inform you of your punishment when the time was right," he told his son. "For one hour each afternoon, starting today, you'll read to the patients from that book."

Finding Cuffe on a flat rock in the grassy area outside the kennels, Wynne waited while his son considered the penalty. The lad had been reading with a newly weened pup asleep on his lap.

"Perhaps it would be best if we started tomorrow, Captain. I'm certain I've heard the vicar say something about laboring on the Sabbath."

"He was speaking theoretically."

"He mentioned yawning gates and a fiery pit."

"I'm willing to risk it. Up, lad. Time and tide wait for no man."

A steady rain had fallen over the past two days, but

the sun had broken through by mid-morning. During that time Wynne had been quietly impressed by the influence of Jo's presence on the fabric of life at the Abbey. And that included her suggestion regarding how to ease Cuffe into his new responsibility.

When he returned to the Abbey after their walk to Knockburn Hall, she'd been waiting for him with the book of African fables. When he gave it to Cuffe and explained what it was, the boy had taken an immediate interest in it. Yesterday, Wynne mentioned the volume to Cameron, and the bookkeeper said the ten-year-old was spending every free moment he had reading through it, and that Jo had stopped by to talk about the stories and tell him how they came to be in the book. Seeing how much the collection appealed to Cuffe, Wynne intended to talk to her about possibly having a copy made.

Cuffe closed the book and hugged it close to his chest. "What good would it do? They won't understand what I'm reading."

"How do you know?"

The shrug was familiar, but Cuffe got to his feet and carried the squirming pup back into the kennels. A moment later they were walking side by side toward the Abbey annex.

Jo had also been offering that fawning dog McKendry ideas about the ward. He couldn't walk by Dermot without having to hear him sing her praises. As they neared the door to the annex, Wynne realized he would have been joining in if he wasn't so annoyed by the doctor's blasted wooing of her.

Since the morning of Wynne's walk with Jo, the scoundrel had been herding her about like a prize cow. Wherever she went, the caw-handed sawbones was there beside her. When she wanted to meet with the vicar in the village to ask him what he might know of the Barton family and their history, Dermot had piped up and volunteered like a wet-nosed landsman on his first sea voyage. When she wished to bring Charles outside for an hour in the mid-morning sun, the doctor had changed his schedule to sit beside her. At dinner, he made sure she was seated at his end of the table. Whatever rules still existed regarding courtship, the villainous rake was ignoring them all.

All of this should have meant nothing to him, but Wynne was highly annoyed just the same.

When he and Cuffe entered the ward, they paused by the door. The noise level was high, for all of the patients were still inside. Some were milling about aimlessly while others were standing at the windows. A few were sitting at tables, but no cards or dice boxes were out, this being Sunday.

Wynne's attention was drawn to Charles Barton, who was sitting beside Jo as she read to him.

Jo's delicate chin lifted after each passage, and she looked at the patient as if to reassure him that she was there. Her world centered solely on the fortunate man.

Wynne recalled what she told him the morning of their walk. *Begin again as strangers.* Pretend they'd just met. No history.

To agree to her wishes meant that Wynne would have no chance to say the words that would free him of the burden he'd been carrying. Also, to agree meant that he'd have no more hold on her than Dermot.

He wondered if she knew how much she tormented him by asking such a thing.

At that moment her head turned in their direction

and she smiled. Wynne wasn't the only one affected by her acknowledgment of their arrival. Cuffe held the book up for her to see.

Dermot noticed their arrival, as well, and abandoned an attendant he was speaking with and crossed the room to Jo. Clearly, he couldn't stomach the idea of a competitor vying for her attention. Wynne seethed inwardly when the jackal bent his head over hers solicitously, smiling at whatever she said.

"This is foolishness," Cuffe complained. "No one here cares to listen to these tales. No one will even hear me."

Wynne motioned to a long table. The only person occupying a chair was a patient named McDonnell. A blacksmith of about thirty years of age, he'd sustained a head injury from a horse he was shoeing. The man absorbed directions, but was unable to string words into a sentence. His inability to communicate and his difficulty in controlling his limbs severely frustrated him and left him wretched.

"Come with me. Mr. McDonnell will appreciate the stories."

The young boy's feet dragged as Wynne led the way, but he followed, honoring the promise he'd made.

At the table Wynne spoke to McDonnell and introduced Cuffe, but other than a small spasm causing a muscle in his cheek to jump, the patient made no response.

"I won't stand on a table or a chair," the ten-year-old whispered. "And I won't yell. I don't care if they hear me or not."

"As long as McDonnell and I can hear you," he told him, adjusting a few of the chairs to face the spot where he told Cuffe to stand. Leaving him to it, Wynne sat next to the patient.

"And you'll keep the time."

"I'll tell you when your hour is up," he assured his son.

"What if I'm in the middle of a story?"

"You'll finish it."

The lad shook his head. "But some of the tales are short. It wouldn't be fair if—"

"Cuffe," he warned, cutting him off. "Begin now."

A frown, some shifting from one foot to the other, and then he opened the book, paged through it, found a page to his liking, and started.

Wynne was here to see his son through the task rather than to listen to the story, but Cuffe's posture changed as soon as he began. He became animated, energized by the text.

"Why the Sun and the Moon Live in the Sky," he read. "Many years ago the Sun and Water were great friends, and both lived on the Earth together. The Sun used to visit the Water, but the Water never returned his visits."

Cuffe paused and looked up at Wynne and the patient, seeing if he had their attention.

"At last the Sun asked the Water why he never came to see him in his house. The Water replied that the Sun's house was not big enough, and that if he came with his family, he would drive the Sun out."

Cuffe showed no hesitation or difficulty with the reading. To Wynne's surprise, he was more than proficient. He spoke in a clear voice with no shyness whatsoever. The boy's grandmother taught Cuffe to read and write back in Jamaica, but Wynne had never imagined he'd be so good at it.

Captivated by the effort, he watched and listened to

the story as his son read dramatically, speaking in various voices to portray the characters.

"Yes, come in, my friend," Cuffe said in a high-pitched voice for the Sun.

Wynne heard what sounded like a chuckle from the man sitting beside him and realized McDonnell was engaged in the reading.

"When the Water was level with the top of a man's head, the Water said to the Sun . . ." Cuffe paused as another patient took a seat. "Do you want more of my family to come?"

McDonnell shook his head in response for the Sun.

"Yes," Cuffe replied emphatically. "For the Sun did not know any better. So the Water flowed in, until the Sun and the Moon, his wife, had to perch themselves on the top of the roof."

Several more patients joined them, and Wynne saw another had left the window and was standing close enough to hear. Someone made a noise behind him and was hushed as Cuffe continued.

"The Water very soon overflowed the top of the roof, and the Sun and Moon were forced to go up into the sky, where they have remained ever since."

Immediate words of praise and "Hear, hear!" echoed from the gathered patients. Cuffe looked up, a smile tugging at the corner of his mouth. Wynne nodded his approval, and he saw the boy beam at someone standing behind him. He looked up and saw Jo. He immediately rose to his feet.

"Cuffe's reading was wonderful," she whispered. "You must be proud."

"Thank you," he said, meeting her shining brown eyes. "I'm grateful to you for—"

"He's starting again," she interrupted. "May I join you?"

"Of course." Only two seats remained at the table, and as he held the chair for her, he saw Dermot approaching. Wynne looked around him at every occupied chair and sent the doctor a feigned look of sympathy before sitting beside her in the last chair.

"'Clever Jackal Gets Left Out,'" Cuffe said, announcing the title of the next story.

❧ 12 ☙

Wᴴᴇɴ Jᴏ ʀᴇᴄᴇɪᴠᴇᴅ Dr. McKendry's invitation to travel to the Highlands, she never imagined her sojourn to the Abbey would result in friendship with the doctor. They conversed easily, sharing opinions and ideas, but their relationship ended there. Although he pretended to pursue her when they were in the presence of others, no spark of attraction existed. They were friends and only friends. But she was beginning to feel that others were not seeing their rapport in the same light.

Sitting at dinner on Tuesday night, Jo squirmed at the discussion between the Squire and Mrs. McKendry regarding the virtues of matrimony. Their opinions were seconded by the vicar, who went on to extol the doctor's fine qualities. As they talked, the three of them continually sent Jo knowing and meaning-laden glances. Clearly, the only matter left to be concluded was the decision on a date and the reading of the banns.

She would have tossed the topic off as being in keeping with the jocular nature of the family, but Wynne's fierce demeanor across the table told her that he too had bought into the misconception.

It shouldn't have mattered. She could have ignored it and allowed the conversation to follow its delusional path until it ran its course and dissipated into nothingness. However, having her name ensnared or even bandied about in rumor never sat well with her. Jo held the doctor in high esteem, but she wanted it known to those around the table that no understanding existed between the two of them.

"Doctor," she said during a momentary lull, "I hope I'm here long enough to meet this exceptional young woman your family is so exceedingly enthused about."

McKendry was about to speak, but she cut him off.

"I can just imagine her virtues." She paused for only a moment, feeling the company's eyes upon her. "Aside from her beauty, I envision her as a young lady in the spring bloom of life. A man of your age and position would certainly want a partner who shares his desire for a houseful of children." As opposed to a spinster getting to an age beyond childbearing years, she thought. This was a fact of life she'd accepted. "I'm also thinking she must be a local lass from a good family, for I'm certain the isolation of the Highland winters could prove wearing on one not as hearty as the McKendrys."

Jo raised her glass of wine. "If I may be so bold . . . To the McKendrys. *Slàinte mhath . . . Slàinte mhòr.*"

Surprised laughter and comments immediately followed her tribute to the family and to their Jacobite ties. She'd hoped her words would lay the subject of matrimony to rest and redirect the conversation, but the doctor raised his glass in her direction.

"The lady I have my eye on is beautiful indeed.

Regarding age, whether she be in the spring or autumn of life or anywhere between, it makes no difference to me. I seek no heirs, Lady Josephine. I'm committed to this hospital. My time is consumed by patients who need my care and attention."

"Hear, hear," the vicar began. "A man's work is—"

Dermot interrupted his uncle and continued. "My future wife's qualities of intelligence and empathy for others are unparalleled. In all my travels, I've never met another lady quite like her."

Rather than feeling flattered by the compliments directed at her, Jo was embarrassed and disconcerted. Dermot's family, however, having received all the encouragement they needed, only ramped up their matchmaking efforts.

Dinner's conclusion could not have come soon enough.

Later, while the women waited for the men to join them in the drawing room, Jo stood by the windows staring out at the gardens. She couldn't bear to join Mrs. McKendry and her guests for fear of becoming the victim of foolish questions regarding her phantom engagement.

Ridiculous, she thought, gazing at the shrubs and hedges in the dying light. But there was no point in scolding Dr. McKendry about any of it. Everything he said was innocuous; it was only in the perceptions of the listeners that his words gained specific meaning. Besides, she'd be gone by the end of the week.

Jo had already been here six days. Sending another letter south to Baronsford and one north to Torrishbrae, she'd promised her family that she'd continue on her journey in a few days. It pained her that there'd been no improvement in Mr. Barton since the first day. He stared at her. He drew. He held her hand. Still, deep in her heart, she felt a connection between them. Or she imagined it.

Jo's trip to the village and her talk with the vicar had produced no information. No record of the Barton family history existed at the kirk in Rayneford. Tilmory Castle was four miles away, but the estate had a small village and a church of its own where births and deaths and marriages were registered. As much as she wanted to, though, she had no right to go there and inquire into the family's private affairs.

The men entered the drawing room just as Jo espied the distinctive figure of Captain Melfort outside in the gardens.

Her desire to speak with him edged out any concern about courtesy toward the others. Not wanting to make a grand exit, she whispered a hastily made-up excuse to Mrs. McKendry and escaped.

Hurrying out to the gardens, Jo saw him down a long alley of tall privet. She half ran, half walked to catch up to him.

He must have heard her, for as she turned a corner, she ran straight into his broad chest. His hands caught her, steadying her.

"What are you doing out here?"

"I needed to speak with you."

His face was concerned but calm, and she was struck by the similarity of this situation to another long ago. Jo suddenly became aware of his touch on her arms. In spite of the long sleeves of her dress, she tingled where he held her. Heat from his hands traveled through the velvet as if it were gauze, caressing the skin beneath.

They were too close. With little effort, he could draw her to him in the fading light, press her against his chest.

Suddenly, she wanted it to happen. She wanted to raise her lips to his and discover if the taste and texture of his mouth was as she remembered. She wanted to feel his body move against hers. She wanted to hear the rumble of desire in his throat.

Her face grew hot and flushed as she realized, regardless of what she said or how she acted, she was still under this man's spell. And she wanted him.

"What do you need to speak to me about?"

Perhaps it was her imagination, but his fingers traced a slow intimate path down the length of her arms before his hands dropped to his side.

She moved back a step and was relieved to find a stone bench near them. She sat down, distrustful of her knees. She held her palms to her cheek to cool the burning.

"Are you unwell?" he asked moving closer. "Should I call for help? Should I get Dermot?"

"For heaven's sake! Not you too?" she scolded. "I don't need to see Dr. McKendry. I am perfectly well. I'm only trying to catch my breath from running after you."

"You don't need to run after me," he replied gently. "I'm here."

Jo gazed up at him. A sly smile tugged at his lips, conveying deeper meaning behind his words.

"But what do you need to say that requires private conversation?"

"I wanted to tell you about what happened with Cuffe this afternoon."

His demeanor hardened. "Was there a problem? Did he leave early? I received a communication about a potential client that I needed to answer immediately. Otherwise I would have been there for his reading."

"Nothing unpleasant occurred," she said quickly. "I was about to sing his praises."

He let out a relieved breath and sat beside her. Although he was a respectable distance away, he was still too close for comfort. She could feel the warmth of his body radiating through the night air.

"Then tell me," he said softly, as his eyes trapped hers in their spell again. "I like hearing good things; I'm just not accustomed to hearing them of late."

Memories flickered again and she recalled a bench in a garden, his arm around her waist. In the sweet darkness of that summer night, Wynne drew her onto his lap and kissed her as time ceased to exist.

A glint of amusement flashed in his eyes, and Jo feared he might be thinking of that moment too.

She tore her gaze from his face and forced cool air into her lungs. "Let me see. Cuffe arrived at his appointed time and, as before, stood by the table. Today four patients were waiting."

"Four?" Wynne asked, obviously delighted.

Jo named them and continued. "He read three stories with the same dramatic flair. At one point he had the entire room silent and waiting to hear the end of the tale."

"I'm so pleased," he responded. "I don't know if Cuffe mentioned it to you, but since you gave your permission, he's been spending some of his time with Cameron transcribing the tales for himself into a copybook. And he's making great progress."

"He told me." She smiled. "But I have more to tell."

"More?"

As Jo collected her thoughts before telling Wynne what followed, she recalled the warm flush of happiness that flowed through her that afternoon as she'd imagined herself a part of Cuffe's future. But it was a foolish thought.

"When he finished reading, Mr. McDonnell approached with a stack of letters in his hand."

"McDonnell, the blacksmith? He can barely speak."

"I wasn't near enough to hear what was said or how the man communicated with him, but the two went over to a table. For quite some time, they sat beside each other as Cuffe quietly read each letter."

"McDonnell has a mother who is too old to travel to the Abbey," Wynne said. "I knew he receives letters, but I never thought he might not be reading them."

This morning, as she sat with Charles Barton, Jo kept an eye on the two at the table. She was impressed with how patient Cuffe was with Mr. McDonnell.

"Your son was there far longer than you required him to stay," she said, pleased to be able to put Wynne's mind at ease.

He waited for her to say more but she'd reached the end of her story.

"Thank you for coming out here."

A window opened in the drawing room and the melodies of a pianoforte drifted through the night air. It was time to go, but she stayed.

"Why did you need to tell me all of this tonight?"

If she were only strong enough to voice the truth of what was in her heart. The denial in the dining room wasn't for the sake of the McKendrys but for Wynne. Staying out here, she was adding fuel to an inferno that was building between them.

"I thought you'd want to know."

He leaned forward on his knees. His face moved

closer. His intense blue gaze caught and held hers. "You could have mentioned it when we were all going in to dinner."

"It would hardly be my place to share something publicly about your son," she reminded him. "I didn't know the McKendrys' guests. And besides, the story should be yours to share."

A lie, in part.

"I saw you defend him and *his* mother quite publicly when you thought the Squire and his wife were being unfair. You didn't know them either."

"Now that was not exactly the same thing." She glared at him. "What are you trying to say, Captain Melfort?"

He entangled his fingers in hers. She watched the dance, forgetting to breathe until he withdrew his hand.

"I'm saying you had an ulterior motive for coming after me tonight."

He was daring her to speak the truth, but she was a coward. Jo wanted him, and yet she was too afraid to act, even hidden with him here in a maze of privet. She'd started a dangerous game, but she was an amateur. She didn't know how to finish it.

Jo resigned her wildly impulsive, half-formed plan, and turned toward the candlelit windows of the drawing room. It was time to go and she came to her feet. He immediately followed her lead.

"Mrs. McKendry will be wondering what's happened to me," she lied. "I should say good night, Captain."

"Not yet."

Her heart fluttered with alarm when he took a step toward her. He knew the truth. He saw through her. She could have shared the story about Cuffe tomorrow or the next time she'd seen him.

His height and strength gave him an overpowering advantage, but it wasn't Wynne that Jo feared. It was herself. She *did* have an ulterior motive.

"Cuffe has been here for over two months now," he said. "And despite me asking him on numerous occasions, not once has he come with me to see what I'm planning for Knockburn Hall. He's agreed to go tomorrow."

"I'm so glad to hear it," she responded brightly, all the while chiding herself for imagining a romantic liaison in the garden while he just wanted to tell her about an outing with his son.

"But he has one condition."

"A condition?" she asked, daring herself to look up into his eyes.

"You."

"Me?"

"Actually, we both want you to come," he said, lifting her chin when she tried to look away. She could not seem to find her balance in this conversation. All she knew was that her heart was about to hammer through the wall of her chest.

"Don't you think this might be the perfect chance for a father and son to share a walk together? You really shouldn't ruin it by bringing a stranger—"

"*I* want you there," he said, stopping her.

Jo knew this was her last chance to retreat to a safe haven of respectability. She couldn't do it. Her heart wouldn't allow any more denials. Not now. Waiting and wanting, her gaze fell on his lips.

He slowly lowered his head until his lips brushed hers, and the floodgate of memories opened. His kiss was warm and subtle, as gentle as their first time, yet it moved her in wholly unexpected ways.

The touch of their mouths reawakened feelings Jo had thought she'd never experience again. The pounding beat of her heart, the pooling warmth in her belly, the scorching fever of her skin.

And she welcomed them. She wanted more.

As if reading her mind, Wynne bent forward again and brushed his lips over the sensitive skin of her brow, her cheek, her chin. He was teasing her, pushing her to smash the constraints that bound her, to give in to the impulses that seemed so natural at this moment, to kiss him back.

Jo's undoing came when the tip of his finger caressed the edge of her ear and moved slowly down her throat to the neckline of her dress.

She kissed him.

Even as her lips pressed against his, she tried to fool herself with the thought that one kiss would be enough. It was rash, indulgent, an attempt to slake a thirst that she knew deep down would never be satisfied. But before she could withdraw from him, she felt his hand cradling the back of her head. And then he was kissing her with such passion that Jo felt overcome with a melting desire.

Whatever shred of control she'd been clinging to crumbled. She wrapped her hands around his neck, her fingers threaded into his hair. She nipped at his lower lip, challenging *his* control, wanting him to show her more.

He groaned as he deepened the kiss, his tongue teasing the corners of her mouth. Her lips opened to his advance, and she became aware of a pulsing heat emanating from her belly. She heard a satisfied sound in the back of his throat as his mouth became more demanding.

Jo couldn't get close enough to him. Her arms moved higher around his neck, her body pressing against his until no breath of air existed between them. She was running a race and stopping was not an option.

Wynne's hands slid down her back and over the curve of her bottom, pressing her against his arousal. She should have been frightened. Somewhere in the back of her mind, a muffled alarm was sounding. But she wasn't afraid. The mating of their mouths thrilled her. The touch of his capable hands as they caressed the sides of her breasts made Jo wonder if he might just take her here in the darkness of this garden.

And then it occurred to her that wondering had somehow become hoping.

A door opened and closed somewhere in the distance, and she gasped. Pressing a hand against his chest, she drew back, horrified by her actions, shaken by what she was about to do, and breathing hard.

The passage of years meant nothing. Their passion still burned, hot enough to consume them. The innocence of youth was gone, replaced by a firestorm of need.

"Wynne, I can't do this." Her voice shook. "We shouldn't."

"I'm sorry." His ragged breathing matched hers. He ran a frustrated hand through his hair and looked in the direction of the sound.

"I . . . I have to go." She tried to back away, but he caught her hand.

Jo was starving and he was her sustenance. She was dying of thirst and Wynne was the only one who could quench it.

"Come with us tomorrow."

Her treacherous heart had already decided.

"I will," she whispered.

13

WYNNE WASN'T certain if it was a matter of wanting to do the honorable thing or if it was the devil in him.

Finding Dermot in his office, he leaned in at the door. The place had more piles of books and journals and scraps of paper every day. The doctor had clearly given up sitting while he worked because his chair, like every other one in the room, was piled high with more volumes and ledgers and medical equipment than Wynne could even begin to identify.

"If we ever have a fire, they'll be able to see your office burning in Edinburgh."

Dermot was standing at the desk by the window, writing in a notebook. He grunted in acknowledgment.

Wynne made no attempt to enter. There was no discernible path through the mess on the floor. "Of course, you'll go up in flames as well. We'll remember you as the Jeanne d'Arc of the medical profession."

Another sound came from the area of the window.

"I'll be out this morning, Joan. Just wanted you to know."

Another grunt.

"I've told Mrs. McKendry already not to expect us back before noon."

"Us?" The doctor's head lifted from his work, his eyes curious. "Who is going with you?"

"No worry about me?" Wynne frowned. "You don't ask where I am going or the reason?"

"*You* can go to the blazes. If you were swallowed by a loch monster, no one would miss you," Dermot declared before a half smile broke over his face. "Since when have you become such a delicate flower? Wait, I don't care to have an answer to that either."

He wondered if his rival knew why Jo left their dinner guests early last night and where she went. Wynne knew, and that was a kiss he'd never forget.

"Very well, then. We'll be off."

"*Who* is going with you?" Dermot repeated the question. "And what does Joan of Arc have to do with any of this?"

"I'm taking Cuffe and Lady Jo to Knockburn Hall."

The doctor threw down his pen and searched for a way to the door. "Wait for me to get my hat. I'll come along."

"Stay where you are," Wynne retorted. "Hat or no hat, you're not invited."

"But I insist."

"You can insist all you want. You're not—"

Dermot stepped over a barricade of medical journals onto a smaller mound of newspapers which immediately shot out from underfoot.

On instinct, Wynne nearly dived in to help, but it was

too late. Dermot landed on the floor in a very awkward position amid the avalanche of fallen books and papers.

"Bloody hell. Help me up. I think I may have sprained something."

"I wouldn't be surprised if you did." Wynne crossed his arms over his chest and leaned against the doorjamb. "But not being in the medical profession, I wouldn't know."

"I've definitely split the seam in my pants, I can tell you that."

"That sounds quite serious. In fact, it's the final nail in the coffin. You're not coming."

"See here," Dermot snapped, planting his hands on the floor and glaring across the room. "Have you forgotten our conversation?"

"We have many, Doctor. Fortunately for you, I don't recall most of them." As he began to back out of the office, Wynne paused, deciding his rival needed clarification. "But I do remember the conversation you're referring to. And to amend the concluding remarks of that discussion, you will *not* be standing with her at the church door. That is, if you can ever stand again."

Dermot's face was the very picture of surprise as he searched for a response.

"But while we're gone, try to do something useful for this hospital you're so committed to." Wynne closed the door and started for the stairs as the sound of another crash and a muffled curse came from the office.

Six days ago, when the Highlander expressed his intentions, Wynne didn't know his own mind about Jo. He certainly couldn't articulate to someone else what she meant to him. But watching her, speaking with her, getting to know her over these past days, and especially after their kiss in the garden last night, he was in a far better place now. He still didn't know what the future held for them, but he wasn't about to let her be pressured into a marriage with his scoundrel of a friend.

Sixteen years ago, he'd done a poor job of breaking off his engagement with Jo. Unforgivably poor. Wynne didn't care one whit about her parentage, but he had no choice in doing it. He still believed he was protecting her from abominable treatment at the hands of his family and horrible unhappiness during his long periods of absence. With the war on and his naval duties, he couldn't have given her the life she deserved.

Their lives were different now, but as he left the house, Wynne wondered what was motivating him. Was it Dermot's actions or an awakening in himself that was driving him? She was beautiful and accomplished and wealthy, a woman any man would want. But to him, she was Jo. Just as he'd known her. It made no difference if they'd known each other six days or sixteen years. Something had reignited between them. All their yesterdays and today were one. But he believed they couldn't move forward from here, not until she allowed him to explain the past, and forgave him.

Her initial offer, to pretend they'd just met, no longer suited him.

Wynne admired the woman she'd become. He was drawn to her as sure as the bee to the flower. And if her reaction in the garden was any proof, she wasn't immune to him either.

Their kiss had started a fire in him that had been nearly impossible to contain. If it weren't for the slam of a door and the threat of someone coming upon them, they could have gone too far. And that was wrong because they still hadn't put the past behind them. Taking Jo in a garden or in his bed without offering her a future was not what he'd intended to do.

Thankfully, reason and respectability reared their stern and forbidding heads, and she couldn't get away from him fast enough. In spite of all she'd said, he sensed that the past was still wedged firmly between them. The botched retraction of his offer of marriage. Her family. His own family. His duel with her brother Hugh.

Jo had changed and so, Wynne realized, had he. Until she arrived, he thought he knew himself and what his future would be. Now he wasn't sure exactly what he wanted. Over the past few days, an ache deep in his gut had begun to gnaw at him, and it was getting worse. As if he were a young bull in springtime, stirrings of desire afflicted him, and he would not stop in his pursuit. But to what end?

He needed to win her, but he would not hurt her again.

Cuffe and Jo were waiting for him by the fish ponds. As Wynne approached, his focus shifted to the two. His son stood so confidently as he spoke to her. He was meeting Jo's gaze directly, something he still rarely did when speaking with Wynne.

For her part, Jo glowed with the sparkling water behind her. Enthusiasm lit her face at whatever the lad was conveying.

The image was perfect. A vision of harmony. The two were more at ease with each other than either was with Wynne.

His relationship with Cuffe had improved tenfold in this past week alone, but the boy's decision to speak didn't make him feel like a trusted father. The lad continued to complain and question his authority and negotiate what Wynne said needed to be done. He had no doubt his son still wanted to get back to Jamaica, the place he considered his real home.

The conversation stopped as they noticed his approach. Undeterred, Wynne asked them what they found interesting to talk about on such a fine morning.

"Cuffe was telling me that between late last night and early this morning he finished copying out Ohenewaa's stories into a volume of his own," Jo replied as they set off toward Knockburn Hall.

One more reminder of his failure as a parent. He'd missed so many rungs in the ladder of fatherhood. Last night, rather than a hastily said "good night" from the doorway, he could have gone into Cuffe's room and talked to him. He could have already heard from his son's lips about this accomplishment.

Too late now, he thought, still managing some belated praise as they walked along.

Cuffe slowed down when they reached the second fish pond. A lad from the kitchens was net fishing in the shallows. Drawing in the lines, the young man closed the net around his catch and hauled in a dozen good-sized trout that were destined for the Abbey's dinner table. Wynne realized this was one of the boys his son had fought with, and he was relieved to see there was no open hostility between them.

"Now that I've finished reading them all," Cuffe said, addressing only Jo as they continued on, "I can't decide which of the tales are my favorites."

"The story of Lightning and Thunder was one I particularly liked when I was growing up," she replied.

From a marshy area at the top end of the pond, the

sound of a thousand frogs filled the air, causing Cuffe to glance in that direction.

"'Getting Banished to Sky,'" he said as they continued to walk. "The stories have a lot of banishing in them."

"They are tales people told each other to explain nature, while keeping the young ones' attention."

"Almost all them teach a lesson," he noted. "And they're learned painfully."

"True in life as well, isn't it?" she asked. "But some of the tales are uplifting and quite funny."

Wynne decided to venture into the conversation.

"What about your grandmother, Cuffe?" he asked. "She must have had stories that she told you when you were growing up."

The old shrug was back, but Wynne wasn't going to be put off so easily.

"What were those stories like?"

Cuffe picked up a stick, hitting it on the ground as they walked, and Wynne and Jo exchanged a glance over the boy's head.

"How did they compare?" Jo asked. "Were any of the lessons in Ohenewaa's stories similar to your Nanny's?"

"She always said her tales were about wisdom," he answered with a smile. "'You smarter now?' she'd say after a story. 'Ol' Hige is out tonight. Better to stay in.'"

"What is Ol' Hige?" Wynne asked.

Cuffe ignored him and dragged his stick along the ground.

"Ol' Hige is a witch," Jo told Wynne. "She sheds her skin and flies by night. Sometimes she turns into an owl."

"How did you know?" Cuffe asked, looking up with admiration.

She shrugged and smiled. "Go ahead, tell your father what Ol' Hige does."

Too excited about the story to remember he was trying not to be nice to Wynne, Cuffe rattled off his explanation. "She sucks out people's breath while they're sleeping. She especially likes the babies."

"How do you protect yourself?" Wynne asked. "Can she be killed?"

Cuffe looked first at Jo, but when she shrugged, he decided to continue.

"She sheds her skin when she flies. And that's when you can beat her." He talked as if this was information everyone knew. "If you find her skin, you put salt and pepper on it. Then she can't put it back on because it will burn her. That's how she dies."

Wynne smiled and looked at Jo. "You've heard this before?"

"A version of it. I've heard Ol' Hige stories under different names. In Ohenewaa's tales, she was called the Sukuyan, and she traveled not as an owl but as a ball of light, looking for blood to suck."

"But your sister didn't put it in the book," Cuffe said, holding out a hand to help Jo around a low wet place in the path.

"I think Phoebe was too frightened to write it down on paper." Jo smiled. "Even as an adult, she spends most of her time living in her imagination. I wouldn't be surprised if she still lies abed at night looking at the window and expecting Ol' Hige to swoop in and steal her breath or her blood."

They reached the log that traversed the brook and Cuffe ran across before quickly coming back to hold Jo's hand as she crossed.

As they started along the path again, Wynne tried to keep his son talking. "Maybe you should add the stories your Nanny told you to this collection. Or perhaps you could make a separate book."

Jo's nod told him he'd made a good suggestion, so he was surprised when his son's eyes grew sad.

"I didn't hear them enough to keep them in my memory," he said in a low voice before turning to Jo. "You were able to listen to Ohenewaa for years and years."

"No, I wasn't, though I wish I could have. We lost Ohenewaa when my sister Phoebe—the one who set the tales down on paper—was younger than you are now."

"How did she remember them?"

"She put down what she could and embellished them as she wrote. The ones you read are retellings of retellings."

"So they're not exactly as you heard them?"

Jo shook her head. "No, but we were all so relieved that she did it, because now a woman we loved will stay in our minds and hearts forever. And the next generation of Pennington children will know her too."

Cuffe seemed satisfied with the answer, but he said nothing of Wynne's suggestion about writing down Nanny's stories.

They walked in silence for a while until the stone walls of Knockburn Hall came into sight. As they were passing the orchard, Cuffe spoke up.

"How did you lose her?"

Jo glanced over the lad's head at Wynne before she answered. "Ohenewaa died of old age."

"In Scotland?"

She nodded. "Yes, she's buried in a cemetery at our home in the Borders."

Cuffe stopped, facing her. "Why? Didn't she want to go back to her own home?"

When Jo hesitated, Wynne knew she was beset with her memories of the old woman. He'd heard so many stories of her. In every way that mattered, Ohenewaa had been a member of the Pennington family.

"She chose the place she wished to call home," Jo said finally. "Ohenewaa was a free woman since before I was born. She came from western Africa originally, suffered the brutality of slavers in the West Indies, and came to live with us when she was free. She could have gone anywhere she wished, and she guarded that freedom fiercely. But she chose to remain with us. It was her choice to live the rest of her life where my mother and her children were, to be part of our lives. We loved her and she loved us."

Cuffe shrugged and drew a pattern in the grass with his stick before meeting Jo's gaze again.

"But what about her other family, the people she left behind in Africa or in the islands? Don't you think they missed her? Didn't they need her too?"

The ten-year-old didn't wait for an answer, but turned and strode away from them.

Wynne saw the concern in Jo's face as Cuffe trudged toward the massive building.

"He is still struggling," he whispered, touching her hand.

"I know." She smiled sadly and linked her arm with his. "But he has a point. My brothers and sisters and I, my parents, my grandmother before she died—everyone who knew Ohenewaa—felt so fortunate to have her in our lives, but we were only thinking of ourselves."

There was nothing Wynne could say to console Jo. He

had no answers, no wisdom to share. He felt the same helplessness that he had been experiencing for months in the face of his son's unhappiness and anger. There were no other choices for Cuffe but the life he was offering him. Jamaica was not a safe place for him. But to say the words or to argue them wasn't enough.

The walls of the house glistened in the morning sun. It occurred to Wynne that he could have moved here with Cuffe before now. He could have had windows installed and purchased the furniture, and that would have been enough. But he'd held off, making excuses, telling himself he was waiting for the addition to be completed. All lies. They weren't living here because neither of them was ready. How could he move his son from the Abbey—as flawed as the living arrangements were—to a shell of a house that had no heart?

As he considered this, he saw his son walk directly to the door, push it open, and disappear inside.

At one time his life was all about keeping those he loved under control, protected, safe. It had driven his decisions about life with Jo. About who would raise his son. But what did that get him? He felt no fuller than the empty house looming ahead.

While they were climbing the last short rise to the door, Cuffe reappeared. Without giving them so much as a glance, he walked around the side of the house to where an overgrown greensward dropped away to a pond. There, he plunked himself down, hugged his knees to his chest, and looked across the water into the murky depths of the Highland forest.

Wynne's air of sadness and defeat was palpable to Jo as she stood with him outside the door of Knockburn Hall. He said nothing but continued to gaze at his son sitting alone on the knoll.

She understood his feelings. Cuffe made a forlorn little figure, sitting in the dense shadow of the chestnut trees, his head resting on his knees. He'd tossed his tam somewhere and was yanking out clumps of the long grass.

Wynne roused himself and took a deep breath before turning his attention to her.

"We're here," he said quietly. "We may as well go in. Would you care to see the inside of the house?"

She shook her head and placed a hand on his arm. "Go to him. Talk to him."

"Cuffe doesn't want to talk to me. He already knows I won't give him what he wants. I can't send him back."

He was aging before her eyes, lines of concern creased his brow.

"Go sit with him then," she suggested, motioning in the child's direction. "He needs to know that you understand he's in pain."

"To what purpose?"

She could hear the naval commander in the utterance of those words. He was frustrated. She knew what worked with some men, instilling obedience in their children, was not Wynne's way. Her own father, though gruff and short-tempered, was a loving man with very different ideas about what a parent's role should be.

"Simply to let him talk about the life he left behind. Coax him to tell you in his own words what hurts," she said. "Perhaps you may learn how to make things better for him and for yourself."

Gently and without warning, he lifted her chin and

placed a chaste kiss on her lips. The look of tenderness in his eyes took her breath away.

As he walked toward his son, Jo remained where she was, hoping they could break down the walls between them.

Wynne reached Cuffe and the two exchanged a few words. From his gestures, it looked as if he was asking for permission to join his son. She felt the world stand still. Finally, she saw the slight shrug, and she let out a sigh of relief as he sat on the grass.

Not wanting to intrude on their privacy, she went into the house.

Like so many tower houses, stone stairs ran along the outside walls, and she went up to a landing and through an arched doorway into a large great hall with a cavernous fireplace at the far end.

A carved stone medallion above the fireplace depicted two unicorns holding a shield that bore the rampant lion of the Stewarts, and Jo found herself staring vacantly at it. No matter how hard she tried to focus on the stonework or the plan of the building, her mind continually returned to the conversation they'd had on their way here and the one that was happening now.

She couldn't recall a question about her childhood jarring her the way Cuffe's had done. For all the years that Ohenewaa had been a part of her life, rarely had she imagined the old woman's life outside of the world they lived in. Hertfordshire and London and Baronsford comprised the entire universe for Jo until she'd grown. It was where they lived, where they belonged. She didn't remember ever asking Ohenewaa if she had another family, people who waited for her and hoped someday she'd return, as Cuffe put it. After she died, Jo recalled no conversation about where she should be buried, only that her mother wanted Ohenewaa interred with the family. Whether her adoptive parents ever asked the older woman's wishes, Jo didn't know.

Jo tried to shake off these thoughts and made her way back to the stairs. The smell of stone and ancient fires filled her senses as she climbed to the next level, and she thought of all the people she'd known who lost their families and their homes through acts of violence. The freed Africans and islanders she'd lived with at Melbury Hall who had seen unspeakable crimes against them. The Scottish women and children, shunned by society, who found sanctuary at the residence she established in the tower house near Baronsford. Even her sister-in-law Grace, who'd witnessed her father's murder at the hands of assassins, in desperation hid herself in a crate being shipped to an unknown destination. All of them severed irrevocably from their past, with only the slightest chance of surviving the present, facing a world in which the future was dark and bleak.

Upstairs, Jo entered a long corridor, lit by a construction opening in the stone at the far end. Doors led to what she guessed were bedchambers. As she walked in and out of rooms, she thought about her own birth mother. She'd spoken to servants and farmers who were around at the time of her birth. Everyone had a story, even haughty people like Lady Nithsdale, and Jo had etched them into her memory.

None of them added much to what Jo heard from her adoptive mother: the words of an old woman and a few utterances of a dying, wild-eyed girl whose only fears were for her newborn bairn.

All the poor creature ever said was that her name was Jo . . .

Don't know if she was a faerie child or just cast out on account o' the child swelling in her . . .

Reckoned she had no man she was a-going to, and no husband left behind. Leastwise, she never mentioned any . . .

Terrified . . . kept that muddy plaid pulled over her like a shroud.

"Those poor people, cast out of their homes in the Highland clearances, had been stripped of everything," Jo's mother told her. "And what awaited them at the end of their journey looked to be nothing but more misery, if they didn't die on the road itself. They were torn from their kin, their land, and their homes. And still, they were proud. Jo died with her tiny, tartan-swaddled daughter in one arm while her other hand clutched mine. You were her child."

Jo wiped away the tears on her face and looked out a small window at the father and son sitting on the knoll below. Her life was a story of displacement too. Without the woman who took her home and raised her, she too would have surely died in a muddy ditch on a road to nowhere.

But to someone, somewhere, Jo's birth mother belonged. There had to be people who cared about her, who loved her, who worried fearfully about what had become of her.

Perhaps, she thought, a man still lived who cared for her. A man who—years later, in spite of a badly damaged mind—continued to sketch endlessly the woman he'd lost.

As she watched Wynne and Cuffe sitting together, rays of sunlight spilled over the tower house and lit the grassy area around them. The child's shoulders were shaking while his father spoke steadily. Then Wynne placed an arm around his son and drew him close.

A single tear slid down Jo's cheek. She loved Wynne. And she'd never stopped loving him. Never. Not through all the years when hope was gone.

***

When Wynne first approached his son, he thought they wouldn't speak at all. But Jo was right. Cuffe wanted to talk to him, to someone, and once he began, the floodgates burst open.

He only needed to ask about Jamaica, about the village in the mountainous forests above Falmouth. About the house Cuffe lived in with his grandmother. He didn't need to say anything else, for his son talked of Nanny until homesickness and grief nearly choked him.

The trees, the grass, the pond, the dark hair resting against Wynne's shoulder became a blur as he struggled against the raw emotion his son's words and tears unleashed in him. He waited, allowing the tranquility of the woods and the water to calm Cuffe's sobs before he spoke.

"You want to be there with her, I know. You feel your place is to help your grandmother." Wynne forced the words out through the tightness in his throat. "But Nanny's last letter before I sent for you convinced me that her sole hope, her greatest prayer, was that you come to live here."

"But why?"

"Because she was worried about you."

"But I'm worried about *her*!" he cried.

"Your Nanny saw more trouble coming on the island, and she was afraid you'd be caught up in it."

"I'll stay out of it. I won't do anything to make her worry."

"Nanny has lived through troubles before. She knows how young men and boys get swept up in it, whether they mean to or not. It's the nature of war, and she said war is coming between the Maroons and the plantation owners." Wynne rubbed his son's back. "Nanny told me she'd die if you were taken by the authorities or hurt for tagging along."

"If you let me go back, I swear I won't do any of those things." Cuffe pulled away and turned his pleading eyes on him. "I'll stay close to her, I promise. I won't even leave the village."

He knew his son was mature far beyond his years. Cuffe had grown up hearing about or witnessing with his own eyes the ruthlessness of the landowners. The injustice would inevitably drive him to resist.

It had been more than seven years since slave-trading was made illegal, but little had changed in the islands. Wynne was a military man and he believed in the Maroon's fight. He too had seen the evils of slavery first-hand. Too many in England profited by the exploitation of human beings, and too many turned a blind eye to it.

More than the fair-weather abolitionists and the idealists in Parliament, the Maroons were the strongest force resisting the evil of slavery in Jamaica. In the sugar islands, they were known as the Children of the Mist. And they were feared. Emerging from nowhere, they'd attack a slave trader, free a shipment of slaves bound for a plantation, and then disappear. When retaliations came, everyone was dragged into battle—every man, woman, and child. And this is what Cuffe's grandmother feared most.

Wynne respected the fight, but he couldn't allow his son to take part in it at his age.

"I'm not saying this well," he said, searching for the words that might help Cuffe understand. "The decision to bring you to Scotland was to give you a safe home, but that's not all. Having you here is as much about your Nanny and me. It's about being a grandmother and a father. It's about caring so much that you would die before allowing your son to be hurt."

He pulled Cuffe to him again, and to his relief, the boy allowed it. Wynne hadn't been the father he should have been, but he would make up for it now.

"Until you're grown," he told him, "your place is with me. But I promise you this, I'll teach you all you need to know to survive in the world you choose to live in. You'll learn to think and ride and fight. You'll train your mind and your body. You'll become strong and sharp and clear thinking. You'll be a leader that men can trust. And when you're ready, when you're old enough, you can choose where you want to be."

Wynne knew this wasn't the answer Cuffe hoped for.

"I know you miss your grandmother," he said softly. "You can write to her. I know she'll write back to you."

"But the time between is slow," Cuffe said, pulling away again. "If I don't see her, I'm afraid I'll forget her."

"Never. Nanny raised you. She made you the fine, strong lad you are. For as long as you live, she'll be a part of who you are and a part of all you'll do."

Cuffe stretched his legs out in front of him and stared at the line of trees beyond the pond. His tears had dried and the sobs had subsided, but his sorrow still showed on his face.

Jo told him to listen and talk to his son. He'd listened and then he'd talked, as well. He hoped Cuffe knew that he understood his son's pain.

They'd made a great leap forward in a very short time, but he knew that this moment was just one step on a long road.

"So much of life requires making difficult choices," Wynne said quietly. "You have many ahead of you."

He was surprised when Cuffe's gaze swung around to him.

"What difficult choices have you made?"

"Too many to count."

"Was it a difficult choice bringing me here?"

Wynne pushed the shock of hair to the side to see his son's alert brown eyes. "No. That wasn't difficult at all."

"Tell me one difficult choice you made. One that changed your life."

Wynne's gaze drifted toward the stone edifice behind them. "I broke off my engagement with Lady Jo sixteen years ago."

Cuffe twisted around to glance back at the house. "You and Lady Jo? Why would you do that? What's wrong with you? How could you let her go?"

Wynne could not disagree. *What was wrong with him?*

"I gave her up because I feared for her," he replied finally. "I let her go because I couldn't protect her."

❧ 14 ❧

By Thursday morning Jo still hadn't informed her hosts about her difficult decision to leave in two days for Torrishbrae. She'd only intended to stop briefly as she passed through. But as she looked at the patients enjoying the spring sunshine and busying themselves around the pond closest to the Abbey buildings, Jo could almost feel the invisible ties that had already formed.

Sitting on a blanket on the lee side of a large boulder, she looked at Charles Barton. The bruises from last week's attack were fading, and thankfully, there were no lasting effects. He was drawing furiously beside her. Her task was to put each drawing on the growing stack beneath the rock they were using to secure the sheets of paper against the breeze. Mr. Fyffe danced by, sawing away at his imaginary fiddle, and Mr. Stevenson was sitting calmly by a host of daffodils, an attendant lounging on either side of him. A dozen other men were spread along the edge of the pond, fishing poles in hand.

The peculiarities in the behavior of the patients in the

annex had become less and less strange to her. Jo was surprised how quickly one came to accept their quirks and their difference. While she was watching them, a shout drew her gaze across the pond as a patient landed a trout, which flopped and flashed on the grass in the sunlight, to the delight of all.

Hamish, the farm manager, greeted her as he and an assistant went by, inspecting the banks of the pond as he made his way toward the small dam. Normally, Cuffe would have been with him on such an occasion, but he was otherwise engaged this morning with his father.

Her companion interrupted her thoughts, handing her another drawing, which she dutifully secured.

The Squire and his wife were unrelenting in their efforts to press their nephew's matrimonial case, but Jo sensed that Dr. McKendry was having too good a time playing the role of a rejected suitor when he had an audience. The air of exaggeration in his suffering reminded Jo of comic performances at the theatre in Drury Lane. Still, his family's warmth and hospitality were exceeded only by their unintentional social blunders and their fondness for local gossip.

Jo had formed attachments here, to be sure, but more than any of the others, it was almost unbearable to think of leaving Wynne and Cuffe. They needed time, however, for themselves.

The father-and-son conversation they'd shared at Knockburn Hall had marked a new chapter for both of them. Last night, Cuffe even decided to join the family for dinner. And now this morning, they had ridden together to the village for the Thursday market.

Jo was glad they had gone alone. They'd both asked her to accompany them, but as much as she wanted to go, she couldn't. By not going, she was giving the two a chance to build their relationship. These times together were critical for them, and she would not allow herself to intrude.

The ache that gnawed at her when she thought of leaving was back. The brief time she and Wynne spent together had rekindled the spark inside that had never died. But perhaps this didn't need to be a permanent farewell. She felt better thinking that nothing was to hinder her from stopping back here in a month or so when she was returning to Baronsford.

Twice a day she'd been sitting with Charles Barton, searching for any clue he might have about her mother, but nothing more had revealed itself. She wasn't giving up, though. She could only hope he would continue to improve by the time she returned.

And when it came to Wynne, she wasn't about to interpret his behavior toward her as anything more than friendship. The momentary burst of passion they shared in the garden was simply a fleeting impulse on both their parts. It was a good thing that he'd made no further overtures, because she didn't trust her own heart. Perhaps when she was gone, however, distance and a month's time apart would afford them a clearer perspective on the reality of their situation.

She was deep in these meditations when Charles Barton tried to hand her another drawing. Without warning the paper flew off in the breeze and went sailing toward the water. Jo jumped up, waved off a nearby attendant, and scrambled after the sketch. She chased it down and grabbed the paper at the top of the embankment before it flew off across the glistening surface.

Looking at this latest drawing, Jo was astonished to

see that for the first time, the depiction was not of a young woman who resembled her. It was Jo herself. The braid pinned at the back of her head, the lines around the smiling mouth that indicated her age, the style of the clothing. Charles had drawn the dress and spencer jacket and shawl she had on today. Even the matching velvet and lace cap that was presently sitting on the blanket was discernable in her hand.

Hope softened the clenched fist of disappointment she'd come to accept. She turned and found the older man watching her.

"You see me," she said, smiling. "You're drawing *me*."

Maybe it was her imagination, but she would have sworn she saw the slightest of nods and understanding in his eyes.

He *was* responding. Could it be the fog he'd been lost in was lifting?

Suddenly, the dancing fiddler came out of nowhere and inadvertently grazed Jo's shoulder as he whirled past.

Her flailing arms were of no use as she slipped backward. It was too late. Her heel caught on something and then she stepped back into space. She hit the water like a felled tree and sank beneath the surface. The coldness of the pond shocked her and she swallowed a mouthful of water. Jo was a capable swimmer, but there was no need for such skills. Once she got her legs under her and stood up, the water barely reached her chest. She would have had no trouble getting out of the pond if it weren't for two men leaping in after her.

The wild shouts from the nearest man stunned her.

"Jo . . . Jo . . . save Jo." Charles Barton yelled, waving his arms in desperation. Right behind him, Hamish was up to his waist and shouting to the attendants to fetch blankets and help.

"Save Jo," Barton cried out, driving through the water to reach her.

He'd seen her. He was calling her name.

"I'm right here," she said, pushing hair and grass out of her face and taking the man's hand. "Nothing has happened. I am with you. Right here with you."

Hamish grabbed the older man from behind and tried to steer him toward other attendants rushing over to help.

Barton fought him and cried out in an anguished voice. "No . . . Jo! Garloch!"

She waded after him, not wanting to let him go. It broke her heart to see him so upset.

Hamish and an attendant dragged Charles toward a more gradual bank to help him out of the water. All the while, the older man continued to cry out and she struggled to get to him. Jo was about to climb out of the pond herself when Wynne was there, splashing into the water and wrapping a blanket around her shoulders.

In the distance, Jo could still hear Charles Barton shouting the same words over and over.

"Garloch! Garloch!"

"Captain Melfort is pacing the hall like a bear, m'lady," Anna said, not even trying to hide her delight as she hurriedly braided Jo's wet hair. "The man may take the door down if we don't hurry. And the doctor is out there too, arguing that *he* should see you first, him being the medical man and all."

They'd both have to wait, Jo thought. She was

perfectly fine. A quick dip in a fish pond in the month of May was no worse than swimming in the chilly waters of the River Tweed, and she'd been doing that since she was a child. She was made of hardier stock than these two gave her credit for.

Dried and dressed and again presentable, she stepped out of her room a few minutes later and found the two men still patrolling the corridor. Dr. McKendry was the first to reach her.

"You look terribly pale, m'lady. This has been a shock. You should undoubtedly be in bed. The last thing we want is this turning into brain fever. Allow me to—"

"Brain fever? Now I *am* certain that Edinburgh medical college taught you nothing about treating humans," Wynne barked, shouldering him out of the way. "You can leave Lady Jo in my hands. She looks perfectly well. But I believe one of those shaggy red cows wandering about may need you."

"Being governor of the hospital hardly makes you a medical expert."

"And what kind of expertise allows you to jump from a dunking in a fish pond to brain fever? Have you even spoken with the patient to ask how she is?"

"There it is," Dermot crowed. "You admit she's a patient. In which case Lady Josephine is under my care."

The door behind her opened and Anna appeared with her arms full of Jo's wet clothing. Seeing the gathering in the hallway, she quickly changed her mind and disappeared inside again.

"If I may, gentlemen," Jo said, using the momentary pause in the men's bickering to interject. "I'm in perfect health, Doctor, and I assure you there is no need for medical treatment. But far more important, I'm worried about Mr. Barton. How is he?"

Wynne stood next to Jo and glared at Dermot, as if demanding an answer on her behalf.

"Other than his frenzied concern for you, he appears to have weathered the incident fairly well. Hamish brought him back to the ward and stayed with him until he became calmer. As I was coming up here, one of the attendants was helping Barton into dry clothing."

The door behind her opened a little, and her maid peeked out. Before Jo could tell her that it was safe to go by, she popped her head back in and closed the door again.

"Is there a more suitable place where we can speak?" she asked.

The change in Charles Barton's sketch this morning. The way he'd jumped into the pond when he'd thought she was drowning. And the word he'd been shouting. She had a number of questions for the doctor, but this was not the place to pose them.

"Of course." Dermot motioned down the hall. "We can go to my office."

Wynne's muttering indicated that he didn't think of it as a good idea, but he stayed close as they followed the doctor. Arriving at the doorway, Jo watched the young man scurry around the office, trying to clear some space on the floor for her to walk. The place looked as if a tempest had recently blown through. Finding a chair free of parcels and books and stacks of paper would be an entirely separate matter.

Wynne's voice over her shoulder was a curious mix of derision and triumph. "Never mind this scene of chaos. Come with me."

When he took her hand, Jo allowed him to lead her down the hall, assuming the doctor would follow.

Wynne's office was the epitome of neatness and order. She couldn't help but smile at the contrast. Everything had a defined place in his work area. The desk and chairs and bookshelves appeared to be exactly where they were meant to be. A terrestrial globe stood in a corner with a framed map of the world on the wall above it. Over his desk, a colorful print depicted the Battle of Trafalgar being waged, and it was clear the French were being badly beaten.

Jo was impressed but not surprised. She knew Wynne well enough to see the orderliness of this room reflected his personality. He liked planning. He enjoyed order. Satisfaction came only when the pieces of a puzzle lined up and met his expectations. Even as a young man, he was put off by unforeseen events. She recalled him telling her that the key to a well-ordered ship depended on discipline and training. The sea was often unpredictable, which made it the duty of a commanding officer to control what he could by keeping his men and his equipment in top form.

Jo thought of his relationship with Cuffe. His son was already teaching him a few lessons about the unpredictability of a growing child, and the importance of flexibility.

Wynne offered her a seat near the desk, but she glanced back at the hallway.

"What happened to the doctor?" she asked. "Wasn't he going to join us here?"

"He's probably already forgotten we were there. I imagine right now he's standing in his office, one book tucked under his arm as he reads through another book he picked up from the floor." He sent a pained look at the doorway. "And when he's finished with whatever passage caught his eye, he'll see his logbook or ledger lying in a corner beneath a ream of paper and recall that he intended to look up a journal article having to do with melancholia or phrenology or some such thing. And then, of course, he could just possibly find a parcel of letters he'd intended to ask me to answer a month or so ago. The man is incapable of keeping order."

Jo's mind flashed to her youngest sister, Millie, and her obsession with creating order. Dr. McKendry would provide a worthwhile challenge for her talents.

Wynne paused as Jo sat in the proffered chair.

"Pray don't let on that I told you this, but in spite of my badgering and complaining, I know the man is as fine a doctor as you'll find anywhere. Many a sailor owes McKendry his life."

"You don't think he'll join us?" Jo asked.

"I was only half jesting. He'll be down here shortly, I assure you."

They were odd friends, she thought, but they definitely complemented each other's strengths.

"How did your trip to the village with Cuffe go this morning?" she asked.

The crease in his brow disappeared as Wynne settled into a chair. Satisfaction registered on his face. Jo already knew that look meant he was pleased with his son.

"The vicar told Cuffe recently of an old widow who lives on the outskirts of the village. He had a mind to purchase a few things to take over to her." His blue eyes met hers across the room. "He's a good lad."

In her mind she saw the father and son sitting together by the pond at Knockburn Hall. She'd known it then and she knew it now. With Wynne's commitment, their relationship would flourish.

The momentary silence in the room was broken by Dr. McKendry charging in, carrying a parcel that he tossed on Wynne's desk. He drew a chair close to Jo and threw himself into it.

"I'm quite relieved to find you here, m'lady," he said with a note of apology that didn't match the mischievous glint in his eye. "I was fearful this villain may have absconded with you."

"You can call off the search party, McKendry," Wynne responded. "The only danger she faced was from some feral creature living in that wilderness you call an office."

Ignoring his friend, Dermot focused solely on her. "Are you certain you're feeling well enough to be up and about?"

"I assure you, I am," Jo told him.

"What's this?" Wynne demanded, holding up the parcel.

"Inexplicably," the doctor replied, "it was somehow misplaced in my office. I'm not certain when it arrived, but it's addressed to you."

Wynne sent Jo a conspiratorial look and inspected the packet before putting it aside. "Yes. Golf balls I had sent from St. Andrews as a gift for the Squire . . . about six months ago."

"But I am happy to see you're not any worse for your adventure this morning," Dermot said to her.

Coming out of the fish pond, Jo had been too agitated about Charles Barton's welfare to be concerned about herself. Wynne had been there to support her, immediately ordering the others to see that the patient was taken to the ward and that Dr. McKendry was informed. As he escorted Jo back to the house, he'd murmured words of assurance and stayed with her until Anna had taken over.

"About that adventure," Wynne said, drawing his friend's attention, "Fyffe's actions—"

"Were completely unintentional," Jo broke in. "It was an accident and largely my own fault. I was standing too close to the edge and paying no attention."

"Fyffe is exuberant but harmless," the doctor acknowledged. "That's why we don't assign an attendant specifically to watch him. However, considering today's events, we'll need to be more watchful."

"Of course, you must do what you think best, but he was hardly a threat," Jo asserted, conveying exactly what happened and then going on to tell them about the sketch she'd been holding when she fell into the pond.

The doctor was particularly interested in her observation about the change in Charles Barton.

"No doubt, Mr. Barton is now accustomed to your company. And enough people have been addressing you as Lady Josephine or Lady Jo in his presence. It's possible your name has registered with him," Dermot mused. "But the shift of sketching you instead of what he holds in his memory is very exciting. More and more, the curtain separating the remembered from the real appears to be falling away."

"But what is Garloch?" she asked, thinking of the words he shouted. "Barton kept saying 'Garloch.'"

"Garloch?" Wynne repeated, looking at the doctor. "Isn't that the name of a village north of here?"

Dermot nodded. "Yes, about three hours by carriage if the weather is good. The place isn't even half the size of Rayneford. Most of the farms have given over to raising sheep, I believe. Haven't been there since I was a lad. A fine river runs through it that my uncles used to fish in before they were seized with their golfing fever. Beyond that, I don't know much about the place. I can ask the vicar or the Squire; they may know more."

"But why would Mr. Barton shout the name?"

The doctor shrugged. "Difficult to say. Garloch is quite a way from Tilmory Castle."

"You say it's about three hours north of here?"

"Indeed," Dermot answered. "Are you thinking of going there?"

Jo decided it was time to tell them of her decision to leave. "Since you say this village is in the direction I'm traveling, I'll make a stop there on Saturday while I resume my journey to Torrishbrae."

The doctor's protest was immediate and pronounced, but Wynne's darkening expression was what Jo fixed on. He held her gaze. She imagined the questions running through his mind. He abruptly stood and went to the window.

"But you can't leave right now," Dermot exclaimed. "We need you here. Mr. Barton's progress clearly depends on your presence."

The doctor continued to protest. Watching Wynne's profile, she saw the clench of his jaw.

"My family expects me in Sutherland," she said in a reasonable tone, her words directed at Wynne. "And I believe I've accomplished all I can here."

"Hardly. We have finally broken through his silence. And another week's delay in your departure could make substantial difference in Mr. Barton's condition." Dermot turned to the captain as if he was noticing his silence for the first time. "Talk to her, Melfort. Talk reason. You're good at that sort of thing. Don't you want Lady Josephine to stay?"

He glanced over his shoulder at her. His penetrating blue eyes revealed his wishes before the words left his lips. "I do."

"There you have it," the doctor announced as if that were all she was waiting for.

Jo shook her head, still thinking it was wiser to put some distance between them. They were moving too fast.

Wynne turned from the window and joined the conversation. "That village is not on your way. You'll still need to travel toward the coast to go north to Sutherland. But if you stay, I'll go with you to Garloch and return here. This will give you the opportunity to investigate and see what connection exists between Barton and the village."

Wynne's offer to take her had its merits. An unknown Englishwoman stopping at an out-of-the-way village in the Highlands made less sense than having him traveling with her, considering his connection to the Abbey and the McKendrys.

"But what shall we do once we get there?" she asked him. "We don't even know if there's a tavern or an inn where we can ask about Mr. Barton."

"Most every village in the Highlands has a church." Wynne looked at Dermot, who nodded confirmation. "That will give us a place to start. We can ask the vicar what he knows. Perhaps even get a letter of introduction from him."

"I hate to think of you leaving your duties here," she persisted, her pulse rising at the thought of being alone with him for a full day.

"She's quite right," Dermot agreed. "I'll take care of

this. I can have my uncle write a letter and I can escort Lady Josephine to Garloch."

Jo thought the captain's response most interesting, for he first sent her a questioning look, as if seeking her approval, and she nodded.

"My dear McKendry. Over dinner recently, I heard you eloquently affirm your commitment to this hospital. About your devotion to the patients who need your care and attention. Lady Josephine would never allow you to sacrifice your valuable time." Wynne turned his attention back to Jo. "I happen to be at my leisure on Saturday, m'lady. We can leave at dawn and plan on returning before dark, if that suits you."

Jo accepted the offer, somewhat astonished at how easily she'd been persuaded to extend her stay once again. She'd need to send off another set of letters to her family, inform them of her plans, and try to avoid any reference to Captain Melfort.

❄   15   ❄

ON FRIDAY NIGHT, Wynne stopped in Cuffe's room to ask if he'd care to accompany them on their excursion in the morning.

"What does she hope to find in Garloch?"

Cuffe's astuteness constantly surprised him. In fact, the more time Wynne spent with him, the more he saw how far advanced the lad was for his ten years.

"She's hoping to find out who she is. It's possible someone in that village can explain the linkage between her mother and Mr. Barton."

"Why does it matter?"

"Because she still needs to know where she came from. It matters greatly to her, even though she was raised in a family that loves her deeply." Wynne recalled his son's fear of forgetting his grandmother. "You and I know where we came from and who our parents are. That knowledge anchors us in some way. It gives us a bond with a certain place and certain people. Lady Jo would be greatly heartened to have a portion of what you and I have."

"She's a good person," Cuffe said. "I see how upset she gets sometimes when she is sitting with Mr. Barton and he doesn't respond. She's always trying, always asking questions. But he's in a world of his own."

He sat cross-legged on his bed, studying Wynne in silence. In recent days, the difficulties of others had been injecting themselves into the lad's life. He'd begun to help McDonnell with his letters, reading them to the blacksmith at first. But he was now answering the mother on the man's behalf, and that was no easy task. In addition, the vicar told Wynne that his son had been asking about others who were in need in and around the village. He seemed particularly keen on helping old women, and young mothers who didn't have enough food to feed their families.

"Just the two of you should go to Garloch, Captain," Cuffe said finally. "And maybe while you're there, you can convince her to stay at the Abbey. I think that'd be good for her and for you. For all of us."

The following morning, as he packed his sword with his pistols under the seat of the carriage, Wynne was still thinking of his son's encouragement to pursue Jo.

No doubt existed, in either his mind or his heart, that he wanted her. He'd dreamed of her a thousand times. Since her arrival, he continually sought her out or kept an eye on her whereabouts at all times. She was back in his life, and her effect on him was stronger than it had been sixteen years ago.

His blood pulsed each time he recalled riding back from the village with Cuffe and coming upon the pandemonium at the fish pond. When he heard her name cried out with such anguish along with the heartrending entreaties to save her, he'd become a madman himself until he saw her standing upright and wading through the water.

Later, her announcement that she was leaving wreaked havoc in Wynne's mind. He was struck with the fear that he'd found her only to lose her again. He dreaded that once she returned to the protective arms of her family, his connection with her would be severed forever.

As a widower at his age, with wealth and a place in society, Wynne could probably have entered into marriage again. But he'd never been prepared to take that step. He would never consider a foolish match. He had no desire for a child bride, regardless of her dowry or her position. His sights had always been set higher. His devotion to his son dictated that he choose a woman with a strong mind and a kind heart.

On the list of women he wanted, Jo Pennington occupied the first and only place.

Leaving the driver and groom with his coach and four, Wynne went back up the half-dozen steps into the north annex.

Jo was the woman for him, but he feared a proposal right now would only invite rejection. He could make his feelings for her known; he could reveal the true workings of his heart, but their future lay in her hands. He'd withdrawn from her already when they were young. This time, it was up to Jo whether they should try again. All he could do was to be here. She needed to decide if a future with him was worthy of a second chance.

As he reached the bottom of the stairwell, he saw Jo coming down the stairs alone.

"You're not bringing your maid?" he asked after they'd exchanged greetings.

"As you know, sir, I'm well past the age of thirty," she answered lightly. "I have little need to worry about a damaged reputation."

"Your courage does you great credit, Lady Jo," he said in mock seriousness as he led her out into the courtyard.

"And you, Captain? Are you worried?"

Wynne pretended he was resigned to fate as he handed her into the carriage. "On more than one occasion, Dr. McKendry has said I'm a delicate flower in matters of my own reputation. But in your case, m'lady, I'll make an exception and try to bear up."

Climbing in and sitting across from her, he admired the smile tugging at Jo's lips. She was a woman who seemed ready for any situation. The black velvet hat and the deep-green carriage dress she wore beneath her cloak were as handsome as they were sensible, he thought.

In spite of the early hour, she was fresh-faced and ready for their adventure. Today was an unexpected gift. The two of them alone together on the road.

The serving men climbed up top, and the driver was heard calling to his four-in-hand, "Walk, walk on." As the carriage rolled on, Wynne saw Jo looking out the window back toward the Abbey.

"Please don't tell me that moonstruck suitor of yours is running after us in his nightshirt?"

"Don't tease me," she scolded, although the reprimand didn't reach her deep-brown eyes. "The doctor is not moonstruck. At least not because of me. And he is *not* my suitor."

"Well, he's mastered the woeful look," he told her. "I'm sorry to tell tales out of school, but last night after you ladies left the dining room, the rogue tried everything he could think of to get the vicar to give *him* the letter of introduction. His performance would have outshone Garrick himself."

"But you were able to get the letter?"

"Happily, I still have the ability to outwit McKendry." Wynne patted his pocket with the letter. "I promised the vicar I'd bring him a new set of Denholm golf clubs the next time I come back from Edinburgh."

"You didn't," she gasped. "You need do no such thing. I'll see to it. I'll make the arrangements to have the clubs made as soon as I get back. I'm so sorry to impose on—"

"All of this was in good humor," he said softly. "The vicar expects no reward."

Her cheeks reddened prettily and her eyes flashed reproachfully as she slapped his knee and smiled. Time again ticked backward for him. She'd often acted exactly this way any time he'd tease or fluster her. Wynne recalled how he'd then pull her onto his lap and kiss her, begging her forgiveness.

He was tempted to do it now. This was the first time they'd really been alone since their kiss in the garden.

Her flushed skin matched the color of the rising sun, and she leaned toward the window. He wondered if she too was recalling those bygone moments.

While she was distracted, Wynne studied her profile. The shape of her face, from the high cheekbones to the fullness of her lips. She was more beautiful than his memory served. His gaze moved to the dark curls escaping the velvet hat and slipped lower to the dress, momentarily lingering on her breasts. He'd felt their fullness when he'd brushed his fingers over them in the garden.

The two of them were close in age, but not in experience, he was certain. He'd been married. And during the years before and after his late wife Fiba, he'd had liaisons with women. Wynne's gaze once again moved over her body, her face, her parted lips, and he wondered if it was possible that she was still as innocent as she'd been years ago. It made no difference to him. Her passionate response to his kiss stirred that desire in his loins even now. She'd wanted more, as he did.

He shifted in the seat, suddenly uncomfortable with the direction of his thoughts and the reaction of his body. He needed to put his attention elsewhere and quickly found a topic more potent than any other to curb his body's wanton response.

"Your brother," he said. "Viscount Greysteil, Lord Justice of the Commissary Court in Edinburgh. Does he know I serve as governor at the Abbey?"

Her dark eyes relinquished the view of the rolling hills and turned to him. "Dr. McKendry failed to mention you when he first communicated with me."

"He was acting upon my recommendation. But since your arrival, you've sent a number of letters to Baronsford, have you not?" He cocked one eyebrow, waiting for an answer.

"Does it matter to you if my brother knows?"

Wynne patted the seat. "I always travel with a brace of pistols, so I'm prepared, just in case he decides to pursue you here. Greysteil missed my heart the first time. If he has a second chance, he might not feel so generous."

He was joking, but Jo's eyes clouded at the memory. "I thought we weren't going to speak of the past."

"That was before," he said softly. "Now I find it unavoidable."

Her brows knitted, and she returned her attention back out the window.

"I didn't blame him then. I don't blame him now. He was defending your honor. If I was gifted with a sister like you, I would have done the same thing."

She continued to sit in silence, but Wynne knew he didn't have days or weeks or months to pursue her. She could decide tomorrow to leave the Abbey, and he'd be left with only memories and regret. This was his opportunity to speak.

"My manner of breaking our engagement was badly done. Leaving you a letter instead of meeting with you and telling you in person—"

"Did you know Hugh lost his wife and son during the war on the Peninsula?" she interrupted, her voice grave. She was forcing a change in the topic. "They died of camp fever."

Wynne knew this. His sister-in-law sent him not only news of Jo. He was also regularly informed of Greysteil's successes and losses.

"He suffered terribly. The entire family mourned their deaths for years." Her words were marked with sadness. His reference to the past reawakened more than just the tragedy of their own separation.

"This past year, however, another chance at happiness came into his life. He's married again, and he and his wife now have an infant daughter."

Studying Jo's imploring look, he nodded and accepted her entreaty to cease his attempt to speak of their break, at least for now. She wasn't ready to have the wound of their past reopened. At the same time, he knew neither of them could fully mend until the scar had healed.

"Is it true," he asked instead, "that his new wife arrived at Baronsford in a crate?"

Relief reflected in her eyes and in the smile that suddenly graced her lips. "Who are your spies, Captain Melfort? How could you know this?"

"My brother John and his wife purchased Highfield Hall near Baronsford not long ago," he explained. "They are not among the Penningtons' circle of friends, justifiably, but there is very little news of you and your family that doesn't reach me through their letters."

"Then you must know about Gregory's marriage too?"

"That must be fairly recent, for I hadn't heard it. I only learned of it when you told the Squire and Mrs. McKendry that your younger brother now lives in Sutherland."

Perhaps he wouldn't mention this in *his* letters. His sister-in-law was well aware of the history between the Melforts and Penningtons. She understood why they were the only family in that part of the Borders who were not invited to Baronsford's summer and Christmas balls. Nonetheless, her disappointment at being excluded from the more public celebrations of the viscount's wedding in the village of Melrose came through clearly in her letter. It wouldn't be very kind to tweak her nose about this wedding as well.

The carriage rolled on, climbing higher into the hills above the Don river valley, and Jo appeared preoccupied with her thoughts as she gazed out at the rugged forests and gorse-covered countryside. Still thinking of his brother, John, and his wife, Wynne now pondered their repeated invitations to bring Cuffe south to Highfield Hall. They wanted him to meet the rest of his family. They had a son who was twelve, or thereabouts, and a nine-year-old daughter. A fortnight ago, he would never have seriously considered bringing them all together. Now he was actually feeling quite sanguine about it.

And all because of the woman seated across from him.

"If I may ask, Jo, how are your parents?" During the time when they'd thought Wynne would soon be joining their family, the earl and the countess had shown him only kindness.

Her eyes lit with pleasure. "My father pretends to be hard of hearing to get more attention, but my mother is a master at the game. Their arguments and their affection for each other still provide a great source of entertainment for the family."

As a young man, Wynne had considered the Penningtons the model of a happy family. So different from the Melforts.

Her voice was solicitous when she continued. "I know it has been years since you lost your own parents, but I was sorry to hear of their passing."

He tipped his head in acknowledgment, but all he felt in his heart for the old baronet and his wife was pity.

"I had been estranged from them for a number of years by the time they died. He went first, my mother a year later. It sounds harsh for me to say it, I know, but they were lonely and bitter people to the end."

She didn't press him for more, but Wynne felt she deserved to know the truth about them.

"You're very kind to mention them, but you must have known that they were against us. It was less at first; slighting your family has its perils. But their opposition only became worse, privately, as the talk became more poisonous."

He recalled so clearly the arguments, the threats, the

daily torment of repeating whatever malicious gossip had been circulating in one social circle or another. Jo's dowry had been enticing, but they'd changed their minds faced with the talk regarding her past.

Wynne studied Jo in silence. She'd been too generous to complain back then about their subtle slights, and she was too polite to acknowledge now what they both knew to be the truth.

"After I recovered from my wound and went to sea, my brother fell in love with a minister's daughter from Cornwall. She was a young woman of no social consequence and very little dowry. As you can imagine, their disapproval was fierce. They threatened to strip him of his inheritance, but John was much stronger than I. He spurned their efforts to intimidate him and called their bluff. He married the woman he still loves."

"I'm glad that Sir John has found happiness."

Wynne nodded. "Two lively children and a good life."

Gazing across at her, he wondered how she must have felt when she learned that he'd been married and had a son. She didn't want to speak of the past, but these were the events that had steered both of their lives to this place. And time was running out to tell her the things he needed to share.

"After my father died, my mother wrote to me and told me that my marriage to Fiba, Cuffe's mother, had been the cause of his demise."

"Oh no," she murmured, touching his knee.

He shrugged. "At the time her words wounded me, but I'd been burned by them before. I had no regrets about marrying Fiba. My plan had been to leave the navy and establish myself in Jamaica. I didn't think I'd ever return to England. In my mind they'd ceased to exist a long time ago."

"I am sorry."

Wynne understood how deeply heartfelt Jo's words were. She had spent her entire life in search of her true parents. He had celebrated the day he could finally turn his back to his own, free and unencumbered.

"I still have my brother," he told her. "And our friendship gives me great pleasure."

"Please, accept my sincere apology," she said. "My family and I have treated your brother and his wife unfairly. You can be certain I shall call on her and introduce her to Grace, my sister-in-law, when I return to Baronsford."

Wynne watched her closely. The blush blooming on her cheeks, the dark eyes swimming with compassion, the kindness that he knew permeated the very fabric of her existence.

He'd mentioned Cuffe's mother by name. He'd admitted that he readily walked away from his family to marry her, even though he'd been too weak only a few years earlier to face Jo and let her be a part of any decision regarding their future. He'd robbed her of a life. He'd taken away her voice. He'd done what he thought was best without thinking through how his choice would affect her life.

And yet she was apologizing to *him*.

"I couldn't protect you," he said, speaking the words in his heart. "I was going away to war. I never cared about the vile gossip. None of it. But I knew how monstrous my parents would behave toward you. In marrying you, I would be throwing you into a den of lions."

"Please, Wynne. Let's not—"

"We must," he interrupted, watching a single tear escape the corner of her glistening eye and slide down her cheek.

"You kept yourself aloof and removed from the lies while I wanted to tear to pieces anyone who said a wrong word about you. You were kind and forgiving while I raged inwardly at those smiling vipers who were not worthy enough to buckle your slipper. But I was not worthy either. I was helpless, Jo. I was helpless in shielding you from the sadness that you so courageously hid in the face of each assault."

"Wynne, stop," she whispered. "I pray you—"

"I can't. You must hear me out." More than anything else, he wanted to move across and sit beside her. Take her in his arms and ask for her forgiveness. But he couldn't. Not when there was more that needed to be said.

"My youth, my pride, my assumption that you wouldn't be able to survive unless I was there to act as your protector led me to the selfish act of walking away. I decided for both of us that you'd be much better off without me, without our marriage. And I did it poorly. But I can't lay the blame at my family's door. I bear the blame. In the end, I was really only thinking of myself. As if I were the one injured by all that happened. The way I left you, Jo, was wrong and hurtful. I know I caused you more heartache than you ever deserved."

Since the day she'd arrived at the Abbey, Jo thought her heart would break if they spoke of their past. But she'd been wrong. Two hearts were at stake here.

As he spoke, raw emotion was laced into each word.

His frustration over the situation they had been facing was still so alive to him. She saw it in the set of his shoulders, in the turn of his head, in the searching gaze that constantly returned to her face. He'd carried the blame for so many years, and she knew she could not allow that to continue.

"Two young people were involved, Wynne. Two," she repeated, forcing the words past the knot in her throat. She paused, summoning her strength and willing herself to continue.

His hand reached for hers and their fingers entwined. He always knew when she needed him. Whether it was in a ballroom when malicious rumor was destroying her or in the ward of an asylum when she found herself faced with the Barton family's hostility.

"Over the years," she said, "I've looked carefully at my own actions and my own character. In the eyes of my family, I was the person injured, the one left behind, the victim. But as I've searched my soul, I've come to realize that I was greatly responsible for bringing an end to our engagement."

Wynne started to deny her assertion, but this time Jo silenced him.

"I was timid, ashamed of my past. And I allowed the rumors and the innuendo and the slander to affect me. I withdrew rather than challenging the hateful people who spread the poison." She met his troubled eyes. "My excuse was that I had no firm ground to stand on. I didn't know what was true myself, so how could I fight the lies?"

Long after their breakup, Jo continued to avoid confrontation with the rumormongers. In her mind, she always found a way to diminish the insult, back away, and retreat into silence. It pained her now to know that she'd forced the men in her family to become that much more protective. To this day, no one dared whisper a word about her in the presence of Hugh or Gregory or her parents. But when they weren't present, the behavior of many others of their acquaintance was quite different.

"I know that in my hesitation to fight the insidious backbiters so prevalent among the ton, I hindered you from defending my honor and speaking up for me. I wasn't strong enough myself, and I rendered you helpless too." She spoke the truth that had taken her years to see. "I know now you could never stand by and allow that. I asked you to be something you could not be. In doing so, I pushed you away."

His hands were warm when they closed around her icy fingers.

"You can say all you like, but the blame still lies with me," he said. "I was young and impatient. I was nearly mad with thoughts of war and dying, and I couldn't think past tomorrow. When the orders came that I would soon be sailing, I panicked. My duties would not bring me back for some time, that I knew. What would happen if we married and you found after I left that you were with child? I certainly didn't trust my parents to treat you as they should. And what would happen if I died at sea? I had more questions and insecurities than I could convey."

"We were both so young."

"But rather than giving you a voice in what our decision should be, *I* chose for both of us. *I* decided that our marriage would be a disaster."

And yet, Jo thought, she would have made it work, even in his absence. She loved him and what she wasn't willing to do for herself, she would have done for him. But there was no point in saying any of that now.

"I wanted everything to be ideal," Wynne continued. "In the rashness of my youth, I thought if I couldn't make things perfect, I couldn't subject you to what I was certain would be a harsh reality. It took years for me to realize that the ideal is a goal, but falling short of it is not always a disaster. To be honest, I still struggle with it when it comes to Cuffe and his life here in Scotland. I had to learn all over again who my son was. I needed to remember his mother and what she would have wanted for him."

He sat back.

Jo kept her eyes on his face. Wynne's apologies had been on behalf of a youth who'd proclaimed his love to her and then faltered. Since that time, another woman had helped him grow into someone better. What she saw now was a man firmly in control of his own destiny.

"Will you tell me about Fiba?"

He stirred in the seat. A moment of unease darkened his expression.

"Forgive me. I'm not asking to pry into your life. I shouldn't have—"

"No. You *should* know," he told her, relaxing. "When we met, Fiba had been married to an English naval officer but was recently widowed. I was taking command of the *Carnatic*, which was being fitted out for duty at the time."

Wynne's gaze moved to the window, and Jo almost felt the groundswell of memories rushing back at him. Cuffe was an extremely handsome child, and she could only imagine how striking his mother must have been.

"She came from a Maroon family, and in spite of being part of English society during her marriage, she maintained her allegiance to her people."

Jo knew that the number of those like Fiba in Jamaica was only a fraction of the multitudes enslaved there.

"Cuffe comes about his fighting nature honestly. After Fiba and I became involved, I realized she had another life from the one she lived openly. I closed my eyes to what I saw. She was relaying to the Maroons living in the Cockpit information about the traders and the plantation owners."

"She was so brave," she said admiringly. How different her life had been from Fiba's. How meaningless her aspirations were to a champion like Cuffe's mother. "I can understand why you would turn away from your family to marry such a special woman."

His intense blue eyes found and held her gaze.

"Marriage was not part of our plan. Neither of us wanted or needed it. Fiba was financially independent after the death of her first husband, and she cherished her newfound freedoms. And my duties would rarely bring me back to Jamaica. To be honest, I had a very difficult time convincing her to marry me after we found out that she was with child."

Jo would have expected nothing less from him. His sense of honor had never changed over the years. In their own relationship so long ago, he'd never taken advantage of Jo.

"Carrying your child didn't influence her to marry you?"

"Fiba's refusal wasn't about me. For the first time in her life, she'd been able to help her people. Marrying another English officer only complicated matters. As far as our child, she planned on raising him herself, and argued that the island had a large number of mixed-race children."

How sad that Cuffe lost a mother of such strength before having a chance to know her.

"How did you finally convince her?"

"I told her about you."

"About me?" she asked, confused.

"I told her about a child who grew up searching for answers. About a young woman who couldn't fathom the value her own qualities and character simply because of questions about her origins. I told her I did not want a child of mine to suffer as you had suffered."

Jo thought of all he'd said about Fiba. A rival. A woman she should dislike, perhaps even hate. She'd married the only man Jo ever loved. She should envy Fiba for the multitude of days she'd had to spend with him. She had so many reasons to feel the deepest antipathy toward her. And yet, she could not. They'd loved the same man, and what Jo felt instead was nothing but kinship.

❧   16   ❧

GARLOCH HAD MORE to offer than the vicar had suggested.

The rough Highland road they'd been following descended into a valley town, protected from the north winds by a rugged ridge of mountain. A coach road, no doubt built by the army for moving troops during the Jacobite Rising, followed the shore of a long, narrow loch that stretched to the west, and a number of shops, cottages, and a venerable coaching inn clustered around the market cross in the village center. A second river converged here at this end of the town, cascading from the higher elevations and flowing beneath a stone bridge that appeared fairly new. The small stone church, the object of their journey, sat in a shady flower-studded glen below the confluence of the waters.

Going directly to the church, Wynne got out to speak to an old man bent over a well-tended plot in the kirkyard.

"That'd be Mr. Kealy," the villager said in response to

his question about the priest. "Ain't here but once a fort-night, but yer in luck, sir. The young fellow's arrived for the service tomorrow."

After a few more questions, Wynne was able to ascertain that Kealy was the curate who divided his time traveling between two churches in area, the rector of the large parish keeping to a single church in a distant village.

"If ye've a mind to stretch yer legs along the river path or take some refreshment at the inn, he should be back bye 'n' bye. Off visiting one of the parishioners, he is," the older man suggested.

Wynne conveyed this information to Jo as he assisted her out of the carriage. He admired her profile as she raised her face to the sky and closed her eyes, taking in a deep breath.

A great deal had been said between them. She finally allowed him to speak of the past, and she asked about his wife, but that wasn't where her questions ended. Among other things, she wanted to know if Fiba had a chance to hold Cuffe and for how long she lived after delivering him.

Three days, he told her. She'd lived for three days after giving birth.

A child losing a mother at birth was very personal to Jo, and that fact wasn't lost on Wynne. It was the reason she'd come to the Highlands. Their journey to Garloch was based on long odds; the incoherent cries of Charles Barton could hardly be considered definitive. But she was not about to leave a stone unturned in her search. Here in this village, she believed she would find answers about her own mother.

"Would you care to go to the inn, or shall we walk?" he asked when she turned her beautiful brown eyes on him.

"Let's walk," she replied, linking her arm in his.

Following the stone wall that bordered the kirkyard, they made their way toward the river. The path was well-used, and they passed pine groves and cottages. Green fields dotted with sheep and adorned with yellow flowers stretched out over rolling meadows on either side of the wood-lined river.

The sun was shining, and Wynne wondered if she knew how much he appreciated the gift she'd given him. A burden had been lifted from him now that he'd had the opportunity to explain his actions and apologize for them. Jo's absolution was more than he'd ever hoped for.

"I know this is a monumental day for you," he told her when they paused on a prospect above a bend in the river. "You believe you'll find a key here that will unlock the past. But regardless of where the day leads, I hope you know that I'm here with you. And I'm not only talking about this village or today. I mean, whatever you need, whenever you call on me, however you allow me to help."

Wynne didn't want any misunderstanding to linger with regard to his intentions. He didn't want to lose Jo. At the same time, he understood she had much on her mind. He took her hand in his and looked into her eyes.

"Jo, there's so much more that I want to say."

Unexpectedly, she slipped her arms around him and pressed her face against his heart. Wynne's arms closed around her and he held her. How often in their youth would she do this! When they were alone and she was shaken or upset, she would suddenly turn and embrace him like this. Holding him for even a moment seemed to reassure her that he was there with her.

"I'm sorry," she murmured, releasing him quickly as she always did.

But Wynne wasn't ready to let go. His arms remained around her, keeping her against him.

"I'm not," he replied, smiling down into her upturned face. "Does it still make you feel better?"

"Much better. Thank you." Her bright eyes glistened with unshed tears. "I've put so much hope into finding an answer. And now, as the possibility of learning the truth becomes stronger, I feel so unsure. It's no longer simply an issue of knowing. What happens if I don't like the answer?"

"Does it matter?" he asked. "Whatever you learn today or tomorrow or next year, it doesn't change who you are. And it won't change anything for those who love you."

Jo smiled and nodded.

"We all need to do what we know is right," he continued. "Travel the road that we must. Even say the words that we should have said long ago. You're doing it. You're chasing an answer that means something important to you. But if you find nothing at the end of this journey, you've lost nothing in the search."

He lifted her chin and wiped away a tear from her cheek.

"You are closer now than ever before, Jo."

"I know," she agreed, appearing to be satisfied.

Retracing their steps, they'd just reached the stone wall of the kirkyard when a thin young man wearing a dark suit and waistcoat came hurrying down the path toward them.

The curate hailed them and introduced himself. The old man they'd spoken to earlier had informed him strangers were waiting for him.

Wynne handed Mr. Kealy the letter of introduction

provided by Dermot's uncle, and the curate quickly scanned the contents.

"It will be my pleasure to assist you in any way I can, m'lady," he said, directing his words at Jo as he glanced at a pocket watch. "Unfortunately, I have only a few minutes at present. I have a previous commitment I must honor, but I can help you once I have fulfilled that obligation."

"Of course. But could you tell us if you do have records that might help us?" she asked.

"We do indeed. And I've been particularly diligent during my tenure here." Kealy paused and looked at Wynne. "I must say, however, that hasn't always been the case. Sadly, I know of one curate in recent years who was . . . well, less devoted, shall we say?"

Wynne and Jo exchanged a look as the young man motioned for them to follow him up the path toward the church.

The curate turned to her again. "What is it exactly that you hope to find, m'lady?"

"I'd like to start by looking up the name of a gentleman who may have some connection with Garloch. I can also supply the gentleman's age if that helps."

Passing through a gate into the cemetery, Wynne was struck by the inordinately large number of graves.

"We keep records of birth, baptisms, marriages, and burials in a secure box with two locks," Kealy told them. "Everyone in the parish is there. Since the change in the law six years ago, we've used the official registers from the King's Printer, and once a year I send a duplicate copy of our records to the office in Aberdeen."

"And how far back do these records date?" Wynne asked him.

"Well, with the exception of my predecessor, the

curates and rectors have kept exceptional records going back to the years before the Union. So, well over a century, I'd say."

The young man paused and looked thoughtfully at the graves around them. Many of the older stone markers nearest the church had fallen or were askew.

"But of course, one must discount the damage caused by the great flood. And there's no telling how accurately the records were kept immediately following it."

"The great flood?" Jo asked.

"Not Noah's flood, m'lady, but a terrible version of it that struck Garloch, folks say. It was well before my time, but parishioners talk of it still. The churchyard was inundated. You can see the damage to the stones here. The water even reached the church, and the vestry was badly damaged. Actually, we're fortunate the record box wasn't lost entirely."

"When was this flood?" Wynne took Jo's hand in his, remembering Charles Barton's agitation about Jo drowning.

"Let me see." The curate stared at the sky for a few moments as if trying to recall the year. "I'm embarrassed to say I can't tell you, but—"

"Do you have an approximate year?" Jo persisted.

The young man glanced past the older graves.

"This way, if you please." He motioned for them to follow. "Quite a few died in that flood. And not just villagers, so I understand. Innocent folk traveling through were caught unawares and swept away. Many were buried in that section over there."

Wynne put a hand on small of Jo's back, urging her to follow the curate.

Kealy went down on a knee beside one of the first

graves they reached and pushed away old leaves and debris.

Wynne read the inscription aloud. "Here lies the body of John Campfield. Departed this life May 4, 1781."

The curate moved to the next grave. "The same date. May 1781. That must have been the month and year of the flood. I'm quite sure of it."

Wynne turned to Jo, whose face had taken on an ashen hue. Both of them well knew the significance of the date.

In May of 1781, her mother would have been nearing her time. A month later, in the Borders far to the south, she delivered her daughter in the mud beneath a cart.

Jo trailed her fingers down Wynne's arm, and he understood, immediately engaging their guide in a conversation.

Sentiments accompanying the lost and found. A fearful surge of emotions. The beat of Jo's heart echoed in a hollow space carved in her chest. She walked away. She needed to breathe, to make peace with the information she'd received. There was still no sure connection. Nothing firmer than the cries of Charles Barton.

Jo walked past grave after grave, some bearing names and ages, others adorned with ancient Celtic symbols and crosses. Some were carved with worn shapes her watery gaze could not focus on. The names on the stones meant nothing to her.

She looked up at the village beyond the river and wondered if her mother had lived here. Perhaps these names meant everything to her. A childhood friend. A nursemaid. A clerk in the milliner's shop. Or perhaps she was only a traveler passing through. She turned around to see the curate hurrying off and Wynne striding toward her through the grass.

Where would she be today without him?

"Kealy is certain we'll find no record of Charles Barton in the books. From the information we were given when he arrived at the Abbey, I know he was born at Tilmory Castle," he told her. "The curate claims they have their own parish and church. Still, I asked him if we could take a look in whatever he has of the older ledgers."

"The coincidence is jarring," she said. "The date."

Wynne nodded. "He's agreed to let us search through the records of births and baptisms and marriages." He offered her his arm as they walked. "If she came from here, how many people do you think we'll find with the name Josephine?"

"But we don't know if she was born in Garloch." She took a deep breath, trying to remain calm.

"We're here. We should pursue every possibility."

He was right. Jo was letting her nerves get the better of her. This church. This might have been her mother's church.

"You said Lady Millicent always spoke of her as being quite young," he went on. "I gave the curate a range of about six years or so that we'd like to look at."

She looked up, feeling admiration for him and gratitude that he was here. "When can we search the records?"

"Mr. Kealy has promised by the time we walk to the inn and have something to eat, he'll have concluded his business and be ready for us to proceed."

"Are the records here in the church?" she asked.

"No, he told me since the flood, the books have been kept in the rectory, up the hill, away from the river."

She followed his gaze to a small stone cottage. The place looked tidy but unoccupied, and she remembered that the curate only came here twice a month. The church itself looked better kept.

After Sir John Melfort purchased Highfield Hall, Jo had often wondered if she would run into Wynne at the church in Melrose Village. She never went without thinking about it. The same fear haunted her at social gatherings with their neighbors. In her imagination, he was happily married and would be aghast at seeing her. The incident would be terribly painful and tear at her heart all over again.

How wrong she was.

"I can't tell you how thankful I am for you," she said without a tinge of embarrassment. "You're thoughtful, considerate, dependable, and wise. In short, you're indispensable, Captain Melfort."

He smiled, running a thumb caressingly over her hand before bringing the palm to his lips. "I like the last one the best. It gives me great pleasure to think you find me necessary in your life."

But he was so much more.

"What are you saying?" she dared herself to ask.

"I'm asking if—once we have returned to the Abbey— I may have the honor of calling on you and making my intentions known."

She studied the smile creasing his handsome face. "Let me see. We have conversed privately many times, have been alone in a room, traveled unchaperoned in a carriage, called one another by our given names, corresponded with one another and exchanged gifts, danced more than two sets on any evening—"

"And touched intimately, if I may be so bold as to

recollect." He lowered his head and brushed his lips against hers, making Jo's breath hitch, before straightening again.

"You are indeed bold, Captain."

He bent his head. "I bow to your reprimand, m'lady."

"And *I* recollect that we have exchanged a great many smiles and sighs."

"And becoming blushes," he said, caressing her cheek. "Tell me, though, that you are inclined to accept my proposal."

Jo felt as if she'd stepped into a dream. Wynne wanted her.

Sixteen years ago, her happiness with him had been destroyed because of her unknown origins. Today, here in Garloch, where she might find the truth of her mother, she was also being given a second chance at happiness.

"I am so inclined, Captain," she said, slipping her arms around him. "But pray, don't write for my parents' permission to visit and pay your respects. I have a great deal of explaining that I need to do first."

17

Jo and Wynne returned from the coaching inn to find the door of the rectory open and Mr. Kealy starting a small fire, despite the warm weather. Neither did much to diminish the damp and stuffy smell of the little cottage, but the curate's efforts on their behalf were greatly appreciated.

After seating them at a table by a sunny window, he disappeared into another room and then returned shortly, carrying a large wooden box. Jo watched his every step, studied the curate's pale hands as he started to pull out the old parish record books. Her heart climbed into her throat.

"The most recent registers are far better organized," he told them. "We now use a superior system with ruled pages."

"Are the years we discussed here, Mr. Kealy?" Wynne asked.

"Of course, Captain," the young man replied, taking out the books containing prior years and checking the entry dates until he found the two relevant volumes. "Here we are."

He opened one and laid it on the table, giving the other to Wynne.

"No last name. Only Josephine, you say?"

The difficulty of the search became immediately clear. The volumes containing the years surrounding her mother's birth had been soaked during the flood, and it didn't appear that anyone had opened them for decades. The smell of mold rose from the stiff pages, many of which were stuck together. In spite of the curate's extreme care, edges of the paper cracked and crumbled as he handled them. The water damage had caused the ink on the pages to blur and run. Whole pages were illegible. The register Wynne was looking through was in no better condition.

Jo began to feel queasy as she tried to read the entries along with them. She'd been given the task of writing down any relevant information, but nothing had as yet turned up.

"Are there any copies of these?" Wynne asked.

"Very likely not," Kealy told them. "Though I believe this far back, the procedure was to have each year's records copied out and sent to offices of the bishop in Aberdeen. Yes, I'm certain of it."

"And whose job was that?" Jo asked hopefully.

"The parish clerk, I should think. But looking at the condition of these registers and the untidy handwriting, I have to think they were as short on qualified help as we are now." He shook his head. "I would not be surprised if very few of the records from this time were copied out and sent along to the bishop."

Several times, they were interrupted by parishioners coming to the door with problems requiring the curate's attention. Three separate times, he left them alone to continue reading the entries. Jo imagined Mr. Kealy was required to perform all the duties of the rector, and for a meager salary. She'd already noticed that he could not afford a maid.

As the afternoon began to wear on, Jo took strength in Wynne's presence and his attentiveness to her. Their earlier conversation, his offer of marriage, and their time together at the inn had provided new life and new hope for her.

As they'd walked through the village before going to the rectory, he told her about Cuffe's words of encouragement about winning her over. She, in turn, suggested perhaps the three of them could return to the Borders. While she spoke with her family, Wynne could be introducing Cuffe to his brother and wife and children. She hoped they could sufficiently mend the rift between the Melforts and the Penningtons. Though she didn't mention it, the prospect of Hugh and Wynne coming face-to-face did give her heart palpitations.

Before sitting down to search the registers, Jo hadn't imagined that so many children would have been born and baptized during the six-year span of their search. When she posed the question, Mr. Kealy explained that since the village was on the coach road, many families continued to straggle through Garloch because of the ongoing tragedy of the clearances occurring farther to the north, in particular. For this reason, the number of names in the books was far greater than one would expect.

Another problem that slowed down the search was that occasionally two or more children were baptized together, and their details were entered at the same time.

Wynne shared an entry where a family's older sons and daughters were mentioned alongside their youngest.

It was some time before the curate stopped, his finger pointing to a page.

"Finally!" he exclaimed. "Josephine. Do you see? This entry is difficult to read because the ink is blurred and faded, but I'm certain of it. Josephine Young."

For a moment Jo lost the ability to breathe. Unlike Mary and Elizabeth and Margaret, Josephine was not a common name.

Almost immediately, Wynne pointed out a second Josephine.

"The name mentioned in this volume refers to a child born in 1764," he told her. "Josephine Sellar."

Her heart racing, her mind churning with all the possibilities, she copied what she could read from both registers onto her paper.

The name of the child. Lawful or natural birth. Date of baptism. Father's name and occupation. Names of witnesses and the minister who performed the baptism. The name of mother was illegible in one of the two entries.

"Ah, here's a Josephine that I know," the curate said soon after, excitedly showing her another mention. "I'd quite forgotten that Mrs. Clark's Christian name is Josephine."

"She lives in the village?" Jo asked.

"Yes, she runs the circulating library. You should stop and see her. A delightful woman and very knowledgeable about the history of the parish. More than happy to share it too, if you know what I mean. She's lived in the village her whole life, I believe."

Mrs. Clark could certainly not be her mother, Jo

thought. But perhaps she'd be a good source of information not captured in the church registers. She glanced out the window at the late afternoon sun and recognized the irony of hoping to glean information from a village gossip.

By the time they finished going through the books, the records of four children named Josephine were written down on Jo's page. Five, if she included Mrs. Clark.

"Young, Sellar, Scott, and Brown," the clergyman read the names aloud. "I'm not certain how they may relate to you, m'lady, but we do have parishioners with these family names still living in the area."

Jo didn't know if there was enough cause here for celebration. Pieces of the puzzle were revealing themselves, but the background where everything might fit was murky.

"Do you keep your marriage records here?" Wynne asked.

Mr. Kealy had begun to replace the volumes in the box.

"Yes, of course. What years are you interested in seeing?"

"For 1781, the year of the flood, and for 1780," Jo told him.

"If you'll excuse me a moment, I believe I have them on a shelf . . ."

As the clergyman went to retrieve the records, Jo sent a look of gratitude Wynne's way. She was satisfied to find a possible surname for her mother. But he thought beyond it, unwilling to leave any stone unturned while they were here.

When Mr. Kealy returned and placed the book on the table, his face already showed his dismay.

"How unfortunate," he said, laying it open on the table. "These should have included the years you're interested in, but I'm afraid we have very little left."

The flood had nearly destroyed this volume, and age had done the rest. Vermin had chewed sections of the cover and the paper. Pages were torn and many appeared to be missing. The ink had run and what was left was often blurred beyond legibility. They looked over what they could but found nothing of use.

The curate glanced at his watch. It was nearly five already. "I am sorry, m'lady, but I believe we've done all we can do here."

Picking up her list, he studied the names they'd collected and proceeded to explain where each of the families lived in relation to the village. Two of the names had several branches of the family in the area.

"I know the time is growing late and you wished to return to Rayneford tonight, but tomorrow is Sunday. All these families should be attending church," the young man suggested. "If you care to stay, I can introduce you to all of them tomorrow after the service."

Wynne's look at Jo caused a reaction in her that had nothing to do with their search and everything to do with the two of them staying in the village tonight. No Squire and Mrs. McKendry to break into their conversations and endeavor to keep them apart. No dinner guests. There was the question of propriety, but what did she care about her reputation?

And Wynne had proposed to her already.

The press of his knee against hers under the table was her undoing, and her insides melted.

"The inn where you took refreshments earlier offers comfortable accommodations. I would invite you to stay here, but as you can see, I have little to offer. Since my housekeeper left, I'm afraid the house is hardly suitable for guests."

"Thank you, Mr. Kealy," Wynne replied. "We'll think about it."

Because a group of army officers traveling through had already engaged the private dining room at the coaching inn, Wynne and Jo were seated in the public room, which suited them perfectly. He'd convinced her that they should have their dinner in Garloch before making a final decision about staying or going back to the Abbey.

"But what about Cuffe?" Jo asked, speaking over the noise of the villagers, as well as a crowd of travelers who'd stopped to eat while the coach horses were being changed.

"The lad will be fine. I left Dermot in charge of him, and the good doctor takes that responsibility very seriously. I didn't mention it before, but thanks to you and his success reading in the ward, Cuffe has agreed to follow Dermot about as he attends to his duties."

"I imagine Dr. McKendry would be an enthusiastic teacher."

A waiter arrived with their steaks and fish.

Wynne was tempted to make a humorous comment regarding his former rival's enthusiasm, but he could no longer do it. He had Jo's affection, and that was all that mattered.

"Dermot can be relied upon to give my son every attention."

As they ate, Jo grew silent, and that worried him. He

didn't interrupt her thoughts, though. He knew her mind had to be roiling with everything that had happened today—from their conversation in the carriage to the information they'd collected at the rectory. And with regard to her mother, she still had no definitive answers.

He'd proposed and she'd accepted. He was only moderately concerned about her family accepting their decision, but they needed to consider how they were going to arrange their lives together. He didn't want her to feel she must make a sacrifice to adapt her life to his, but he didn't want to set the dust of the past swirling about her either. And that would happen if they were to live in London or the Borders.

Sixteen years ago, the uncertainty of her birth was the source of her unhappiness. Today, they were looking at many doors, and Wynne would do whatever was necessary to help her open every one.

"If we were to stay, meeting all these people tomorrow could produce nothing," she said finally, laying down her knife. "All I can ask them is what happened to *your* Josephine. But what would induce them to answer such a question? I have nothing to offer in return for their family confidences."

Wynne could understand her hesitation. Still, he found himself arguing against it.

"You might never come this close again," he told her. "And time will inevitably diminish your chances of finding the truth. Tomorrow—if we stay—we can attend the service, go through some introductions, ask the questions, and return to the Abbey. I've already spoken to the innkeeper, and he's put aside two rooms for us if we choose to take them."

Jo began to say something but stopped. Her gaze was

fixed on something behind him and a faint blush was rising into her cheek.

"I'm being stared at."

Wynne turned and looked. Sure enough, a middle-aged woman stood by the door, clutching a large canvas bag and gaping in their direction.

"I believe she knows me," Jo said, getting to her feet.

Wynne stood as the woman approached.

"My apologies for being so forward, m'lady. Captain." She curtsied, and they learned she was Mrs. Clark.

"I happened to run into Mr. Kealy just now, and he told me about yer interest in the name. Told me ye'd likely be here. Naturally, I had to take a peek." The woman pressed a hand to her chest. "Laying eyes on ye from a distance, m'lady . . . for a moment I was dead certain. You're so much younger than her, of course. Ah, but I know it must be a mistake. My eyes ain't what they once were."

"Would you care to join us, Mrs. Clark?" Wynne offered his seat.

She glanced back at the door. "Thank ye, Captain, but no. I've two more deliveries that need to be made, and my old man is waiting outside. The curate said ye might be coming around to the service tomorrow. Perhaps we can chat then."

"Will you at least tell me who it is you thought I resemble?" Jo asked as the woman turned to leave.

Mrs. Clark studied Jo's face in silence for a few heart-beats before she spoke.

"Josephine. Josephine Sellar. A lass from my childhood years."

The older woman shook her head and held up a wrinkled hand before either of them could ask more.

"I'm sorry, m'lady. But it's all just an old woman's fancy. She can't possibly be any relation to an English lady. Can't possibly be. Never mind my foolishness. Till tomorrow, then."

Without another word, she hurried off and disappeared through the door, ignoring Wynne's entreaties to stay.

When he looked back at Jo, tears were running unchecked down her face.

$\approx$ 18 $\approx$

Josephine Sellar.

She had a name. Her mother had a name.

Josephine Sellar.

Her mother had a village. A family. People who cared for her. They remembered her.

Jo's eyes burned from her tears. Locking herself in the room Wynne had taken for her, she gave way to the rip current of emotion that she'd stifled for so much of her life. She cried for herself. And she cried for the young woman who'd not lived to hold her daughter past the first day.

Josephine Sellar. Seventeen years old when she gave birth. Frightened, hungry, sick, alone.

The women and girls who arrived at the Tower House were often broken, solitary, and afraid. For Jo, every one of those women was her mother. She sat with them. She cried with them. She listened as they gradually crept past their shame and their fear, and revealed to her the details of their lives. As they spoke, Jo wondered which painful journey ran parallel with her mother's path. And as she listened, she silently swore the same oath to each of those women—not one of them would die as her mother had, clutching her newborn in the mud while an unfeeling world looked away.

She paced the room—cold and shaken, recalling the insinuations, lamenting the lost years when she'd failed to fight for her mother. Guilt squeezed her heart and choked off the very breaths in her chest.

She thought of the grave in the Melrose churchyard. The grave she visited every Sunday when she was at Baronsford. The only true connection she had with the past.

JO. Two letters and the date her mother died. Nothing else. No acknowledgment of a life, only a death. No reference to when or where she was born. No family name. No husband. No parents.

But now Jo knew more.

A maid knocked at the door, saying the captain sent her up to help her get ready to retire. Jo sent her away. Sometime later, the same young woman came up to check on her. The captain was worried and asked if she needed anything. Jo sent her away.

She didn't know how long she sobbed in misery before the realization came to her. Sellar. Sellar. Why was she sitting here? She had to see the family now. She wanted answers that only they could give.

With no care about how she looked or the disheveled condition of her dress, Jo left her bedroom and rapped on Wynne's door. He appeared in the doorway immediately as if he'd been expecting her.

"Take me to them," she demanded, his face a watery blur. "Please take me to the Sellar farm. I need to speak to them."

"My love, I understand," he said gently. "But the hour is late. Tomorrow—"

"I'll go by myself," she exclaimed, turning on her heel. She didn't make it more than two steps down the hall, however, when Wynne caught her and drew her back to him.

"I need to do it, Wynne. I need to go now." She struggled to free herself. "I need answers."

The sound of boots coming up on the stairs startled her, and Jo let him pull her into his room and close the door.

"I know you need answers. And you'll have them. I swear to you. But not tonight," he said, his voice thick with emotion. "Tomorrow, we won't leave Garloch until you meet and speak with everyone you need to. I promise you that. I give you my word."

"But tomorrow might never come," she sobbed as he pulled her tightly into his arms.

The rush of tears, the pain rising from the cracks in her battered heart, the need to empty the boundless well of sadness was like no grief she'd ever experienced.

He whispered soothing words, tried to wipe away the tears, and as she felt calmer, another wave would begin, overwhelming her, drowning her.

"Talk to me, my love," he murmured against her ear. "Tell me what you're feeling. Perhaps it would make this heartache easier to bear."

She pressed her face against his chest. The steady beat of his heart, the warm strength of his arms around her, made her troubles fade for a moment. For just an instant, the pain was gone. She tried to pull away, but he held her there.

"Stay. Let me."

Jo's tears soaked his linen shirt, and she realized he wasn't wearing his coat and waistcoat. His hands massaged her back. His lips pressed kisses into her hair. He enveloped her with his soothing warmth. She didn't know for how long they stood there, but gradually the sobs lessened. The tide of tears ebbed until only a few runaway drops were left.

"What happened?" he asked softly. "I thought the discovery of your mother's family name would be cause for celebration, but your reaction breaks my heart."

It was some time before she could trust her voice.

"I found her," she whispered. "I've learned her name only to realize that she is truly lost forever. For all of my life, I was told she was gone. Still I looked for her. I searched for someone that I resembled. Creating a world of my own, I imagined a woman who shared my hair, my eyes, someone who spoke like me. Deep in my heart, I carved out a protected space for the belief that she wasn't really gone. When Charles Barton's drawings arrived, that belief exploded within me."

"I can only imagine the shock." He continued to hold and caress her.

"Tonight, giving her a name, a village, people who knew her made everything finally, irrevocably real. I mourn because she was gone before I ever knew her."

Jo pulled herself out of his arms. She felt horrified to have fallen apart like this in front of him. Her eyes were nearly shut. The room was small, a bed and a dresser comprised all the furnishings. There was no space for her to pace.

She took his hand and pulled him to the bed and sat on the edge.

He remained standing.

"Sit with me."

He hesitated. She wasn't so far gone in her grief not to understand why. He was trying to be a gentleman, even now.

"Hold me, Wynne."

She was relieved when he sat next to her and gathered her to him.

She was calmer, more in charge of her wits, her mind clearer. She leaned her head on his shoulder, inhaled his scent, took comfort in his warmth.

"When did you first learn that Lady Millicent wasn't your mother?" he asked.

The leaves of time flew back to a day that she'd never forget.

"Lord Aytoun's younger brother Pierce and his wife, Portia, were visiting Baronsford. She was with child and close to term. The women were gathered in my mother's favorite room, the upstairs library in the west wing. Hugh and I were very young. We were playing with some toys on the floor."

She told him how the golden rays of sun angled through the open windows. The women were laughing happily at the active nature of the unborn babe in Portia's belly, its movements clearly visible through the material of her dress. Jo walked to her aunt, amazed by the display.

"My curiosity made me ask Lady Millicent, 'Did I move like that when I was in your belly?'"

To this day, Jo recalled the sudden silence that fell

over the library. It was as if the air had been drawn from the room.

"Did she answer you?" Wynne asked. "Did she tell you in front of the others?"

"Before she could say a word, Portia's mother answered. 'You aren't hers, child,' she said."

He pulled her closer. "Why people insist on cruelty—"

"It wasn't cruelty," Jo told him. "She was battling dementia. She'd become less and less responsible for the things she said."

She was finished with her tears, but the vividness of that memory wouldn't leave her.

"I recall throwing a tantrum in front of them all, demanding to know whose belly I grew in. And where was my *real* mother?"

"What did Lady Millicent do?"

"If I shed one tear, she shed ten," Jo told him. "She took me out of the library. She kissed me and hugged me and wept over me. She explained that my mother was in heaven. But that was only the start of my questions."

Jo told Wynne about the crippling anxiety she felt any time she had to be separated from Lady Millicent as she grew up. She began each day worrying if her parents were going to be gone. Or if she might be separated from her siblings.

"She was my mother as truly as any birth mother could be," she whispered, sitting straight and pressing her fingers to her swollen eyes. "She and my father were always there. They always loved me. They protected me, even when the rumors during my first Season made me want to run in shame to the Antipodes. They never made me feel like an outsider."

Jo took some deep breaths, trying to recover from her earlier breakdown.

"My reaction tonight . . ." She shook her head.

"I was telling Cuffe last night that part of knowing who you are is knowing where you came from." He tucked a curl behind her ear. "Your search has been about finding your history. Histories have a beginning. Today you made a fine start. But I understand your sense of loss and I am sorry for it."

He was so loving, so perceptive. Years ago this was the way it had been between them. Their minds and hearts were so open, so much in harmony. She could tell him anything. Pour out her heart. Share with him her struggle to belong and feel connected to a society that kept her at arm's length. He always understood. He always made her feel complete.

A weight had been lifted from her chest. She could breathe again.

"I am sorry I've behaved so badly."

"You haven't." He raised her chin, and his gaze caught and held hers before placing a kiss on her brow. "But you're allowed if you choose to."

"I must look a fright."

"You look beautiful," he whispered, his lips kissing the wetness from her cheeks as his fingers combed the loose tendrils of her hair.

Jo studied the line of his jaw, the sensual shape of his lips, the deep blue of his eyes as they caressed her face before focusing on her lips. A reckless hunger pounded through her. She wanted him. She needed his kisses. Where sadness had ruled before, hunger now reigned.

She stood up and moved between his knees, looking down at his surprised expression.

"Kiss me."

He smiled, closing his eyes for a moment and shaking his head. "Jo . . . this room. The two of us alone. This might not be the best . . ."

She recognized the change in his voice. He wanted her too.

"Very well. Then I'll have to kiss you." She pressed her lips to his.

Wynne's mouth immediately took hers, and sparks exploded within her. The kiss was scorching. So different from those they'd exchanged in the garden. Coaxing, shaping, exploring. He was now a man with all the time and all the patience in the world.

She was aroused and welcomed the light touch on her spine as he reached for her. She pressed closer and his mouth became possessive. Lost in the kiss, Jo moved her hands over his shirt, feeling his chest and broad shoulders, and then slipped her arms around his neck.

The moment she molded herself to him, his mouth opened further, his tongue becoming more demanding. His hand slid along her waist and ribs, caressing her breast through the bodice of her gown. Their tongues played a seductive dance until they were both shaking with need.

Then, he abruptly ended the kiss and rested his forehead against hers. They were both breathing heavily.

Jo wanted more. "I don't want you to stop."

He pulled her arms down from around his neck.

"Jo," he whispered raggedly. "You don't know what you're doing. We should wait."

She'd waited long enough. No more, she thought. She was thirty-seven years old. Wynne was the only man she'd loved for her entire life. And for sixteen years, he had been the only man in all those dreams from which she'd awakened aroused.

Why should she wait?

"No," she said, pushing him back onto the bed. "No waiting. I want you now."

HE'D DIED and gone to heaven.

After he'd proposed to her today, Wynne's plan had been to do everything right. He was committed to following all the well-established rules of courtship, engagement, and marriage. He'd robbed her of the joys and celebrations of each stage when he broke off their engagement. He would make it up to her this time. But his plans and good intentions went out the door—and took the bloody door, hinges and all, with them—when she pushed her shoes off, climbed onto the bed, and straddled him.

Wynne was happy that Jo had plans of her own.

Jo's hair was a tousled mass of dark curls, and she pulled out the remaining pins, shaking it loose until it cascaded around her shoulders. Her beautiful face was flushed, her eyes puffy, and her lips swollen from his kisses. Her dress . . . his eyes moved down the row of buttons in the front, and the urge to pull every piece of clothing off her body took on religious significance.

She shifted her weight on top of him, and he groaned involuntarily.

She ignored his suffering and began to pull his shirt from his pants.

"Do you know what you're doing?"

Jo had always been passionate. Even when they were young, he'd seen it, felt it. But this exceeded his wildest expectations and dreams.

"You very well know I do." She frowned. "You might be a gentleman and help me remove this shirt of yours."

He held onto Jo's waist firmly to stop her from moving. Any more of this and his cock would punch a hole in his breeches. Then she'd know what kind of gentleman he really was.

Every fiber of his body ached with desire for her. At the same time, he recalled her sadness, her feeling of loss, the river of tears that had stopped only moments ago. She'd had a dreadfully emotional day. He'd be a rogue and a rakehell to take advantage of her and make love to her when she was so vulnerable.

"If you don't take this off, I'll tear it off," she said with remarkable serenity.

Wynne wanted her to feel better. He wanted to see a smile on her face. He told himself he'd go only so far, but he'd remain strong, in control. Yanking his shirt over his head, he tossed it across the room.

He immediately regretted his decision as her shining brown eyes immediately focused on the ugly scar just above his heart.

"So close. He almost killed you."

With a feathery touch, her fingers traced the outline of the place Hugh's bullet had entered his chest. He saw fresh tears spring to her eyes.

"But he didn't," Wynne told her. "There's a matching hole in the back where the bullet came out. I survived. I'm alive and well and yours. All yours."

For today and tomorrow and forever, he thought, reaching and wiping away a teardrop from her silky cheek.

For a long moment, she sat still, her magical eyes studying the scar, his shoulders, his chest. He never imagined a look could be so powerful that it could make his body react as it was right now. When her gaze finally returned to his face, he was a lost man. She wanted him.

She sat back and slowly, ever so slowly, began to undo the buttons of her dress.

"Jo," he whispered, reaching up and trying to take over. Her fingers wrapped around his wrists and she pushed them back to the mattress.

Leaning over him, silky locks of hair trailing across his chest and belly, she turned her attention to his scar again, pressing a kiss on it. From there, her lips followed a meandering path across his burning skin, kissing, tasting, breathing gently, and gradually driving him insane. Her hips moved against the rising bulge of his erection. He wanted to dive beneath those layers of skirts. He wanted to touch her, taste the sweetness of her delicate sex.

He fought to retain some degree of control on his imagination, for his thoughts only worsened his condition. She was driving him mad with desire.

His hand reached for the bunched hems of her skirts, but she caught his wrist and pushed it away. "Don't move, Captain Melfort. I'll do it."

Another half-dozen buttons came apart and the front of her dress opened to reveal the curve of her breast above the top of her shift. A moment later, her lips were back on him.

His skin sizzled with her touch as her hand trailed downward across his stomach.

Wynne reached deep, commanding himself that these pleasures must have their limits. He tried to think of sea battles he'd fought, of bloody boardings, of rough seas, broadsides, and burning ships. Anything but the softness and beauty of the woman sitting on top of him. His muscles were flexed, rock hard, and he ached with the primal need of a male.

He didn't realize he was holding his breath until her mouth returned to his.

"You're killing me, you know," he murmured raggedly. "But this game of yours has dire consequences, so perhaps we should stop."

Stopping was not an option.

Jo's kisses silenced him once again. She teased him, running her tongue across his flesh. And as she'd asked, he didn't move. Waiting. This position of control was arousing. She let her lips move to his neck and kiss their way to his ear. She bit at his earlobe. He growled in response. Smiling and feeling bolder, she kissed a path back to his lips. She let her tongue play across their fullness again, and this time they opened for her and her tongue delved in and began its voyage of discovery.

The unrestrained desire to do as she wished, the power of being in charge, having decided that neither of them would walk away from this night unscathed, was thrilling.

Jo feared he would be scandalized if he knew that her virginity was intact. Never had she given herself to a man. But she would give herself to Wynne tonight.

This boldness made her feel . . . strong. She was in command, except that the pleasure was sliding through her too fast. She could feel a tingling in her limbs, and an urgency was building.

Jo sat up again, taking deep breaths. She painstakingly unfastened what was left of the buttons on her dress. His eyes were fixed on every movement of her fingers. His hips moved every now and then, building her awareness of the massive bulge she sat astride.

She loved the taste of him, the texture of his skin under her tongue. The magnificent chest, his strong neck and jaw, the lips. She pushed the dress down one arm, then the other, then to her waist. The ties at the neckline of the shift came undone with one tug and the material fell open, baring her breasts.

Her gaze moved to his eyes, and he was an animal unleashed.

He couldn't wait. He wouldn't wait. The flawless skin exposed and the perfection of her breasts took his breath away.

"Take me," she whispered.

He sat up abruptly, taking possession of her mouth. His tongue plunged into the soft recesses of her mouth. She arched against his body as his palm closed over the firmness of her breast. She moaned, driving him insane.

He had to go slow and take his time. The urge to tear off her clothes and bury himself deep inside her was too great. Wynne took her by the waist and the next instant she was on her back, staring up at him.

Leaning over her, he studied her eyes, the curve of her cheek, the delicate coloring of her lips, the play of dark hair on the sheets. She'd finally stepped out of his dreams into his life. He would love her for eternity.

He kissed her more gently this time, and their mouths continued a dance of love as their souls joined.

"Make love to me, Wynne," she whispered against his lips.

"I will . . . in time."

He slid his lips slowly down her neck and to her breasts. He pushed the shift to her waist and he heard her gasp as he tasted and teased her nipple.

He wanted to see all of her. Moving back onto the floor, he slowly undressed her. As he worked, his hands grazed across her skin, over her quivering belly, down the leg and up the inside of her thighs until a finger brushed against the opening of her sex.

A moment later, still standing beside the bed, Wynne looked down at the incomparable splendor of her naked body. She was the huntress Diana come to Earth to take her pleasure and grace the world of mortals.

He tossed aside his boots but didn't trust himself to remove his breeches when he lay beside her on the bed.

"Why?"

"Later," he told her. "After I am done with you."

Before she could object again, his hand slid over the symmetrical perfection of her breasts and then moved slowly downward. His mouth recaptured hers, again muffling her gasp when he touched her center of pleasure.

"Close your eyes and feel every sensation," Wynne whispered in her ear, and she arched her body in response.

Jo closed her eyes as his mouth trailed down to her nipple. She felt a blissful madness coming on as his lips tugged at her. Waves of heat swept from her breasts to her core. She lifted her hips, desperately wanting his hand there again.

He was an expert. He knew what she wanted. His warm and magical hand slowly skimmed down her belly, leisurely exploring until it reached the junction of her thighs. She moaned as his finger gently slipped between her legs and found the delicate spot.

"Wynne." His name escaped her lips in wonder.

He began to stroke her, and Jo forgot her own name. His palm pressed at the mound, his fingers retreating and entering again. He caressed her so softly, so perfectly. Her legs tensed, and she felt the slick wetness beneath his touch. Jo found herself short of breath. Her body was suddenly humming with brilliant new sensations.

All the years of dreaming, of imagining this man in her bed, in her life, and the real experience of this moment so much surpassed all those visions.

His fingers circled and stroked, and an unbearable pressure was building within her.

She was possessed by him. He had enthralled her body in a timeless, frenzied world of sensation and passion. When she thought her release was imminent, he surprised her again by moving down her body and kissing her stomach and moving still lower.

Her eyes opened. She stared, not allowing herself to breathe. Praying that he wouldn't stop. Jo gasped when he covered her sex with his mouth.

His tongue replaced his finger, nudging at her so gently, lightly sucking, prodding.

Jo's hands tangled themselves in Wynne's hair, trying to pull him closer, wanting it to never end.

Suddenly her world splintered into unfathomable pleasure she'd never known before, and she heard herself cry out.

The climax exploded within her with the awesome power of a summer storm. The air around her lit up and she could not breathe. And then she was simply sailing through a crystalline sky, colors she had never before seen flashing around her as she soared. She cried out his name and fought fiercely to reach for him.

Wynne held her as she descended, kissing her softly until she found she was still in his arms.

The sensations in her body continued to recede in waves, but as he worked at removing what was left of his own clothes, she felt her excitement and desire growing once again.

She heard him curse. His breeches were too slow coming off. She shivered in anticipation when he stood gloriously naked beside the bed.

"Make love to me, Wynne." She lifted her hips, offering herself to him as he joined her.

The discomfort as he first entered her was sharp and quick and soon replaced by the wonder of their perfect fit. The haze of frenzied delight that followed, swept her up in wave after wave, lifting her, shattering her, until her bones dissolved into liquid, her flesh tingling and spent.

Lying together, they banished every specter of sadness and loss. Right now all that mattered was the two of them. All that existed was the affinity of two hearts and minds. Two bodies and souls. Tomorrow would be a challenge. And the day after. And many days after. But they would have time—a lifetime together—to face the world that awaited them.

For now, for tonight, each lived only for the other and basked in the afterglow of love.

$$\text{❦} \quad 2\,0 \quad \text{❦}$$

GREY MIST ROSE from the river, the sun only a dull smudge of light above the phantom fields and cottages. The worn and battered graves in the kirkyard were dark with the damp. Beads of dew clung to the tufts of grass on either side of the path, and here and there a patch of daffodils hung their heads, waiting for the day to brighten. Jo needed to keep a hold on her emotions. It was as if she were going to the funeral of a friend, and she could not allow herself to break down when she needed to be strong.

They arrived early for the Sunday's service and walked on in silence for some time until she became aware of the sound of the river running over shallows. A cuckoo called from a grove on the far bank, and the feel of Wynne's arm linked with hers fortified her will.

It was time to go in.

They were the last ones who entered the church. As they seated themselves in the back row of the congregation, a spectral arm wrapped around her, surprising her with the comfort and encouragement it conveyed. Ghostly hands pressed her arm and gently touched her cheek, filling her with an unexpected sense of welcome. Jo knew it was her imagination, her anticipation of meeting those who shared with her the blood of the same fore-bears, of having long-held questions answered. But only in part. Her mother had been here.

The curate started the service, but Jo's mind couldn't comprehend the words. Instead, she wondered how many times a little dark-haired girl had sat in this church, perhaps in this very pew. Perhaps her wandering attention had been caught by the dark wood of the seat in front of her and she'd run her tiny fingers along the swirling lines of the wood grain. Perhaps she had practiced her counting on the rows of grey stones that shaped the arches of the windows and been distracted by the thought of spring flowers outside in the kirkyard.

Maybe, as she sat here with her mother and father, the worn coat of the stern old farmer sitting in front of them drew her eye, and she'd been tempted to pull the ribbon that held his hair back. The droning voice of the minister might have caught her attention, and she'd wondered why he wore such funny clothes and had such a strange hair when he looked nothing like that during his visits for dinner.

As she grew older, her gaze may have wandered from neighbor to neighbor. Her friend Josephine, who had the same name and loved to read. The two horrid boys from the next farm who teased her in the tiny schoolhouse at the end of the village. Perhaps those boys became less horrid as time passed.

Her mother had been here. Jo could feel her presence. As she studied the backs and the occasional profiles of the people in the congregation, she wondered which of them had known little Josephine Sellar, loved her, pined for her, puzzled over her disappearance.

Wynne's hand closed around hers, their fingers entwined. She thought of Charles Barton. Had he come here too? Sat with her in this church, their arms linked together, her hand pressed against his side, as Wynne was doing now? What was the relationship between them?

The candles in the sconces and on the altar flickered and flared as a slight breeze wafted through the church. Mr. Kealy concluded the service, and Jo and Wynne stayed in the last pew watching the parishioners leave the church in clusters of twos and threes.

Old and young, women and men, children and old people. Many passed, deep in conversation with friends. Some paused and nodded. But the pleasantry was neighborly and gave no hint of recognition. Mrs. Clark saw them and stopped to introduce her husband. The four of them were among the last to leave.

"Ye should know, m'lady, I thought of our meeting for much of the night," Mrs. Clark told her as the women walked out ahead of the men. "Jo and I were bosom friends when we were but lasses. Always had our heads together, we did. But her family circumstances drew us apart. My husband says my memory ain't what it used to be, but yer resemblance to my dear old friend set me back on my heels, I don't mind saying. And now Mr. Kealy tells me ye might just be a relation to Josephine Sellar. I'm thinking it must be a blood tie."

"This is the reason why I'm here, to discover if we're kin or not," Jo said, unwilling to offer more.

The sun had broken through the clouds during the service, and they found the curate standing in the midst of a small assembly outside. Jo decided they must be the families he'd promised to introduce to them today. Since last night, however, it was only the Sellar family that she cared to meet.

"Do you know which of those people are Mr. and Mrs. Sellar?" she asked Mrs. Clark.

"The missus is homebound these days. Turned an ankle in the garden a fortnight ago. As far as her husband, let me see." She squinted at the group and shook her head. "Can't find him, m'lady. But perhaps Mr. Clark recalls if the gentleman was attending today or not."

She turned to ask her husband and brightened, noticing a man coming out of the church.

"Just looking for ye, Mr. Sellar," Mrs. Clark called to him. "This English lady and the captain here come all the way from Rayneford to make yer acquaintance."

Wynne stopped next to Jo. But the older gentleman's immediate reaction told them no introductions were needed.

"Josephine Sellar? Truly? I don't believe it. It can't be you!"

Cuffe saw the two old people roll up in their ancient carriage. When, a few minutes later, a footman announced the arrival, Dr. McKendry's sudden frown told him trouble had come knocking.

The doctor asked him to stay with Mr. Cameron while he took the guests up to the captain's office to speak with them.

The bookkeeper was busy with his accounting books, so Cuffe went downstairs. Listening to the muttering between the attendants, he heard the name Barton mentioned. When he asked, one of the former sailors told him it was the mother and uncle, and he'd be "best off tacking well away of 'em, for a storm's a-blowin' in."

Mr. Barton was the reason Lady Jo had come to the Abbey, and the sweet old man sketched her likeness every day.

Treading lightly on his way up the stairs, he heard the sound of loud voices coming from the captain's office, and he edged toward the open door, pressing himself against the wall.

A woman's harsh tone pierced the quiet of the hallway. "We didn't give him into your care to put him at risk, Dr. McKendry."

"Mrs. Barton, Graham," the doctor said. "Taking him now would jeopardize the advances he's made. The accidents that occurred—"

"Don't try to pass off what's happened as *accidents*," she hissed. "We've heard the truth, so don't try lying about it. They were attacks, pure and simple. A madman going after Charles while he was sleeping. And now I hear the lunatic is still housed in the same room, free to attack again."

"That patient was provoked by someone who has since run off," the doctor explained.

Cuffe's chin sank to his chest in shame. *He* was the person responsible for what happened to Mr. Barton, having allowed himself to be tricked by Abram. And now Dr. McKendry was being blamed.

"And then," the grating voice scratched out, "we find out my son was nearly drowned, cast into the fish pond by yet another patient, as you call them."

"Nothing of the kind happened," Dr. McKendry

asserted hotly. "Mr. Barton jumped into a waist-deep pond after someone who'd fallen in—"

"Two attacks and you can't protect him."

Cuffe remembered the chaos he and the captain came upon when they rode back from the village that morning. Mr. Barton had gone in after Lady Jo because he thought she might be drowning. He cared for her. He was worried. Since when was trying to save someone's life considered an attack? These people knew nothing.

"The progress your son has made has been astounding," the doctor asserted. "Not only has his health improved dramatically, his mind is—"

"Don't you be talking of progress," she barked, cutting him off. "We've had enough. We're taking my son with us today. We shan't be leaving him at the mercy of vultures. The asylum in Aberdeen is ready for him, and they have bona fide keepers there."

"Sending him there would be a terrible mistake," the doctor argued. "Do you know how they treat their patients?"

"We've made all the arrangements," the woman announced in cold indifference.

"Charles will be beaten. Mutilated. Starved. Dunked in ice-cold water," the doctor exclaimed. "They'll tie him to a chair that's been hung from the ceiling, hoist him up and spin him until he vomits, wets himself, or defecates. And then they'll beat him for that."

Cuffe shivered, recalling the brutality on the plantations. He'd heard so many stories from the folk that escaped. He'd seen their scars. Their missing fingers and ears. It made him ill to see his own people exposed to such treatment, and he didn't want Mr. Barton to be treated that way, either.

"Graham, please speak with Mrs. Barton," Dr. McKendry pleaded. "Surely *you* see that moving him now is the wrong thing to do."

"She is my nephew's mother," the old man said flatly. "Neither you nor I can say we know what's best. She's the one to decide."

The doctor was not giving up. "Mrs. Barton, patients who are sent there rarely if ever recover enough to rejoin society and their families. Your son would be lost to you forever. Surely you don't want that."

"Save your breath," Mrs. Barton ordered. "They've agreed to take him, and we mean to remove him from this place. The treatment my son has endured here cannot be referred to as anything but evil, and once he's been saved from your . . ."

Cuffe had heard enough, and he backed away from the door. They were correct downstairs. Something horrible was going to happen, and Dr. McKendry was alone to face them. Lady Jo cared about Mr. Barton, and she wasn't here. The captain wasn't here either.

It was up to Cuffe to help.

***

Josephine Sellar.

The older gentleman's unguarded exclamation affirmed what Jo had already come to accept in her heart. She now knew her mother's family name, who her people were, and where she came from.

Mr. Sellar was astonished, but he wanted to know more about her. Jo desired no public spectacle, however, and as the curate and the other families joined them, she asked Mr. Sellar to wait so they could discuss the matter further in private. None of the others appeared to recognize Jo or even understand what the curiosity was about.

Wynne asked permission of Mr. Kealy for the use of his cottage. And as Jo started up the hill with Mr. Sellar, she was relieved to see him head off Mrs. Clark and the others.

"Perhaps I only see the resemblance because the curate mentioned before the service that a visitor in the village was asking about someone named Josephine," the old man said once they settled in at the cottage. "Too many years have passed. Memories fade. But when I first looked into your face, I swore I saw her."

Jo had left the door open, and Wynne ducked his head and entered. She was glad. She needed his strength, his astuteness.

"If I may ask, how was Josephine Sellar related to you?"

"A cousin, twice removed. Not close enough to warrant guardianship when she became an orphan, nor close enough to inherit when she died."

Her mother was an orphan. Of course, Jo thought, understanding the poverty she'd been enduring those last days of her life. She was grateful when Wynne asked about the parents and how they'd died.

"I was a soldier, off fighting in America back then, so I wasn't here to know or help," he said, staring at a streak of light illuminating the stone floor. "What I heard after, though, was that fever ran through the village. It took some lives, including Josephine's parents."

"And what happened to her after the parents died?" Wynne asked.

"She was left no pauper, certainly," Sellar said, his gaze swinging around to them. "She had land and a great house, and once she came of the age, it would have been hers to keep. And it should have been, with Ainsley her guardian."

"Ainsley?" she asked.

"Ainsley Barton. A great, kind-hearted man, bless his soul. He was the brother of Josephine's mother. A tragedy, it was, that he died a year later."

Barton. Jo met Wynne's gaze. There was a family connection.

"Do you know a Charles Barton?" Wynne asked.

"Of course, Charles was Ainsley's son. Another good man, cut from the same cloth as the father."

Cousins, Jo thought, emotions welling up in her. They were cousins. Charles's sketches of her mother. They had to know each other for all of their lives.

Her mind returned to Mrs. Barton's denials. And to Graham's response. They said Jo resembled no one they knew. But Ainsley Barton was her mother's guardian and uncle. She must have been well known to them.

"Did Charles become Josephine's guardian when his father died?" Wynne asked.

He shook his head and his expression showed his disappointment. "No, that couldn't have happened. Charles was close in age to Josephine. Maybe two or three years older. No, Graham became her guardian after his brother passed. He's the one who has made all the decisions about Tilmory Castle since. He was the one I bought the Sellar property from when I came back from the war."

Jo tried to speak, but her voice couldn't push past the knot in her throat.

"Why Graham?" Wynne asked. "How could he sell you her property?"

The old gentleman looked at Jo. "We were told . . . I was told . . . Josephine drowned in the big flood. I don't know why or how she came to be in Garloch. But a gravestone is sitting out there in the kirkyard with her name on it. I can show you if you care to see it."

❧ 21 ❧

THEY FOUND the gravestone marking the final resting place of Josephine Sellar near the wall along the river path. It was plain and similar to a score of others around it, but Wynne watched as Jo studied the markings. A name. A birth. A death.

He wondered what poor soul had been buried there in the place of her mother, and as they stood there, Jo murmured a quiet prayer. As he listened, the thought crossed his mind that someone else may have gone on living, never knowing what had become of their daughter or sister or wife . . . or mother.

In the curate's cottage, Jo had not mentioned what she suspected to be her connection with the Sellar family. When she said nothing to the old gentleman, Wynne had followed her lead and remained silent. He knew as it stood, she had no proof of anything, only a handful of drawings and a series of possible coincidences. Still, he guessed that Mr. Sellar knew the truth.

Back in the village, she visited with Mrs. Clark while

Wynne searched out the curate and compensated him for his time and efforts.

They left Garloch at noon, and for a long time Jo sat quietly beside him, her head resting against his shoulder and their fingers entwined. He knew she had a great deal to think about. This journey had been an emotional whirlwind, and they both were feeling its profound effect.

"Did Mrs. Clark tell you more?" he asked. "Anything that you didn't know?"

"She told me she was living in the village at the time of the flood. She was newly married then," Jo told him. "It was an awful time, she said. The town was full of folk passing through, seeking some place after being turned out of their homes by the landlords. There was a large encampment along the river. As Mr. Kealy told us, when the flood came, so many people were caught in it and carried off by the waters. It took weeks to find some of them and many were beyond recognition. Families were forced to guess at the identities of the bodies."

"That doesn't excuse Graham's false identification of your mother."

"No, it doesn't. Nothing does," she said, her words tinged with anger. "My mother was his ward. She was his kin, his own sister's daughter. But he failed her. Perhaps worse than failed her. When she showed up a month later in the Borders, she was frightened. She would not even tell anyone the name of her family in the Highlands. She gave me to a stranger rather than asking her to send me back to her own people."

Pregnant and alone. Even now, debilitated by a head injury, Charles Barton appeared to care deeply for the young woman he'd lost. But from what Wynne knew of the older man's history, during that time he'd had a commission in the navy. Questions arose in his mind as to the nature of Barton's relationship with Josephine Sellar. More to the point, who fathered the woman sitting beside him now? The woman he loved.

"Last week, Graham and Mrs. Barton saw me in that ward, and they both denied any kinship vehemently. Why?" she asked, frustration and ire evident in her voice. "All they needed to say was the same thing I heard from Mrs. Clark and Mr. Seller—that I resemble someone they'd once known. It would have been enough to put me off and bury the truth. So why reject me?"

Because they had something to hide, Wynne thought.

"Men do vile things for money," he replied. "Graham saw to it years ago that Josephine Sellar was declared dead. In doing so, he took possession of her property and sold it. Right now, he controls the estate at Tilmory Castle. With Charles Barton in an asylum—or dead, as he nearly was when they dumped him at the Abbey— Graham continues to reap the benefits. And then you arrive. What if Charles and Josephine were more than cousins? They were both young when she became his father's ward. We have no proof that they were married, but what if they were and Graham knows it? You would be the heir to everything."

"We have no proof of anything," she said, not denying his assertion. "But what man draws the same woman's face, day after day after day?"

A man in love, Wynne thought. "According to Mr. Sellar back in Garloch, the farm was to be inherited by your mother. The estate was provisioned to allow for a female heir. Perhaps the same condition exists for Tilmory Castle. Why would Graham worry unless he thought you would inherit once Charles is gone? He has a great deal to lose unless you go back to your life in the south."

"But I don't care about Tilmory Castle!" Jo burst out. "Or the money, or any of that. I . . . I'm only trying to find out the truth of what happened to my mother."

Wynne drew Jo closer to his chest and pressed a kiss on her brow. "I know that, but Graham doesn't. And I don't think he'd believe you if you told him."

They rode in silence for a few moments until she spoke, calm again. "You believe it's a possibility that Charles Barton and my mother were married."

"We found nothing in Garloch, but if she married in any of these parishes, we might find some record of it in the offices of the bishop in Aberdeen."

"Married or not, my mother suffered," she said fretfully. "What would drive her to leave the Highlands?"

"I think Graham and Mrs. Barton need to answer that. She was in their care. But Charles Barton may know something, as well, if he ever improves enough to share it."

She nestled closer and tucked her head beneath his chin. "Charles Barton. Could he really be my father? And will I ever know for certain?"

Jo's hand wandered innocently down the front of his coat, and his loins tightened.

"Whatever answers present themselves, you will learn them with me at your side. For that is where I vow to remain . . . except at this particular moment."

He could wait no longer. Wynne moved swiftly to the seat across from her.

Yesterday, Jo agreed to marry him. Last night, overwhelming passion consumed them. Neither had slept at all. Every time they thought themselves satisfied and spent, it took only a look, a caress, and they were young lovers once again.

She looked at him questioningly.

"Which hand?" he asked, holding out two closed fists.

Jo was satisfied with what they'd discovered about her mother at Garloch, but she was also disheartened at the lack of prospects for learning anything else. Wynne read her thoughts. He knew what she was feeling. And here he was, trying to cheer her up.

"What are you doing, Captain Melfort?" she asked, smiling.

"Which hand?"

"If you intend to distract me, you've already succeeded," she said, looking into his handsome face.

"Don't be a coward, Lady Pennington. Pick one."

Jo traveled back in time to a warm evening in London. To the night they met.

"You're being more formal than the last time, Captain," she drawled, biting her lip as she studied her options. "The right hand."

As she'd expected, it was empty. When he extended the left hand in her direction, she saw the right move covertly into the pocket of his coat. This was preposterous, but suddenly she felt young and playful.

"What are you hiding in there?" she cried out, throwing herself into his arms and trying to dig her own hand into his pocket.

"Lady Jo, your impatience astounds me."

"I'm glad." She laughed.

"And I'm shocked by your forwardness."

"Which delights me even more."

Smiling, he gathered her firmly onto his lap, and she met his gaze, reveling in the heat and masculinity he exuded. She wanted him. She wanted to make love to him right now in this carriage. And from what she felt through the layers of their clothing, he wanted it too.

"After," he said, reading her mind. He laid his right fist on her lap. "Which hand?"

If he had a rosebud in there, she thought, he was truly a magician. Jo sighed, turned the hand over and pried open his fingers. There in his palm, an intricately designed gold band gleamed. She looked at him perplexed, but for only a moment. Then her heart soared as she slipped it on.

"I was hoping you'd allow me to put this on your finger when we marry for the first time at the church in Rayneford. The vicar will be officiating."

"Marry for the first time?" she asked, mystified. They'd already spoken of going to Baronsford, having Wynne's family meet the Penningtons, and *then* planning their wedding. She reminded him of that now.

He shook his head. "That will be our second wedding. And we could have a third or fourth as well, if you want," he told her. "After last night, it became clear to me that there'll be no waiting. No long engagement. I'm yours as you're mine. In fact, you told me yourself last night that your younger brother, Gregory, and his wife were wed twice. Do you think I would have you slighted in any way?"

"You're worrying about my reputation," she said, feeling her love for this man rise ever higher.

He held her gaze. "I love you, Jo. And I'll be dashed if I allow anything to jeopardize our future together. Malicious talk, gossip, and lies will never touch us again. We shall forge a bond between us that the world will look on with awe. But if something were to happen to me today, before we marry, I want you—"

She put her fingers to Wynne's lips. She'd die if something were to happen to him. And she understood what he was saying. After what they'd learned about her mother's life, she shared his resolve about the future.

"And I love you, Wynne," she whispered. "We'll marry twice, but this is the only ring I'll ever wear."

The early afternoon sun slanted through the small window, and the older man's eyes were fixed on the angular ray of light on the dusty oak floor of the upstairs room in Knockburn Hall.

"Everything will work out, Mr. Barton," Cuffe told him reassuringly. "The captain is on his way back."

They were supposed to come last night, he thought. He had no doubt they'd be back today.

He got up and went to a south-facing window. When they first got here, he'd seen men in the distance searching the fields. But he saw no sign of them now.

No one was happy to have the Bartons show up at the Abbey unannounced. Cuffe wondered if the doctor knew his patient was here. Perhaps he even approved. In any event, the men never came close to the Hall. They never got the dogs out of the kennels.

The three boys Cuffe approached wouldn't say a word. They were to get a shilling apiece from him for their part in this. In the stables, he told them he needed their help. Mr. Barton was at the pond with an attendant. They'd fallen on the man like highwaymen and taken him unawares. With a satchel thrown over his head, they'd gagged him, bound him, and dragged him back to the barn while Cuffe led the patient away to Knockburn Hall.

It had taken them a long while to reach their hiding place. The older man had grown winded quickly and needed to sit and rest several times. But he was good about following directions. Cuffe looked across the room at him now.

"We'll be all right. You'll be safe here," he said. Mr. Barton was sitting where Cuffe had put him when they arrived, in the niche of a window near the fireplace. "I couldn't let them take you. Not after I heard them talking. That other asylum, the one in Aberdeen, it's a bad one. I've seen people in the islands who suffered. Hurt for no reason. It's not right. Spinning and beatings. Putting you in cold water. The captain wouldn't have let it happen."

The patient said nothing, and Cuffe wasn't sure if he understood a word of what was said to him. His eyes remained locked on the rectangle of light on the floor.

"The captain will be back today," he repeated. "We're safe here. You and I both. Would you care to take a nap? Make the time pass quicker."

He wished Mr. Barton would sleep a little. He usually did at this time of day, but the man made no move to lie down.

It was odd to carry on a one-sided conversation. He thought about when he was doing this to the captain. Not answering. Not looking at him. Acting like he didn't exist, even when the captain was being good to him. Much like Mr. Barton was doing to him now.

Cuffe thought guiltily how much trouble he'd been to his father. His father.

"You've probably been wondering why no one has found us," he said. "I come from Jamaica, you know. I'm a Maroon and we live out where no one can catch us. Not even the soldiers."

He looked out the window again.

"You know the captain. He's Dr. McKendry's partner at the Abbey. The governor. But before that he commanded warships. He's sailed every ocean. Fought pirates and slavers and Americans. And the French. He's smart as they come. He'll know what we should do."

He'd come soon. And he'd know where they were hiding. Cuffe crossed the room and sat against a wall near the older man.

"My father—the captain, I mean—he can fix anything. Everyone depends on him, even Dr. McKendry. They wouldn't have tried to take you if he were at the Abbey today. But he'll be here soon. We'll be all right."

Cuffe wished he were here now. His father.

On Thursday they'd ridden together to the village. He liked how the captain had let him choose a horse as his own. And how he'd gone with him to bring food for the old widow in the run-down cottage at the end of the lane. And how the captain came to his room on Friday night and talked to him about Lady Jo.

The captain . . . his father. And perhaps Lady Jo to make a new family. Maybe it wouldn't be bad to grow up in Scotland.

The touch on his arm startled Cuffe. He turned to see the old man sitting beside him. The eyes were alert, watching him.

"What's wrong, Mr. Barton?"

"Where is Jo?"

�֍ 2 2 ֎

WYNNE KNEW something was wrong before they reached the long drive leading to the Abbey. Groups of men moved along in lines across the fields and the golf links, searching every inch, kicking at patches of gorse and long grass. He could see others by the ponds poking into the water with their sticks. They were looking for something.

"What do you think has happened?" Jo asked.

"I don't know." He paused and motioned toward the carriage and grooms waiting by the door to the annex. "But we have visitors."

There was no point in guessing what was amiss. They'd know soon enough. But as their own carriage stopped by the door, Dermot dashed out the building and climbed in before they could step out.

"Driver, go out beyond the grove of chestnuts and stop there," he called out, and the carriage immediately lurched into motion.

"My apologies, Lady Josephine," he said, bowing his

head in greeting. "But it would be better if you were not to arrive at the Abbey just now."

"What's wrong?" Wynne demanded.

Dermot turned to him. "Graham and Mrs. Barton stormed in here some time ago, angry as a pair of wasps. They want to take her son and deliver him to the lunatic asylum in Aberdeen. They claim all the arrangements have been made. I tried to reason with them, but they're not having any of it. They're demanding that we release him to them immediately."

Jo grew pale and her dark eyes fixed on Wynne. "Is there a way to stop them?"

Dermot's face showed his doubts. "They know about the attack last week. They also know Barton went into the fish pond. She's claiming we've been negligent in caring for him, and as his mother, it's her duty to take him. I managed to keep your name out of any discussion of the events, m'lady. It was obvious to me your arrival and influence on Charles's improvement distressed them."

"Did they ask about Lady Jo?"

"Mrs. Barton did, as soon as we found that Charles was missing."

"What did you say?"

"That she traveled north yesterday."

True enough, Wynne thought.

"What is the asylum in Aberdeen like?" she asked with a quaver in her voice.

"Dreadful." The doctor shook his head. "He won't survive there for very long."

Wynne quickly considered their options. "Where are the Bartons?"

Dermot glanced out the carriage window like a man expecting an ambush. "Right now, they should be in the east wing with my uncle and aunt. I'm guessing the Squire is talking ceaselessly about golf while my aunt buries them with refreshments. But I don't know how much longer they'll stay put."

"And Charles Barton?" Wynne asked.

"That's the other issue facing us at the moment. He's disappeared."

"Disappeared? Where?" Jo asked, upset. "Is that why you're searching the fields? Who took him? What happened to his attendant?"

"We found his attendant in one of the barns, tied and gagged with a bag over his head. He was quite unharmed, really. But there's no sign of the patient."

"Let me understand this," Wynne said, visualizing how the events unfolded this morning. Or rather, how Dermot presented it to the Bartons. "Charles wandered off on foot. Since he cannot have gotten far, he must still be *close by*. And you're not using the dogs because you don't intend to upset him or cause him to injure himself."

"You understand the situation perfectly." Dermot's look spoke volumes. "Once Graham learned his nephew was missing, he was ready to go to the village and fetch the constable and put a search party together himself. But I assured him that no carriage or horses had been taken, and we were confident about finding Charles very quickly. In fact, they assume you're leading the search."

"He was satisfied with that?" Wynne asked.

"For the moment anyway, but yes. Particularly when I mentioned Charles was last seen by the fish ponds."

Jo stared at Dermot and then looked at Wynne. Her expression told him she understood the hinted accusations. After what they'd learned in Garloch, he was beginning to think Graham was capable of anything.

"Where is Cuffe?" she asked.

"He is . . ." The doctor paused with a meaningful look at Wynne. "He's out and around somewhere, but I don't know exactly where. But actually, when I think of it, the lad might have gone missing quite soon after the Bartons arrived and made their intentions known."

"Buy us some time." Wynne leaned over and opened the carriage door. "Read them one of your dissertations on the migration of cuckoos or the structure of the salamander brain. Just hold them. I'll get word to you how we'll proceed next."

The carriage pulled up into the overgrown courtyard at Knockburn Hall. No sooner had they stepped out when, to her relief, Cuffe's face appeared in an upstairs window.

"While you go up, I need to speak to my son."

Jo studied Wynne's grave expression and his purposeful steps as he strode to the house. Before he reached the entrance, Cuffe pulled open the door.

Time stood still. Jo was unable to move, watching as the two faced each other. Finally, Cuffe's chin rose a notch.

"I did the right thing," he said. "Didn't I?"

"Indeed, you did. You've made me proud." He closed the distance between them and took his son into his arms, lifting him up and hugging him tightly.

Cuffe's arms wrapped around his father's shoulders. As Wynne put him down and they walked off a few steps in the direction of the pond, Jo could hear little of what they said. But she knew these two had overcome a great barrier. Father and son were firmly connected. And she was looking at her future. At the men she loved. They were her dreams realized.

Jo turned her attention to the house and hurried inside. She found Charles upstairs where they'd seen Cuffe in the window.

He sat on the floor beneath a window, his legs crossed tailor-fashion. His attention was fixed on a beam of afternoon light at the base of a far wall. Jo studied the lean, angular planes of his face, the narrow shoulders. He had a slight build. Medium height. She tried to imagine him as a young man.

Thinking of what Wynne had said, of the possibility of this man being her father, she searched for similarities. Physically, she'd inherited her appearance from her mother. That fact had been confirmed time and time again since her arrival in the Highlands. But what of her personality? Jo was no gifted artist, but she was quiet and unassuming. She was nurturing and had a giving nature.

She crossed the room to him. He was either her father or simply a kindhearted man who'd never gotten over the loss of a dear cousin. It didn't matter. She was here to help him. If she could reach him at all, she thought he'd want to hear about her journey to Garloch and what she had discovered.

"Mr. Barton," she said softly. "May I join you?"

She didn't expect an answer, so she sat cross-legged on the floor in front of him, their knees almost touching. The beam of light was directly in her eyes, but she wanted to be here where he would see her.

Jo didn't know what Wynne planned to do as far as stopping the family from taking this man to Aberdeen. He'd commended Cuffe for helping Charles disappear.

She knew he'd bend the law if necessary, to thwart the Bartons and their foul plans.

Right now, at this moment, to calm her own nervousness, she had to talk.

"Thank you for directing me toward Garloch. Captain Melfort accompanied me there."

Charles's fingers were drumming softly on the floor by his knee. He was missing the pencil and paper he was accustomed to drawing with. Jo realized her fingers were doing the same thing and she stopped. Reaching over, she took both of his hands in hers. They were cold, like hers.

"We met with the curate there," she told him. "An agreeable young man who was eager to help us and answer our questions if he could."

Jo went on and relayed all they'd learned—the dates they'd focused on, the search for baptisms of girls with a first name of Josephine.

She thought he might know many of the people they encountered, possibly even the curate, depending on when he'd last visited the village. She talked about Mrs. Clark in detail, hoping the name of Josephine's childhood friend might trigger some response.

"Josephine Sellar," she said again. "For my entire life, I've never known my mother's family name until Mrs. Clark revealed it. I didn't know where she came from or who her family might be. The grief . . . the grief I felt after . . ."

Her voice shook. She paused, staring at their joined fingers. She studied the contrast of age in them. She touched the calluses and scars on the weathered hand. When she was finally able to speak, Jo shared how broken she'd felt last night. She told him of the tears, the sense of loss. She explained how, for the first time, she knew who her mother was and that only made her suffer so much more.

Her face was in the light and his was in shadow, so she couldn't see if her words meant anything to him. But if he understood any of what she said or not, it made no difference. Charles Barton and his sketches had been the stimulus, the trigger that had brought her search to the Highlands. He changed everything for her. Finding Wynne again, discovering her mother's origins, even knowing that this silent man was family—it was all due to him.

"I met Mr. Ezekiel Sellar, a distant cousin and a decent man," she told him, reminding Charles of who he was. She conveyed the kind words the older gentleman had said about him and his father, Ainsley Barton.

"So now I know how we're related, the Bartons and Sellars."

Perhaps it was her imagination, but Jo thought she felt a gentle squeeze of her hand.

"You and Josephine were cousins. You must have seen each other many times while you were growing up. Perhaps you shared the same interests," Jo suggested, wondering how many times those two had held hands. "And I now know that she moved to Tilmory Castle when she lost her own parents, which explains why you knew her features so well that you can draw her now, nearly forty years later. We never forget those we care about the most, do we?"

The smile, the laughter, the dark eyes dancing with the expression of a woman who knew she was adored. The sketches of Josephine depicted a young woman who was loved.

"I think you two must have cared for each other deeply."

Jo had no right to assume more than that. She couldn't speculate wildly and persuade herself there was more between them. Her mother was lost to her. She wouldn't convince herself that Charles Barton was her father, only to have it come to nothing. She hadn't come to the Highlands to find him.

"Mr. Sellar showed me my mother's grave today," she said sadly. "He didn't really know her or care for her as you did."

She pulled her hands away and gathered her knees to her chest.

"I didn't tell him the truth about the grave. It would have only unsettled him. But you have a right to know. Josephine isn't buried in the churchyard in Garloch. She didn't die in the flood. She survived. And then she ran from her people as far as she could go."

Her thoughts drifted to the image of her mother from the stories she'd collected over the years.

"Josephine Sellar, little more than a girl herself, turned her back on her home and her kin and traveled, heavy with child, like a pauper with other desperate and friendless folk driven out of the Highlands." The words struggled to get past the fist gripping her throat, but she forced them out all the same. "They said she mentioned no man she was going to, and no husband left behind. She died holding her daughter in one arm and clutching the hand of the kind and loving woman who took me in and raised me."

She stabbed at a tear that splashed onto her face . . . and then another and then another.

"I believe you thought she died and was buried in

Garloch. But someday—when you're better, I'll take you to the Borders, to the village of Melrose. There in the kirkyard, I'll show you where Josephine Sellar, my mother, is buried."

She heard footsteps downstairs and knew Wynne was coming up. Jo lifted her chin off her knees and took a deep breath, trying to calm herself. She couldn't fall apart. Not right now. Not when this man needed her.

The beam of light had shifted with the movement of the sun, and she stared at Charles Barton.

Tears ran unimpeded down his face, and he slowly reached out and took her hand in his.

23

WYNNE STARED at the painting above the mantle of the library at Tilmory Castle. It was a depiction, done in the grand style of the last century, of Julius Caesar being assassinated in the Roman Senate. The irony was not lost on him.

The afternoon sun was rapidly slipping toward the hills in the west, and he wondered how long it would be before Mrs. Barton and Graham arrived from the Abbey. It didn't matter, he decided. He was ready for what lay ahead.

"Cry havoc and let slip the dogs of war," he murmured, moving to a window overlooking the front courtyard.

Tilmory Castle, with its warlike, red stone exterior, presented itself far differently on the inside. The centuries-old castle had been renovated only decades ago, and the interior had clearly been designed to convey the feeling of wealth and power. Reputed to be one the richest estates in the area east of the Grampians, the farms had long ago been cleared of tenants to make room for the more lucrative raising of sheep. The display of artwork, books, fine furniture, and other luxuries demonstrated the success of that strategy, in spite of the sometimes unrestrained shows of force it took to achieve it.

But it was the behavior of the staff that gave Wynne the greatest pause.

In his time in the navy, he'd seen ships commanded by cruel men. The use of the lash and deprivation of rations in the hands of a sadistic captain often made for a disciplined but disheartened crew. Men accustomed to mistreatment did what was required, but with a slack and sullen manner, and they did nothing beyond it. It was the same here.

From the moment he climbed out of the carriage, he'd seen the sidelong looks of fearful, unhappy servants. Without meaning to, they projected the attitudes of whipped dogs, slinking about, disappearing around corners, answering questions when asked in the most hesitant manner, averting their faces when they came in to light candles. The workers at Tilmory Castle were afraid, and they'd been that way for a long time.

Wynne was still standing at the window when the Bartons' carriage rolled to a stop in front of the entrance. Graham stepped out and offered a hand to Mrs. Barton, who ignored him and hurried toward the door with an agility that belied her age.

Dermot was to tell them that Wynne had found their son and was delivering him personally to Tilmory Castle, where he would await their return. He could only imagine how they must have received the message.

Only a moment later, the library door opened, and

Mrs. Barton barreled into the room, with Graham on her heels.

She overlooked Wynne's greeting, her eyes immediately finding her son sitting quietly at the desk near the door.

"I've never been faced with such appalling negligence and ill-treatment. If my son were not waiting for us here, we would have taken the Abbey down, stone by stone. And we may do that yet." She went closer to Barton. "He looks pale as death. What kind of ordeal did you put him through? Why couldn't you bring him back to the Abbey?"

Without waiting for an answer, she turned to Barton's uncle. "Put him in the carriage. I want him taken directly to Aberdeen."

"It's far too late in the day," Graham told her. "Tomorrow is time enough."

Mrs. Barton glanced impatiently out the window at the late afternoon light and then waved a hand imperiously in the air. "Call in the servants. Have him put to bed. Tomorrow at first light, Graham, you'll take him." She whirled toward Wynne. "We have nothing more to do with you, Captain. Our business is finished. Kindly convey our dissatisfaction to Dr. McKendry regarding the management of what you claim to be an asylum. You'll receive no favorable recommendation from us, I assure you. Now get out."

When no one moved, she turned to Graham, who was staring across the room.

"Lady Josephine," he said with a curt bow. "We were told you'd already gone north."

Mrs. Barton swung around, her expression furious as Jo moved away from a bookcase.

"I did go north," she said calmly, holding a volume to her chest. "But only to Garloch."

"You!" the older woman breathed with a tone of accusation.

This was the way Jo wanted it, to stay in the shadows until these two were secure in their own lair.

"After all these years, I was glad to know where my mother was born and baptized. I had to see it with my own eyes. Captain Melfort was kind enough to help me find what I was looking for," Jo said, nodding with gratitude in Wynne's direction. "He's been instrumental in going through the records at the rectory in Garloch and at the offices of the bishop in Aberdeen. Thank heaven we are such dedicated record-keepers in our modern age. One cannot rely on rumor alone."

Silence deadened the room. And then Graham closed the door as she continued.

"In Garloch I visited with some old friends of my mother's, and I had the opportunity of speaking with her cousin Ezekiel Sellar. He sends his best wishes to you, sir. He was heartily sorry he hasn't seen you since you sold Josephine Sellar's property to him."

There'd been a time when Jo would not stand up to her enemies or even allow anyone else to fight her battles. That time was long gone, Wynne thought proudly. A different woman stood in this room now.

"And we stopped at the grave. But we all know she's not the one buried there."

She was ignoring Mrs. Barton's expression of scoffing disdain and kept her gaze on Graham. And when she spoke again, her abhorrence spilled out with every word.

"*How* could you do that to her? She was your ward.

The daughter of your own sister. She was your own blood. How could you not protect her, cherish her?"

"I—" Graham didn't have a chance to say another word.

"Get out!" Mrs. Barton exploded. "Get out of this house now. This very moment."

"Calm yourself," Wynne ordered. "If you would allow Graham and Lady Josephine—"

"No. I'll allow nothing of the kind." She glared wildly at Jo and pointed at the door. "You're no one. Do you hear? No one. No connection. Josephine Sellar drowned in a flood. She's gone. There was no child. You're an intruder in our lives. Remove her from our home, Graham."

"*Your* home?" Jo asked sharply, looking from the irate woman back at Graham. "Look behind you. He is still here. Charles is alive. This is *his* home."

Neither moved. Their attention was on Jo's flushed face.

"Or will you do the same thing to Charles that you did to my mother? Why not? You can save yourself the expense of sending him to his death in Aberdeen. Why not simply dig a grave here and fill it with the body of any poor soul?"

"You're a devil," Mrs. Barton fumed, her eyes spitting fire. "To say such a thing to a mother."

Jo ignored her, keeping her attention on Graham. "Isn't that what you did in Garloch? Isn't it true that you identified the first available corpse as your ward, Josephine Sellar?"

Graham stalked to a desk by a window.

"And what did you gain by it?" she persisted. "A few paltry pounds from the sale of her estate?" Jo shook her head in disgust. "In your vile scheming, is Charles next to die?"

Mrs. Barton took a step toward her.

"*You* are the only vile schemer," she hissed. "You and your clever plans to take everything we have built. Everything we hold dear."

Jo continued to ignore her, keeping after Graham.

"Or were your actions even more insidious?" she demanded. "Did you try to kill her? Did you throw her into those flood waters yourself? Is that the reason she was so terrified of coming back?"

"You're wrong," he retorted, anguish in his voice. "I committed no murder. She was caught in the flood, and I thought she was dead. I was sure of it. No one could have survived those raging waters, certainly not a woman in her condition. And I tell you with God as my witness, it wasn't about her estate. I wanted to bring her back. Save her."

His admission had a more powerful effect on Mrs. Barton than Wynne would have imagined. She crossed the room and slapped Graham hard across the face.

"That's a lie!" she screamed. "You wouldn't betray me. Not then, not now."

Graham said nothing. He never lifted a hand to his face. He simply stood where he was as Mrs. Barton spun and started back toward Jo.

"That harlot deserved to die." The old woman stopped in the center of the room, her eyes wild, unfocused. "It was God's will that she should drown like the Pharaoh and his Egyptian whore. She died as she should. And the devil growing inside her died as well. I wanted them gone. *God* wanted them dead. Both dead."

As if suddenly awakened, Graham started toward her. "Leana. Stop."

She held up a hand, halting him in his tracks.

"From the first moment the little jade stepped foot in this house, all she wanted was to steal the Barton men from me," she sneered. "She wanted to take *everything* from me. Ainsley and his sanctimonious drivel. Speaking of her as the daughter I should have given him."

Backing toward the desk where her son sat, she reached out to touch his hair, but stopped, pulling her hand back as if burned.

"And then my Charles, my boy, fell under her spell."

She glared at Jo, pure hatred in her eyes.

"He turned on me like an adder, and she made him do it. Turned his back on the match that would have made him a man for all of Scotland. Shrugged off the marriage prospect that I'd arranged for him like it was nothing. Nothing! And turned to *her*! Married *her* . . . just to spite me. All my plans for him. All for nothing!"

Married her.

Josephine and Charles. Married. He was her father.

Married her. Mrs. Barton's words reverberated in Jo's mind.

She wanted to go to Charles and hold him. He was her father. But the old woman was standing beside him, her arms askew, her face twitching with fury. And Jo knew Charles's mother would fight her like a wild animal if she tried to get near him now.

Then something changed in Mrs. Barton's face. A glimmer of understanding flickered in her eyes. She scowled darkly at Graham.

"Saved her? You would have *saved her?*" Her mouth opened and closed as if forming words that did not come out. "You wouldn't do that. Not you. Not the man who claimed he loved me. Not the man who had begged me to marry him for . . . how many years, Graham? Not the man who vowed to wait for me till the last breath of life left our bodies."

Suddenly, all the anger and doubt and frustration and helplessness inside of Jo fell away, and pity welled up in her heart. In spite of the knowledge that this old woman was the cause of so much misery, responsible for the death of her mother, she could feel nothing but pity for her at this moment. Another lost woman.

"Leana," Graham began helplessly.

Mrs. Barton shuddered and shot a fierce glance at Jo.

"So you've stolen him from me, as well," she rasped. "You and your whore mother have taken them all. Well, this one's not half the man his brother was. Never could be. So take him. I don't need him or anyone. You *both* should have drowned. I wish you'd never seen the light of day."

"That's enough, Leana," Graham said, crossing toward her.

And then he stopped and began to back away, and Jo glimpsed the small, lady's muff pistol she'd drawn from the drawer of the desk.

The barrel of the gun swiveled toward Jo, and Mrs. Barton moved a step closer. She wasn't going to miss.

Their strategy, devised at Knockburn Hall when Charles haltingly asked Wynne and Jo to bring him here, had degenerated into imminent disaster. Jo had been willing to provoke Mrs. Barton and Graham, and prod them for answers, but right now it looked as if she would die in the effort.

Jo didn't know how he reached her, but suddenly Wynne was standing between them.

"This has gone far enough, Mrs. Barton," he said coolly. "You'll hand me that pistol immediately."

"Do you think for a moment that I'll let her take everything? My family? My home? My position? Get out of my way."

A thousand thoughts and fears raced through Jo, for she knew this woman was capable of pulling the trigger. She'd come to the Highlands to get answers, to find her origins. And now she knew her mother's story. She'd discovered her father. But what about Wynne? He was the one true love of her life. And she could lose him now.

Fear gripped her heart with iron claws. He was her past, her future, her present. Her life and her dreams. He was the happiness that she thought she had lost forever. He was the air that sustained her.

Sixteen years ago she lost Wynne. Here in the Highlands, she found him again. And now he was standing between her and a loaded weapon.

"You can only shoot one of us," he said to Mrs. Barton. "It won't be her, I promise you."

Graham took a step toward the older woman.

"Stop," she barked. "If I had two bullets, one of them would be for you. Now get out of the way, Captain."

She couldn't let him do this. Jo tried to step around Wynne, but he held her back.

"They'll hang you for this as sure as we're standing here. Do you think her brother, the Lord Justice, would allow you to live if you kill either of us today?"

"Do you think I care? Do you think I want to live after this?"

Jo edged around Wynne enough to see Mrs. Barton waving the pistol.

"Then you may as well shoot me," he said. "I've already taken one bullet for her. I'm ready to take another."

"No!" Jo shouted, backing out of Wynne's reach and stepping to the side.

As the pistol turned, she saw the woman's eyes focus on her, and her intent was deadly.

"No, Mother," Charles Barton said as his hand closed over the pistol, pushing the muzzle toward the floor. "You'll not . . . not be killing . . . my daughter."

❧ 24 ❧

Though she hadn't expected to, Jo saw Mrs. Barton every day after the incident in the library.

When Charles intervened, the older woman had immediately sunk into a chair, shocked and staring at him. She'd been defeated, stripped of whatever power she imagined she had over her son, over Jo, even over Graham. When she failed to move or respond to anyone, servants carried her up to her chambers and put her to bed.

Before they left for the Abbey, Wynne had them send for Dr. McKendry.

Struck down by apoplexy from the shock she'd brought on herself, Mrs. Barton was attended by physicians, first by Dermot and then from the village and from Aberdeen. After two days, their diagnosis was hardly optimistic. The old woman was conscious, for she could blink her responses to simple questions even though she could not speak. But she'd been left with no ability to move or perform the simplest of tasks. Leana Barton would lie in her bedchamber indefinitely, stripped of the dignity of living as she had lived, sentenced to imprisonment within her own mind.

After what had occurred at Tilmory Castle, Jo was relieved when her father expressed his wish to remain at the Abbey. Charles had given up Tilmory Castle as his home long ago.

Rooms for him had been arranged near her in the north wing. With the assistance of an attendant, she was certain she could manage his ongoing recovery.

Charles faltered in his efforts to speak, a continuing problem that frustrated him. But when the words failed him, he picked up his pen and wrote out his wishes, for his comprehension was improving daily. His memory contained great lapses, but Dermot told him not to despair. Others before him had recovered fully, and they would keep at it.

Three days later, Graham asked for an opportunity to explain his side of things, so Jo and Wynne took her father by carriage back to Tilmory Castle.

"There could be no punishment worse than what your mother has been sentenced," Graham said to Charles. They were sitting in the library again, and a steady rain was beating against the windows.

"For myself," Graham continued with a glance at the others, "I fear for my everlasting soul."

Jo was stunned by the change in the man in such a short time. Since their first meeting a fortnight ago, his straight back was bent with age, and he favored one leg when he walked. The lines on his face were deeper. His eyes had lost their fire.

"For years you stayed away from Tilmory Castle, from your mother and me," Graham said in a hushed tone. "I know you thought we drove Josephine away. And you were right. Your mother bullied and threatened her until she ran, but I'm as responsible for it. I stood by in silence, tending to my work overseeing the farms, even though I knew what the lass was suffering. I did nothing to stop it. I didn't raise a finger to help her until it was too late."

Charles would not look at Graham, and he said nothing.

"M'lady, your introduction to this family, to your own family has been . . ." The older man faltered and moved restlessly in his chair, searching for the right word to say to Jo. "Ghastly. But before I say another thing, I need to tell you how sorry I am for treating you as I did the day we met at the Abbey, and for wrongly holding my tongue since then."

"What I have to forgive is nothing compared to what you did to my mother and my father. It was their futures that you destroyed."

"I know," he said grimly. "I know."

More than apologies, she wanted answers. "Two brothers and a sister. My father has conveyed to me some of our family history. What he can recall."

Perhaps it was the day Charles jumped into the pond hoping to save her. Or earlier, when Stevenson was released from his night restraints and dealt her father a blow as he slept. Perhaps it was the accumulation of many things or even just the passage of time. There was no way to know, but a fog had cleared in her father's mind and he was undoubtedly improving. And wanting to spend time with Jo, talking of the past, was his favorite pastime these days.

"You were the youngest," she continued. "You've remained a bachelor your entire life, serving the family at

Tilmory Castle. And I know that Mary, my grandmother, was the middle child. She was married and lived on a farm in Garloch, where she gave birth to Josephine."

One day, she'd like to see that place. Ezekiel Sellar had invited them when they met, but there wasn't time then.

"What I can't understand is why Mrs. Barton hated my mother so," she told him. "It can't simply be she was jealous of the attention of other men in her family."

The older man stared into the air for a long moment. Jo's father had hinted to her that Graham never married because he'd always loved Leana Barton.

"It was . . ." Graham finally broke the silence. "You have to understand it was her need to be the center of things, to control everyone. That's what drove her always. She was raised in the fashionable society of Edinburgh. She always threw it in Ainsley's face that she married down in marrying a Highlander."

How much pain in the world was caused by the religious belief in the superiority of the rich with its oblivious ignorance, its warped and misplaced values, and its tawdry fashions.

"Arriving here at Tilmory Castle, she saw all of us as a challenge. Her intention from the very first was to elevate the Bartons to a place that was deserving of her. And that's where she immediately ran into trouble with Mary. She was set on marrying Sellar. He was a gentleman, but still a farmer. Leana had other plans. She saw our sister being sent off to Edinburgh and introduced into finer society. But Mary got what she wanted and married for love in the end."

Jo had learned from her father that the first time he met Josephine was when she came to live at Tilmory

Castle after her parents died. This explained the families' estrangement.

"Ainsley and I thought the bad blood died with the passing of Josephine's parents," Graham told her. "But we soon learned different when your mother arrived here at Tilmory Castle. She had the temperament of an angel. Cheerful and kind. It was impossible not to love her. But of course, Leana saw nothing but our sister, Mary, in her, and she was after her from the very first day."

Thirteen, a difficult age. Not a child and not completely a woman. Jo now knew that her mother lost both parents and came under this roof when she was thirteen years old. A year later, she lost Ainsley, her uncle and guardian.

Graham's attention shifted back to Charles. "I knew about you two. I saw how your feelings for each other grew more with time. I lived in dread of the day your mother saw it too. For I knew Josephine would be facing so much more trouble."

Charles started saying something but, overwhelmed with emotion, he couldn't utter the words. Instead, he scribbled them on a sheet of paper.

"We married on her sixteenth birthday in Garloch," Wynne read as he sat by Jo's father.

He wrote more and passed it on again.

"I was to retire from the service. Return to Scotland," Wynne read again.

Jo knew this already. Her father's plan was to leave the navy. They wanted to settle as soon as her mother was old enough to control her own inheritance.

"War," Charles said, his eyes pooling.

He'd also told her that they were planning to leave

Tilmory Castle and live on the farm her parents had left to her. They wanted to raise a family in peace.

"You were off fighting the rebels in America when your mother found out that Josephine was with child," Graham said. "Of course, the lass proudly told her the two of you were married, that it was your bairn she was carrying. But you knew all along that Leana had other plans for who you'd be marrying."

"*Her*... plans," Charles hissed. "Not mine."

He wrote ferociously on the paper and handed it to Wynne.

"Your job was to protect my Josephine."

Hot and bitter tears welled up in Jo's eyes as she imagined the abuse her mother must have endured at the hands of Mrs. Barton.

Graham's body began to rock forward and backward in his chair, his anguished gaze was fixed on a vacant space on a far wall. He was remembering it all, she thought angrily.

"Why did she run away?" she asked, forcing Graham's attention.

"Leana lied to her. I didn't know what she'd done until after the lass was gone." He stared at Charles. "She told Josephine you were dead. That your ship went down, and you were lost with the rest."

His rocking increased, and his face was about to crumble.

"She told the lass she would take her bairn away from her, fix it so no one would ever know of the marriage. Then she'd turn her out into the fields for a whore. So she ran away. It was just what Leana wanted."

And where would Josephine go, but her own home.

"And I swear to you, I had no part of that. I had no

idea your mother would stoop to a deceit so low. A terrible storm had been battering us for days. The third in as many weeks. When I came back to the castle, the poor thing was gone. And when I heard what happened from servants who were there, I knew what they said was true."

"You went to Garloch after her," Wynne said.

"I couldn't let her go. I had to bring her back. Not to Leana. But to protect her until you returned. I knew perfectly well we'd received no word of Charles being dead. It was all a lie. I had to find her." Graham ran a trembling hand down his face, and his eyes showed the ghosts were still haunting him. "I came into Garloch right after the flood. I looked everywhere for her. The place was a near ruin. Houses in the village wrecked and scattered everywhere. The bridge washed out. Water still lay deep in the fields. I found out she'd never made it to her old house. So many people were killed by the storm. So many bodies laid out on the hill by the kirk . . ." His words were choked out under the pressure of his grief.

"Why identify and bury someone else?" Jo asked.

"It wasn't about taking over what was hers. Not at all." He shook his head. "I waited for days. I searched myself. She wasn't anywhere to be found. And then more bodies were discovered downriver as the water dropped. There was no telling one from the other. I had only one thing I could use to identify her."

Graham's black eyes glistened with tears.

"The woman that I buried in that grave was in a family way. That was enough for me. I told myself it was Josephine. I made myself believe it. God forgive me, I . . . I *wanted* to believe it was her."

❧ 25 ❧

THE FOLLOWING night Wynne returned late from Aberdeen and knocked on her door a few minutes after midnight.

Jo opened the door and threw herself into his arms. Lifting her off her feet, he stepped inside and closed the door behind them.

"Dash me if I haven't missed you," he growled, his arms gathering her close.

The message had arrived last night from the constable in Aberdeen that Abram had been taken into custody. Wynne left early in the morning, and there was so much he wanted to share with Jo about what he'd learned. But seeing her soft, sleepy face, the thin shift exposing a bare shoulder, he was distracted from the real reason he'd come this late to her door.

His lips glided over hers, tasting, sampling, delving into her yielding mouth as her hands eagerly pushed the coat off his shoulders.

"Make love to me," she whispered, pressing her body against his.

They'd stayed out of each other's bedrooms since the night in Garloch. Time had been precious with all that was happening at Tilmory Castle and at the Abbey. While Cuffe was shadowing Dermot more and more, Jo was spending a great many hours looking after her father and getting him settled. But Wynne had spoken to the vicar. Banns or no banns, he was willing to marry them Saturday if they wished it, and no bribing with golf equipment was required. Revealing their news to Dermot had gone easier than he'd expected. As his friend said, he'd known it was to be from the start, and they owed their happiness to him for playing the rival. Wynne had been in too good a mood to argue.

"As desirable as you look at this moment, Jo," he said, "We're to be married on Saturday. Perhaps we should wait until then."

A single tie bound the neckline of the shift just above her breasts, and she pulled the knot and slipped the garment down her arms.

"Are you certain you'd like to wait?" she asked, coyness mixed with challenge.

Wynne's lips were ravenous as they settled on hers. Her breast filled his hand, and his loins caught fire. She ignited a passion inside him that was inextinguishable.

She tore her mouth away as she unbuttoned his waistcoat and went to work on his cravat.

"Saturday is such a long way off, Captain." She pulled his shirt out of his pants and reached her hands under it, running her palms over his burning skin. "But if you insist, we can wait."

"Perhaps we should assess our situation." He took one

of her hands from beneath his shirt and guided it to his groin. "What do you think? Can I wait?"

Her fingers scraped his manhood through the fall of his breeches, and he heard a low moan sound deep in his own throat.

"No, I don't believe you can." She smiled saucily, looking down at the bulge. "But perhaps *I* can wait."

The playfulness in her tone drove him mad with a desire to make love to her right now. Wrapping her legs around him and burying himself inside her against the door had a certain appeal. But that would be only the beginning. There was no question in his mind that she'd want to make love again on the dresser and the chair and on the table by the window . . . and eventually in her bed. This was what their first night together had been like. They were both insatiable in their desire for one another.

"Then perhaps you'll let me try to change your mind."

He slipped his hands over her perfect bottom, picked her up, and set her down on the edge of the bed.

Without waiting, he peeled away her shift and threw it aside. Then he stepped back and took his time undressing as she lay back on an elbow and watched.

As he disrobed, his eyes feasted on the fullness of her breasts, rising and falling with the uneven pace of her breathing. On the pale skin of her stomach and the curves of her belly that he planned to run his tongue over en route to the dark triangle of hair. She was truly breathtaking. And she was his.

"You're taking unfair advantage of me," she whispered, lying back on the sheets. "It's exciting to watch you undress."

Wynne took hold of her knees and pulled her to the edge of the bed. Her eyes were smoky with passion and a low moan escaped her lips as his thumb played lightly over the rosy hardness of her nipples. Pushing open her legs, he stepped between them. His hand moved slowly downward over her stomach and he heard the sharp intake of breath.

"Watching me undress is the only thing that excites you?" he asked, feeling her shiver beneath his touch.

"We'll need to assess that, as well."

He leaned over her and kissed her, his tongue sliding into her soft mouth. He moved to her neck, and then to the tops of her breasts. As he took one nipple into his mouth, her fingers threaded into his hair.

"You're getting closer to an answer," she whispered, breathlessly guiding his mouth to her other nipple.

He slid a finger into her wet folds and watched her eyes open wide. She raised her hips to his touch, rocking gently against it.

The urgent desire to drive his throbbing shaft into her was beginning to madden him. She was perfection. Softness as in a dream. And more willing than he'd ever conceived in his most carnal imaginings.

He was about to put his mouth where his fingers were, but she stopped him, wrapping her hand around his cock and sliding her fingers along the length of him.

"Have you assessed the situation?" he said, trying to stay sane.

"I believe I have." She shifted on the bed, positioning herself. "And I'm proposing a contest."

"A contest?" he asked, looking at the temptress on the bed.

"Who will make the other fall apart first," she said, inching closer to tempt him. "In Garloch, you were certainly the winner. Tonight . . . I'm challenging you."

He had no doubt he'd be a winner in this game, regardless of her enthusiasm or the outcome.

"And no putting your lovely mouth on me or using your magical fingers to drive me over the edge. At least not the first time."

"The same goes with you," he told her, reluctantly removing her fingers from his manhood. "I accept your challenge."

She lay back on the bed, inviting him. This was a vision of his private life with Jo, he thought, his heart soaring. He was the luckiest man alive.

Wynne took hold of her hand and brushed it against her own sex.

"Does this count?" he asked.

She arched her back involuntarily and then pulled her hand away. "You're bending the rules."

"Well, we can't be bending rules now, can we?"

He moved closer until the blunt head of his cock pressed at the slick juncture of her legs. She was ready for him.

"*En garde*," he growled.

"*Allez*," she murmured.

He pushed slowly into her opening, pausing, waiting, allowing the anticipation to amplify the pleasure. For his part, Wynne was going insane, but he held back even as Jo lifted her hips. Every inch of her body seemed aware, craving his next move.

Madness. Lunacy. He wanted to drive deep into her. But instead, Wynne's hands held onto her hips, his skin beading in perspiration as he summoned his control.

With their bodies connected, their eyes met. They were both burning. Ever so slowly, Jo lifted her hips farther, drawing him halfway into her. He moved slowly, in and out, still not embedding himself fully.

She was drawing shallow breaths, and he knew she was feeling the same rising pressure that he was. She reached out for him. He met her halfway, and their open-mouthed kiss was hot enough to set the sheets on fire.

"Take me now," she whispered.

"New rules?" he growled.

Wynne's hands tightened on her hips, his fingers biting into her flesh as he impaled himself fully inside her. Withdrawing his shaft to the very tip, he paused and then plunged into her again. Instinctively, Jo hooked her legs around his waist, urging him on. He kissed her mouth hungrily as their rhythms overwhelmed all conscious thought. Again and again, he slid out and rocked into her, accelerating with each succeeding stroke.

Colors of orange and gold and red flashed in his brain and a roaring filled his ears. Still, he held on, wanting her to come. Her panting breaths were moans and then pleasured cries. Her fingers were digging into his arms and then clutching at the sheets. Over and over he drove into her, filling her with all he had.

And then it came, a blast of glittering passions. Simultaneous, brilliant, mind-shattering, an explosion that consumed them both in a dazzling moment of oblivion. And in that instant, as their bodies melded into one, as they spiraled upward together, a heaven was created . . . a golden place for them alone where a throne was reserved for the winners of such inspired sport.

An eon later, as Wynne held her in his arms, Jo kissed his lips.

"You realize," she whispered happily, "we have two

days left until our wedding, which gives us plenty of time for more competitions."

"Well, I hope you're not planning to forfeit the additional contests we have scheduled for tonight."

"I can't wait to hear the rules, Captain."

"Abram worked at Tilmory Castle before hiring on in the kitchens at the Abbey," Wynne told Jo sometime later, after another round of love-making. They lay face-to-face in the bed, her hands under her cheek, their legs entwined. "Of course, we knew nothing of that."

Jo had almost been convinced that Abram's schemes had no connection to the Bartons, but were the result of an old grudge. She'd been wrong.

"He now says that he was paid by Mrs. Barton to work here and to keep an eye on her son."

"Was it only her, or was Graham involved too?"

"He claims it was Mrs. Barton who called him in and gave him his orders. If Graham knew about it or not, Abram had no idea."

If one ignored all that happened after, Jo could understand the benefit of placing Abram in the Abbey. What better way to keep an eye on the care being given to someone you love? In this case, it was a twisted love, at best.

"Her motivation wasn't concern for her son, was it?" she asked.

"When Abram first came to work in the ward? It's difficult to say. But later?" Wynne's face hardened as he curled a lock of her hair around a finger and looked into her eyes. "The day she first saw you at the Abbey, Abram said she spoke to him as they left. He claims her exact words were that her son was already dead to her because of the state of his mind. Then she told him Charles wouldn't want to live like that and Abram was to end it. Kill him."

She couldn't fathom how a mother could order the end of her own child's life. No matter his age or the condition of his mind, it made no sense to Jo.

But she knew the truth. It had nothing to do with Charles's mind. The trigger was Jo's arrival at the Abbey.

"Why get Cuffe involved? Why the deception?"

"Abram claims he didn't trust Mrs. Barton. She was madder than the patients at the Abbey. He insists Cuffe misunderstood him. Says he intended no harm to come to Charles Barton. He never planned to follow through with her order. Of course, he's only admitting to any of this now because blame needs to be assigned somewhere—and he's pointing the finger at her."

"You don't believe him, do you?" she asked.

"He's a liar," Wynne told her. "Abram was smart enough to realize the likeliness and consequences of getting caught. If Charles's death appeared to be accidental, he'd still get compensated by the mother. If he didn't succeed, he'd play it as he is now."

"What will happen to him?" she asked.

"He'll be locked up for a while. Perhaps transported. But he won't hang for it."

A much better future than Mrs. Barton was facing, Jo thought.

Three Weeks Later

SINCE PASSING THROUGH MELROSE VILLAGE, Wynne and Cuffe had been riding along a road through heavy forests. Only a few cottages had broken the shade cast by the tall trees.

"What's Baronsford like?"

Wynne wasn't at all surprised by his son's curiosity. So far, their visit to the Borders had been a positive experience for him. He'd been made to feel very much at home at Highfield Hall. Meeting and spending time with his cousins had gone exceptionally well. And Wynne's brother and his wife had showered their nephew with affection. Today, however, he was taking Cuffe to the Pennington stronghold for the first time.

"Some say it's imposing."

He tried to imagine how a ten-year-old might see it, particularly one who'd grown up acutely aware of the strategies of running battles and survival.

"One might see it as a fortress, ready to withstand all attacks. The place has miles of footpaths that wind along bluffs overlooking the River Tweed where lookouts can spot an enemy's approach for great distances. And in case of siege, the deer park and the lake would make for a steady supply of food."

Cuffe rode along in silence for a while, contemplating his answer and looking through breaks in the wood for a glimpse of the castle.

Wynne had ridden over earlier in the week to meet with the earl and the countess, and formally ask their permission to marry Jo. It was no secret that they had already been married by the vicar in Rayneford. Still, a second ceremony would be performed at the church here, with a reception to be held the day before Baronsford's famous Summer Ball.

All of this was a matter of formality, but Wynne encouraged it, knowing how much the Penningtons meant to Jo. He was prepared to do anything to smooth over the bad memories of the past. He wanted them all to accept him and his son into their family circle.

And that led him back here this morning, for Jo's brother Hugh, Viscount Greysteil, had been away on legal business the day Wynne spoke to Lord and Lady Aytoun.

"Baronsford has always been seen by Lady Jo as home. She grew up here surrounded by a loving family and scores of people who, regardless of their rank or position, are treated with dignity and respect."

"Is there anything not to like about it?"

Wynne would be able to answer that better after his meeting with Hugh Pennington. Cuffe knew nothing of the duel he'd fought with Jo's brother sixteen years ago.

Today was the first time he and Greysteil were meeting since that misty dawn in Hyde Park.

"Perhaps you can tell me when we ride back to High-field Hall tonight."

They broke out of the woods into the sunlight, and Cuffe reined in his horse. In the distance, perched dramatically on a rocky rise, the castle reared up impressively over the rolling fields and meadows.

"Baronsford?"

"The one and only." He watched a hesitant expression cross Cuffe's face.

"Imposing."

"So I've heard," Wynne said with a smile.

"And why exactly are we going there today?"

"You need to meet your new mother's adoptive parents, her siblings and their spouses," he said reassuringly. "I was told her younger brother, Captain Gregory Pennington, was expected to arrive with his wife and niece from Torrishbrae yesterday."

"But why can't all of this wait until the day of the wedding? Won't there be scores of other people to meet?"

Wynne understood all the questions. In every new place since they arrived in the Borders, with every new group of people, questions and whispers had begun because of the darker color of Cuffe's skin. Questions about the legitimacy of his relationship to Wynne. Every time, he'd resolved the situation swiftly and efficiently, but Cuffe was aware of the tension.

"You shouldn't be nervous. The Penningtons are unlike any family you'll ever meet. They live according to their own values, without any regard for the opinions of society. They've weathered far greater scrutiny in their lives than we ever shall." Wynne reached across and placed a hand on top of his son's. "Besides, I need you there today to help me."

"How can I help you?"

"Be yourself and win their affection. Make sure they can't refuse to take you in as a member of the family."

Cuffe smiled. "That will be easy."

"Good, because *I* might have a difficult time convincing the viscount to accept me as his new brother."

Entering Baronsford's downstairs library, Jo was taken aback to find her father, the Earl of Aytoun, loudly chastising her younger sister Phoebe. It had been some time since she'd seen the two of them so agitated with one another.

"This is too much, young lady. This bruise on your face," he roared. "If you were a man, I'd say someone punched you in the eye."

"I've told you time and time again. I ran into a door, Father. A door." Phoebe threw up her hands in obvious frustration. "Why don't you believe me when I tell you I have my life under control?"

Of all the five children Lyon and Millicent raised, Phoebe was the one most like their father in temperament. 'Explosive' was the way Jo's mother put it.

"Under control?" The earl kept up his harangue. "You come and go as you please. You ignore family obligations. Your mother and I have no idea where you are, who you keep company with—"

"I'm here for my sister's wedding, aren't I? Days before the event." Seeing Jo, she turned to her. "Save me from him. Will you, my love?"

Jo cringed at the bluish-black mark beneath the young woman's eye. Phoebe crossed the room and gave her a warm hug, whispering in her ear, "I need to steal Anna for an hour. There's no one better for hiding ghastly bruises."

Before Jo could start her own interrogation, Phoebe ran from the room.

"I've already told Millicent," the earl said, stretching a hand toward Jo to come and sit by him. "We are hiring a Bow Street Runner to follow her. Your sister is up to mischief again. I know it."

She didn't doubt it. Phoebe was the writer, the adventurer. Growing up, they'd always thought her head was in the clouds, that she was safe in her imaginative world. But lately, Jo had begun to find subtle clues that hinted at a hidden life. Men's clothing stuffed into a corner of her sister's wardrobe. Copied ships' manifests on scraps of paper in a desk drawer. The hilt of a dagger with only an inch of broken blade. And now this black eye today. When confronted, Phoebe simply laughed off Jo's concerns, telling her they were props for dramatic presentations of her plays at an upcoming house party. And Phoebe's confidante, their youngest sister, Millie, stayed silent and tight-lipped in the face of all Jo's questions.

"A Runner might be a good thing," Jo said, taking a seat next to him on the sofa. "But she'll be angry if she finds out."

"I can live with her being angry, as long as she's safe. Each of you is too precious to us."

Each of you. The stress he put on the words, the way he looked at her as he said them, wasn't lost on Jo. The Penningtons knew about the family connections Jo had found in the Highlands. The earl also knew that Charles

Barton had walked her to the church to marry Wynne at Rayneford.

"I know. And I hope you know you're still my father. The father who raised me, prized me, appreciated me, and made certain I've wanted for nothing my whole life. The father who taught me the values I have today," she said, taking his hand and bringing it to her lips. "I'll adore you and love you and cherish you to the day I die."

"I needed to hear that," he said, drawing her into a bear hug. "I was ready to call out Charles Barton and duel with him over you. After all, I've loved you longest and by far the most deeply."

She smiled and stabbed away a runaway tear as Jo's mother hurried into the room.

"What are you doing, making my daughter cry?" Millicent scolded her husband.

Without waiting for a response, she crossed to the windows and peered out into the gardens.

"I can't see them, but it's taking far too long. They didn't take their pistols out there, did they?"

As Lord Justice, Hugh Pennington used his study at Baronsford as his local seat of power. In no way was Wynne planning on groveling before the man, and he demurred at the suggestion of meeting in a room where he would be at a disadvantage.

The viscount's peculiar suggestion of taking a balloon ride while they resolved their past was out of the question too. He didn't trust the man not to throw him out of the basket. And if events turned out otherwise, Wynne wouldn't know how to land the contraption himself.

He had no desire to fly to the moon before this wedding took place.

Walking with Hugh in the gardens was not exactly the manly setting he envisioned for this conversation, but it was the only option acceptable to both Jo and Grace. Neither woman trusted them out of sight of the rest of the family. Both men, smart enough to recognize the value of listening to their wives, accepted the suggestion.

The speech Wynne delivered was the same that he'd given to the Earl and Countess Aytoun.

The viscount listened to the words like a judge hearing final arguments before handing down a sentence.

"Today is exactly ten days before the wedding," he said finally, facing Wynne. "We can still meet at dawn. Say . . . the glen down by the lake?"

His reference to the date wasn't unintended. Wynne had ended his engagement to Jo ten days before their wedding, sixteen years ago. But he saw no humor in the suggestion of another duel.

"She won't receive any letter from me today. I am not breaking our engagement. I love Jo. And in case you've forgotten, we're already married," Wynne told him. "Regarding apologies, her acceptance of mine was the only one required. And she gave her forgiveness freely. She knows what my reasons were then and she shares my feelings now."

The viscount's gaze was steady, and Wynne met it without blinking.

"Does she also know, Melfort, that you meant to die that day? You shifted your aim away from me at the last moment. You had no intention of firing your weapon."

Wynne wasn't surprised that he'd noticed; Hugh Pennington was a cavalry officer then and a crack shot.

"And you could have easily buried your bullet in my heart," Wynne replied. "But you didn't. You chose to spare my life."

Both men were as tall and as broad as the other. Both were secure and confident.

"I respected you for standing up for your sister's honor," Wynne told him. "One way or another, I was leaving her, and I wanted to make sure she had the protection of a good man."

Hugh considered this for a moment before speaking.

"It took me years before I finally came to a clear appreciation of what war and absence and death do to the one left behind," he said. "I understand you now."

Wynne knew Greysteil's first wife had taken their young son and traveled to war-torn Spain in the middle of winter to be with him. The mother and child had died of the camp fever while Hugh fought to get to them. Jo told Wynne that for many years, her brother lived his life with a death wish. Grace's arrival at Baronsford was the light that saved him.

"War takes too many innocent lives," Wynne said, extending his hand. "I'm sorry for your loss. I truly am."

A short time later, while they were discussing Jo's natural father and his road to recovery, Gregory Pennington and Cuffe came hurrying toward them. Wynne saw his son glance over his shoulder as if fearful of whatever was pursuing them.

"What's wrong?" he asked, drawing him to his side.

"I'm helping him hide from Ella," Gregory admitted.

Wynne had already met the six-year-old niece of Gregory's wife, Freya. With enough energy and noise to put a summer storm to shame, the child was a force to reckon with. This morning, upon their arrival, she'd immediately run to Cuffe, declaring that she liked him and asking if she could teach him to dance.

Freya, who was expecting their first child, had been reduced to stammering. Gregory, coloring deeply, had instantly set out to distract the child. From their reactions, Wynne had a suspicion that there was a great deal of confusion with regard to dancing that the couple had no desire to explain.

"What do you think?" Gregory asked Cuffe. "The stables, the kennels, or the lake?"

"Cuffe!" a little girl called from up near the house.

"The stables first," Cuffe said, taking off on a run. "You can show me the lake after."

❧ 27 ❧

Seven Days Later

THE NOTE from Lady Nithsdale arrived as she had expected. Their neighbor would be calling this morning.

Jo asked Grace and her mother not to receive the woman, but rather to have a footman escort her ladyship up to her dressing room where a seamstress and Anna were putting the final touches on her wedding dress.

She didn't have long to wait. Anna spotted the Nithsdales' carriage coming along the drive.

Jo stared at her own reflection in the mirror. The short-sleeve pleated silver dress, embroidered with pearls, was costly in both materials and labor, but her mother had insisted on it. She'd made it known that Jo was her first daughter to marry, and she would have the most elegant dress imaginable, just as she deserved.

Wynne, too, made it clear to everyone that he wanted Jo to enjoy every aspect of preparing for this ceremony, even though they were already married. He wanted the whole world to know about their happiness. He'd gone so far as to have an official wedding announcement printed in all of the London and Edinburgh newspapers, naming the Earl of Aytoun and Mr. Charles Barton as the fathers of the bride, in addition to mentioning the rest of the family.

A few moments later, Lady Nithsdale was announced.

Jo took a second glance in the mirror, surprised at the serenity in her expression. She recalled all the times over the years when she'd feel sick to her stomach in this woman's company. Lady Nithsdale had made a long career of conveying Jo's personal history, true or invented, to whomever she could find to listen. She'd never looked forward to receiving Lady Nithsdale but had borne it with stoic civility.

She nodded to Anna to let her in.

Lady Nithsdale barreled into the room with the grace of an old bull. Stopping short a foot from Jo, she gasped at the sight of the dress. In her usual false show of familiarity, she placed a kiss on each of Jo's cheeks.

"And here you are, my dearest." She stood back to admire the gown again. "Stunning. Regal. Absolutely fitting. You are the picture of the angel that you are. And what a shocking development, finding your natural father after all these years. Shocking. Shocking, indeed!"

Clearly, to Lady Nithsdale, she was beloved by Jo. They were the closest of friends and it suited her to be complimentary at this moment.

"I want to hear every detail of what happened in the Highlands. Especially, you must tell me all about you and Captain Melfort. Together again. Astonishing. A second chance at romance after all these years."

She motioned to the servants to remove the fabrics

and tools from a nearby chair so she could sit, and looked surprised when Jo shook her head and asked the women to go.

"Shall we be taking tea downstairs with the Viscountess Greysteil and Lady Aytoun?" she asked after they were left to themselves.

"My apologies, but my family is not receiving callers today."

"Of course, dearest. You need to prepare. All of you. Only three days left to the wedding of the year. And only four days to the Summer Ball. Such exciting times for us here!"

Jo knew the true reason why this woman was here, and it certainly had nothing to do with taking tea or admiring a wedding dress.

Lady Nithsdale considered herself a Londoner and lived for the wit and gossip of the clubs and salons and theatres and pleasure gardens. Then, when the fashionable crowd moved on, she followed for a month in Bath before her annual pilgrimage to the Borders in May and June. The only reason she came was because she would never dream of missing the ball at Baronsford. Jo had heard her say it a dozen times. The crowd that attended included many from Britain's highest echelon, and Lady Nithsdale could sail about amongst them as if she herself were the hostess.

And of course, many who would be attending the ball had also been invited to come to the wedding the day before.

"I should be home preparing as well, but first I thought I would enquire about our lost invitation."

"Lost invitation?" Jo asked, trying to sound surprised.

"Why, yes," the woman replied shrilly. "I blamed the

servants for having lost it. But Lord Nithsdale said he believed no invitation had arrived. But I told him that Lady Jo will never, *never*, forget her oldest and dearest friends on the most important day of her life. *Us*. Those closest to her. Those who have known her since the first day she arrived at Baronsford. And he said to me it wasn't only the wedding we were not invited to, we'd also received no invitation for the ball!"

"You weren't invited to the ball?" Jo asked mildly, finding it amusing that her sister-in-law Grace—while making certain Wynne's brother Sir John and his wife were included on the guest list—had crossed out some names as well.

"Exactly. Can you imagine? The Earl and Countess Nithsdale not being asked to the Baronsford Ball? I laughed right out loud at the idea. Can you imagine?"

Jo brushed away an invisible piece of lint from her sleeve. "Yes, I can imagine."

"Imagine what?" The woman's shrewd eyes narrowed.

"There is no mistake. No invitation. It means that you and Lord Nithsdale have not been asked to attend either event."

"You're saying . . ." Deep red blotches appeared on Lady Nithsdale's face. "I am appalled! We're neighbors. Friends!"

"You, m'lady, are a challenge," Jo said calmly. "And we are certainly not friends."

She would have been satisfied if Lady Nithsdale had chosen to flee at this moment and spared both of them further discussion. But the woman was, unfortunately, too accustomed to the polite and reasonable Jo she'd been maligning and bullying for decades.

"You had better reconsider your actions very carefully,

young lady," she said coldly, making her threat clear. "I could ruin you. It would be so easy. So tread lightly at this moment. Consider, if you will, what your other guests would think if I am not present to—"

"Please allow me to tell you what the *friends* that we have invited to these events will think," Jo said, cutting her off. "They'll be grateful they've been spared the company of a loud, pushy, intolerant woman and her husband. They'll be relieved, for they will not need to listen to your malicious gossip, your sharp tongue, your arrogance, or your bold and unceasing interference."

The woman's mouth hung open as she searched for a response, but Jo was not finished.

"People *I* think of as friends, Lady Nithsdale, are tired of seeing the pleasure you take in besmirching a faultless reputation or running down something of value with no regard for the truth or for decency. Now, would you care to hear more on this subject, or have I made myself clear enough?"

Lady Nithsdale's face had lost all color, but she managed to close her mouth. When she dropped a curtsy and fled the room, Jo watched her go with no small feeling of surprise. Her ladyship had surrendered the field.

Turning back to the mirror, she examined the expression on her own face. Relieved. Satisfied. In control. Strong. She liked the person she'd become.

And after sixteen years, she'd finally found the right words to say.

EPILOGUE

A Month Later

THEY STOPPED at the kirkyard in Melrose Village before starting off for Glasgow.

Waiting with Cuffe by the carriage, Wynne left Jo to spend some time alone at her mother's gravesite. She'd brought him here many times while they were at Baronsford. And once they'd returned from their honeymoon, he and Jo planned to bring Charles to the Borders. He wished to visit the place Josephine was really buried.

When he came to the south, he would also have a chance to meet the Pennington family. He was continually improving. The news had reached them only a day ago, however, that Leana Barton had died.

Jo was ready to return to the Highlands if her father needed her, but his letter insisted that they continue with their planned trip. He understood the importance of it for them as a family.

Wynne watched Jo stand and place a farewell touch

on the new gravestone they'd had carved. He was relieved to see a smile on her lips as she walked back toward them.

"Are you ready for our adventure?" she asked.

"I still don't know why I need to come with you two. It's your honeymoon," Cuffe complained, following Jo into the carriage. "I can stay with Dr. McKendry."

"We want you with us," Wynne insisted, closing the door and sitting beside his wife.

"But I can look after your father for you." Cuffe turned to Jo, obviously hoping she'd take his side. "Mr. Barton likes me. He asked me to call him Papa. I think I will."

"You're coming with us, sweetheart," she told him.

She'd adjusted quickly into her role as mother of a ten-year-old son. She was stern and yet loving. Strict and yet flexible when the situation warranted it.

"But I'll miss him."

"As will I. But we'll be back soon enough."

She didn't wait for any more complaints but moved across to sit next to Cuffe. She showed him the books she'd borrowed from Baronsford's library. Wynne watched them put their heads together, arguing or laughing over the passages they read.

By mid-afternoon, Cuffe was back to questioning them about the trip.

"You're taking me with you and showing no regard for my education or my teachers," he teased. Cuffe was clearly working on the art of debate. "How is Mr. Cameron going to stay clever with his arithmetic when he has no pupil to teach?"

"I think he'll manage somehow." Wynne smiled.

"And Hamish," the lad said, mimicking the Scottish

brogue of the lead man on the farm. "The man'll have nobody to scold. No laddie to take to task."

"He'll get by, I should think," Wynne remarked.

As Cuffe continued to rattle off the names of all the other people at the Abbey who would miss his company, Jo sent Wynne a pleading look to tell him.

The trip was to be a surprise, but the boy would know their destination once the carriage reached Glasgow's docks at Greenock.

"All this complaining and not once have you asked where we're going," Wynne reminded him.

Cuffe shrugged. "What difference does it make? I'm doomed to travel with newlyweds."

Jo joined the game. "Very well. Then we shan't tell you."

The silence didn't last a full minute before the ten-year-old's curiosity got the better of him.

"Are we traveling by ship or by carriage?"

"By ship," Wynne said.

Cuffe's brows were drawn together as he studied Jo first, before looking at his father and then back at Jo.

"Are we going to visit the rest of the Penningtons? In Boston or Philadelphia or one of those other places in America?"

Jo shook her head. "Not this time."

"We're sailing to the continent to look at paintings and sculptures and snow-covered mountains," Cuffe guessed, looking pained.

"No, try again."

An expression of hope edged its way into the lad's face. He stared at Wynne, waiting, not wanting to ask. "Tell me."

Jo smiled, nodding to him to continue.

"We are going to be gone for three months," he said. "Three weeks at sea to get there and five weeks to return. That should give us about four weeks at our destination."

"Jamaica!" Cuffe squealed, throwing himself into Wynne's arms. "We're going to see Nanny."

Holding his son tight against him, Wynne looked gratefully at his wife. They'd talked about this trip the night of their wedding at Rayneford. They both agreed that if Cuffe was to be at peace with his life in the Highlands, they couldn't allow him to feel irrevocably separated from his past and the grandmother who raised him.

They'd made a vow that every so often they'd make the journey to Jamaica. And if Nanny was amenable to the idea, she could come and spend time in Scotland, as well.

Cuffe went across to Jo next, and he hugged her affectionately, fiercely.

"Thank you," he whispered.

She placed a kiss on his forehead and hugged him back.

They were a perfect pair, Wynne thought, gazing at the two people who completed him. He was the most fortunate man in the world, for he had them and they were family.

His family. His life. His love. His past. His future.

THANK you for reading *It Happened in the Highlands*. If you enjoyed it, please leave a review online.

And be sure to check out the next book in this series, Sleepless in Scotland, the tale of a wounded hero, a woman with secrets, and a killer lurking in the mists.

Scandal, love, and the hand of fate...

Lady Phoebe Pennington risks her life to expose Edinburgh's corrupt political leaders, even descending into the city's seething netherworld. Then one night, she narrowly escapes death and lands in the arms of the brother of her murdered best friend.

Captain Ian Bell is a tortured man fighting through grief and guilt over the loss of his sister, and he still hunts for her murderer.

Fate has thrown them together, but trust is elusive and danger lurks in the dark alleys of the city. But Phoebe is the only one who has seen the face of her friend's killer, and the sinister shadows of evil are closer than she and Ian imagine.

We hope you enjoyed our novel *It Happened in the Highlands*.

As many of our readers know, we rarely let our characters go without a fight, so you get to see them in the numerous stories that spring from our imagination.

Jo's first mention in our stories can be found when she arrived at Baronsford as an infant in *Borrowed Dreams*, the first book in the Scottish Dream Trilogy. Years later, she also played a major role in *Romancing the Scot*, the exciting tale that features Hugh Pennington and Grace Ware.

You might have already guessed that Phoebe Pennington will be the heroine of our next novel. Look for *Sleepless in Scotland* in 2018.

Also, Millie Pennington and Dermot McKendry's tale, Dearest Millie, is not far behind.

As with all of our novels, we have tried in *It Happened in the Highlands* to depict a place and a time in a way that mingles the real and the imagined in an entertaining way.

The story of the Maroons of Jamaica is an important

part of global history, as are the people who contributed to the movement toward freedom and equality. We also hope you enjoyed the references to the folktales of western Africa.

During the time period in which this novel is set, the inhumane treatment of those suffering from mental health issues was prevalent. People displaying symptoms of "madness" were locked away from society and left to suffer and die in the most appalling conditions. Often, society would use these institutions as places to lock away anyone who was seen to be "different." Innovators like Dr. McKendry in our story were at the forefront of treatment.

It Happened in the Highlands is one of ten novels and novellas that comprise the multi-generational Pennington Family series.

If you're interested, here is the complete list:

— The Promise (*USA Today* Bestseller) - Running for her life on a desperate journey to America, Rebecca Neville promises the dying wife of the Earl of Stanmore to raise and care for her newborn son, James. Ten years later, the Earl of Stanmore learns of the boy. He sends to the colonies for his young heir so he can raise him as a peer of the realm. With no intention of forsaking her vow, Rebecca returns to England with James to face a future without her beloved charge, but she must also face her tumultuous past.

— The Rebel - Jane Purefoy, daughter of an English magistrate, takes on the guise of the notorious Irish rebel, Egan, and leads a secret band of revolutionaries against the brutality of the colonial troops. Sir Nicholas Spencer is on his way to Ireland to court Jane's younger sister. When he runs afoul of Egan, Sir Nicholas unmasks the legendary rebel, only to uncover Jane. Bewitched by her, he decides to keep her secret and embarks on a risky plan of seduction that will throw her family into chaos, a country into rebellion, and his heart into the throes of a love that can never be.

— Borrowed Dreams *(RT Award for Best British-Set Historical)* - Driven to undo the evil wrought by her dead husband and facing financial ruin, Millicent Wentworth must enter into a marriage of convenience with the notorious 'Lord of Scandal' Lyon Pennington, the Earl of Aytoun. Lyon is a man devastated by a tragic accident that killed his first wife and left him gravely wounded. Filled with despair, he reluctantly allows himself to be lured into the unwanted marriage. A fresh twist on Beauty and the Beast.

— Captured Dreams - Portia Edwards will go to any length to find the family she's never known. And when she meets merchant Pierce Pennington —the estranged younger brother of Lyon Pennington—Portia has the perfect chance to ask for his help. But her stubborn pride keeps her silent. That is, until she recognizes her strong attraction to the brave man who, by night, is known as the infamous Captain MacHeath, smuggling arms by sea under the pall of darkness, all in the name of liberty...

— Dreams of Destiny - Wounded by scandal and the unsolved murder of his sister-in-law, David

Pennington is outwardly insolent and arrogant. But nothing will stop him from escorting his childhood friend, Gwyneth Douglas, to Scotland to save the Scottish heiress from fortune hunters. But with their arrival in Scotland comes terrible danger. Now, if they ever hope to satisfy long-hidden desires, they will need to thwart the evil that threatens to destroy both their lives...

— Romancing the Scot - Hugh Pennington, a hero of the Napoleonic wars, is now a grieving widower with a death wish. When he receives an expected crate from the continent, he is shocked to find a nearly dead woman inside. Her identity is unknown, and the handful of American coins and the precious diamond sewn into her dress only deepen the mystery. Grace Ware is an enemy of the English Crown. Trying to escape from her father's murderers, she never anticipated bad luck depositing her at the home of an aristocrat in the Scottish Borders. As she strives to keep her identity a secret, a duel of wits quickly turns to passion and romance...until danger comes to the very doors of Baronsford, threatening to tear the two lovers apart or destroy them both.

— Sweet Home Highland Christmas (*RITA©️ Award Finalist)* - Freya Sutherland is a desperate aunt trying to keep custody of her precocious young niece, Ella, even if it means marrying for security instead of love. Recently retired Captain Gregory Pennington wants nothing more than to make it home in time for Christmas, but he's asked to escort some travelers from the Highlands to the Borders. His plans do not include a wife and child, and Freya has responsibilities as Ella's guardian. With Ella conspiring to get them together, Penn and Freya might just experience a little Christmas magic.

— It Happened in the Highlands - Lady Josephine Pennington's life was nearly destroyed when rumors spread about her questionable parentage. Years later, when she receives a package from the Highlands containing sketches of a woman who looks eerily similar to herself, Jo believes she might have found a clue to the identity of her birth mother. When Captain Wynne Melfort was forced to end his engagement to Jo Pennington sixteen years ago, he never imagined he would see her again. More than that, he never expected feelings long thought dead to resurface. As they strive to unravel the mystery of her birth, Jo must learn how to trust Wynne. And as secrets of the past begin to surface, evil forces will stop at nothing to keep Jo from uncovering the truth and reclaiming her legacy.

— Sleepless in Scotland - Lady Phoebe Pennington risks her life to expose Edinburgh's corrupt political leaders, even descending into the city's seething netherworld. Then one night, she narrowly escapes death and lands in the arms of the brother of her murdered best friend. Captain Ian Bell is a tortured man fighting through grief and guilt over the loss of his sister, and he still hunts for her murderer. Fate has thrown them together, but trust is elusive and danger lurks in the dark alleys of the city. For Phoebe is the only one who has seen the face of her friend's killer, and the sinister shadows of evil are closer than she and Ian imagine.

— Dearest Millie - Lady Millie Pennington's future looks bright until fate deals her a tragic hand in the form of cancer. Dermot McKendry is a former surgeon in the Royal Navy who has returned to open a hospital in the Highlands. Providence brings them together, but life's calamities will sorely test the healing power of the human heart.

— How to Ditch a Duke - Lady Taylor Fleming is an heiress with a suitor on her tail. Her step-by-step plan to ditch him is simple. But there is nothing simple about the Duke of Bamberg. Taylor tries to escape to the sanctuary of the Highlands, but her plans become complicated when the duke arrives at her door and her loyal allies desert her. And even with the best-laid plans, things can go awry...

Finally, if second-chance romance with a twist interests you, be sure to check out *Jane Austen CANNOT Marry!*

As authors, we love feedback. We write our stories for our readers, and we'd love to hear from you. We are constantly learning, so please help us write stories that you will cherish and recommend to your friends. Please sign up for news and updates and follow us on BookBub.

As always, if you liked *It Happened in the Highlands,* please leave a review online, and don't miss Phoebe Pennington's story in Sleepless in Scotland.

ABOUT THE AUTHOR

USA Today Bestselling Authors Nikoo and Jim McGoldrick have crafted over fifty fast-paced, conflict-filled novels, along with two works of nonfiction, under the pseudonyms May McGoldrick, Jan Coffey, and Nik James.

These popular and prolific authors write historical romance, suspense, mystery, historical Westerns, and young adult novels. They are four-time Rita Award Finalists and the winners of numerous awards for their writing, including the Daphne DeMaurier Award for Excellence, the *Romantic Times Magazine* Reviewers' Choice Award, three NJRW Golden Leaf Awards, two Holt Medallions, and the Connecticut Press Club Award for Best Fiction. Their work is included in the Popular Culture Library collection of the National Museum of Scotland.

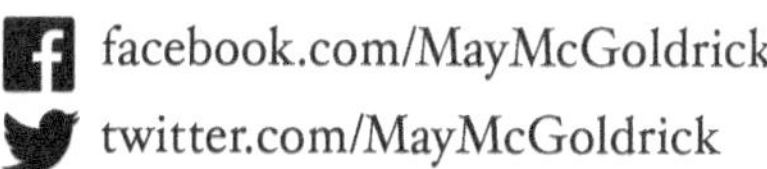

facebook.com/MayMcGoldrick

twitter.com/MayMcGoldrick

instagram.com/maymcgoldrick

bookbub.com/authors/may-mcgoldrick